The Other Side of Us

EMILY COX & NICOLE ALLEN

For Christopher and Jake
365 4-Ever

CHAPTER 1

MID-FEBRUARY

This place either needs an elevator or the shooting pain in my leg is telling me I shouldn't have come back. But I ignore my body's complaints and crutch myself to the third floor one stair at a time. Which gives me way too much time to think. Good thing I've been practicing avoidance techniques the last few weeks. Probably could've just called Dad, but I don't even wanna think about going back down those stairs right now, so I count each one on my way up to The Clubhouse. It helps me keep my mind off being back here and that I just saw Guo in a wheelchair. Even though she said it wasn't my fault, I know the truth and pretending won't change it or anything else right now.

Twenty-three, twenty-four, twenty-five.

Memories hang in the air like spiderwebs, and I wish I could just brush them off instead of getting stuck in them.

I stop to catch my breath, gripping the railing as I lean on one crutch to take the pressure off my burning armpits. Hauling around my dead-weight leg and the load of hurt and anger I brought back to San Francisco has aged me forty years. And it's only been ten days since Mei left me. At this rate, I'll live a couple more weeks and die from old age.

Thirty-six, thirty-seven....

My body yells at me to stop but I ignore it until I'm finally on the third floor, hobbling down the hallway toward The Clubhouse door. I inwardly shudder, remembering the day before I moved to Johnny's, when I used the code and caught Dad and Kenna messing around. Won't make that mistake again.

Taking a deep breath, I knock—loud enough I'm sure everyone on the third floor heard it. The lock clicks and the door swings open to a confused Kenna, her hair piled on top of her head, two pens jabbing out of the mass of dark waves. She's got red lipstick on her top lip but not her bottom, the tube in her hand.

"Marcus—hey!" She frown-smiles and swings the door open wide. "You don't have to knock, you know," she says, grabbing my arm as I hobble inside. "It was your house way before it was mine. But I get it might be weird for you. Right? This is weird? Me living here, answering your door?"

"Uh, yeah. Kinda, but...think I'll always knock. To be safe." I avoid her eyes, but her hand goes over her face.

"Oh. Yeah. That." She shuts the door and backs against it, squeezing her eyes shut. "I'm still so embarrassed about that. Your dad just laughs and says you deserved it, but no one deserves that."

"It's no big deal," I say to the living room, thinking but not saying, '*At least it wasn't Meemaw who caught you, no matter how much I wish it had been her instead of me.*'

"You're nice, Marcus. I'd be horrified if I walked in on my parents. Or parent. Dad. I'm not pretending to be your—"

"It's okay, Kenna," I say, smiling. "I won't call you mom but it's only because I'm not used to having one. And for the record, I'm glad it's you here and not Olivia."

Her shoulders fall and she searches my face, smiling. "She must really be bad, then..."

"Bad's not even a strong enough word. Let's just say

Dad's taste in women has improved by eighty-two billion percent. Took him eighteen years but he finally figured it out. We're slow learners, I guess." I glance around the room, my eyes landing on the throw blankets slung across the back of the couch. The new rug with swirly flowers. The fresh flowers on the end tables and a desk set up in front of the window access to the fire escape, three monitors spread across it.

Kenna turns in the direction I'm looking. "I didn't want to take over your room so when you moved to Johnny's, we set up my office out here in case you ever need a place to stay. It'll always be your room. If you ever need it. Or want it."

"Thanks," I say, glancing over Kenna's desk to the window and fire escape beyond it.

She pauses, then turns toward me, smiling brightly. "Anyway, you look great. How's the leg?"

"Still attached so I'd say, pretty good."

She smiles and turns toward the hall, talking over her shoulder. "Does Ray know you were coming?"

"No. Nope, just…last minute thing. Is he here?"

"Yep—I'll get him. He just hopped in the shower since we're going to a play written by Audrey's boyfriend. Double date."

"Boyfriend?" I raise my eyebrows.

Kenna whirls around and covers her mouth. "I wasn't supposed to tell you." She blinks at me, and I smile.

"Won't say a word. But does he look like Sasquatch by chance?"

"I haven't met him yet, so I don't know what he looks like but I'm hoping not Bigfoot. Why?"

The last time I saw Audrey was my second day back in San Francisco. She never mentioned a boyfriend, but I guess she doesn't have to tell me everything; I took off with Mei without saying anything. Got married. Got left. Now I'm back and Audrey has a boyfriend.

"Just her type, usually," I say to Kenna. "I'm happy for her as long as he's partially normal. None of her boyfriends have been, so…"

Kenna laughs and turns back toward Dad's—their—bedroom door. "I'll report back after I meet him tonight. Take a load off and I'll tell Ray you're here. He'll be so excited."

"I'll be quick. Just need to ask him something."

Before she opens the door and goes inside, she says, "He's really happy you're back, closer to home. I've never seen him so happy. Or heard him whistle so much."

I raise my eyebrows, and she nods. "Ooh. Glad it's you who has to listen to the whistling."

She laughs. "Same song, over and over." She rolls her eyes, hand on the doorknob. "But let the record state that I'm also happy you're here. It makes things feel…complete, I guess. Even though I know you probably don't feel very complete right now. So I'm not trying to take that away from you but I just…I'm glad. That's all." She smiles, then goes inside the room.

My eyes jump around the living room again, picking up memories that I wanna hurl out the window for cars to crunch and smash under their tires. Mei and I, sitting at the table with bowls of Oreos the first time she came to The Clubhouse. After Nick used her as his punching bag. My jaw clenches and my eyes slip to the bar where I sat while Mei pressed frozen peas to my bruised face after Nick's guys jacked me up. The sink I backed her against when we kissed for the first time. The couch where we got carried away and the door behind me that Meemaw walked through and caught us. The same door Mei ran out and disappeared for almost two weeks. If I hadn't gone to Guo's after prom, I never would've found her. None of this would have happened. Mei would've disappeared from my life, and I'd be at Stanford right now, a year of college done, a season of soccer won.

I close my eyes. No crutches. No ruptured heart. No questions and anger and so, so much hurt that it's dripping off me, leaving trails everywhere I go.

I put my hand over my mouth because everything inside me is squirming to get out of the burning, aching, throbbing places. I'm about to lose it all over Kenna's new rug when Dad walks out of his room, rubbing his wet hair with his hands, a towel slung around his waist.

"M.C.!" He smiles and walks toward me like I'm not intruding on his new life, and when he hugs me, I tense because Dad's never been a hugger, especially not when he's practically naked. I grip my crutches because I don't know what to do with my hands.

He pulls away and smiles. "Good surprise."

My eyes jump around the room, then behind him to Kenna, my feet, his face. "Sorry to drop by. Should've called first."

"No, no—this is always your home, son. You're welcome home anytime. Stay as long as you want." His jaw tenses and he swallows hard.

I look away so his emotion doesn't transfer to me; I've got plenty of my own to avoid already. But what I really wanna do is hug him again and cry. Instead, I clear my throat. "Just saw Guo. You didn't warn me."

Dad furiously rubs his hair again. "Oh. Yeah…sorry. I just didn't…"

"That's messed up."

"That's the nice way to say it. Yeah—messed up," he says to the carpet, then glances at me. "You see Charlie?"

"Didn't go inside." I've thought about Charlie every day since I left him at The Clubhouse because I couldn't take him to Johnny's. Dad had to find another home for him because of the no pet policy, and when he told me he'd taken Charlie to Guo's, I'd internally freaked because first Mei had abandoned him, then me, then Dad, and I know what it's like to be left behind. He's been in three different houses in the last ten days, and he didn't ask for any of this either. Kind of like Guo in her wheelchair, acting like it wasn't all Mei's and my fault.

"I know you're going out so, just wondering if there are any new leads on Nick?"

"Uhh, no. Nothing yet. But there will be. He's good but he's not that good, so as soon as I hear, I'll definitely let you know."

I nod to the worn carpet, press my lips together. The words hover in my throat, hesitant, unsure. Once I let them out, they'll start a chain reaction, and I don't know where it'll end. "Know how you told me you'd help me find Mei? I think I'm ready. If your offer still stands."

CHAPTER 2

MID-FEBRUARY

My eyes follow the bustle of scooters, cars, and people thirteen stories below my hotel room window, all with somewhere to be and the freedom to get there. I'm going to be just like them as soon as I can get a passport in my real name—Zhao Xin Yao—even though I don't know her. And neither does Marcus.

I spread my hand across my belly. "Don't worry," I whisper to my tiny travel companion, "we'll both see him soon. Everything's going to be okay." Even though I can't feel the baby yet, knowing I'm not alone is comforting.

Detective Chang said he'd be here at ten to take me to the passport offices so I can start my work on going home. It's been over a week since I showed up at the police station with evidence big enough to lock up Nick. As soon as they find him. Detective Chang asked me not to contact anyone until he gives me the go ahead. He's spent his time trying to track down the origin of the diamonds. He's used what little is left of his time to check on me every day ever since he heard about my cousin, Chaz's, lifeless body washing up in Jamaica.

That revelation shoved me down a twisting emotional slide of memories. We weren't as close as we'd been as kids, but news of his death rattled me. I kept it together long enough for Detective Chang to leave then spent the rest of the day stuck in the past, remembering our childhood, recalling times he'd saved me in the past few years. Nick would have hurt me so much worse if Chaz hadn't intervened on multiple occasions.

I touch the tattoo on the back of my neck. I got it the night Chaz diverted Nick's attention—when Nick took me to his room. But no matter how many times Chaz stepped between Nick and me or withheld information to protect me, he was still one of Nick's guys. Even so, it should have been Nick's dead body that washed up on a remote beach, not Chaz's. If only it were so easy. But I'm not going to wait around any longer. I just want to go home. But before that can happen, I need a real passport and a Visa.

A knock rattles the door, and I snap back to reality, cross the room, and peer out the peephole. Detective Chang's on the other side so I swing the door open and step aside to let him in.

His eyes linger on my face before he smiles and holds up a white paper bag. "Sorry I'm early, but I brought you breakfast."

I take the bag but the look on his face says he has more to deliver than breakfast. "What is it?" I ask, and he moves into the room, then straightens, hands on his hips as he turns to face me.

"Listen, um, I…need to tell you something." Detective Chang hesitates, and it reminds me of when he dropped the news about Chaz. My mind runs through worst-case scenarios until he blurts, "I went to the prison yesterday and spoke to Mr. Zhang."

I stiffen. Last time Detective Chang spoke about the man who, up until a year ago, I thought was my father, I told him I wanted nothing to do with him. I'm grateful Detective Chang calls him 'Mr. Zhang'—it keeps him at a distance and that's where he'll stay.

"And?"

"He talked. A lot. Most of which I can't discuss right now but all of which gives me reason to believe he's telling the truth. It sounds like he doesn't have any loving feelings toward Nick Chao."

I stare at him, not knowing if I want or care for him to say more. I just want all of this to be over and for me, and the tiny life I'm carrying with me, to be on a plane back to Marcus.

"One thing I can tell you is that Mr. Zhang knows you're in Taiwan. I don't know how since Chaz had your flight record deleted, but Mr. Zhang also told me that Nick knows you're here, just as I feared. The only possibility that makes any sense at all is that Chaz was threatened and gave you up as a last attempt to save himself." He lets the sentence hang, and my hand goes to my stomach. His eyes follow before flicking back to mine. "Also…I've confirmed that Nick has a hit out on you. And we don't have much time."

"What are you saying?"

"I'm saying Nick wants you dead, and he's willing to pay a lot for it. Your safety is my number-one priority. I'm going to take you somewhere he won't look for you until we can find him."

My heart collapses and I rasp, "And where is that, exactly?"

His eyes skim the room before landing back on me. "Fo Guang Shan. A monastery not too far from here."

My eyebrows climb, surprise pulling them up. "A monastery. Like, where monks live?"

"Yeah." Detective Chang nods. "We've used their discretion before. You'll be safe there."

I scan the hotel room as the news settles over me, itchy and misplaced in my vision of how my time in Taiwan would go. "How long?"

"Hopefully not long at all." Detective Chang steps closer, places his hands on my arms, locking his eyes on mine. "I am so sorry about this, Mei Li. I know this isn't what you wanted, but you don't need to be afraid. Nick won't even think to come looking for you, I made sure of that. I promise as soon as it's safe, I'll personally get you on your way home. But until then, no one can know where you are. Which means, you can't contact anyone or you'll put yourself and the investigation in danger. And possibly the person you contact."

CHAPTER 3
LATE FEBRUARY

My crutches click on the cement floor as I make my way from the manager's office to the restaurant door. I nailed that interview and will probably be starting work in a few days. I can't keep a wife but I can get a job at a restaurant, thanks to Johnny's hookup. Look at me go. Now if I can just get accepted into Berkeley, a few pieces of my life might finally fit somewhere. Not the ones I wanted, but who's being picky?

As I round the corner, I stop. Dad's sitting on a bench by the employee entrance, and he stands, shoving his hands in his pockets.

"Hey, M.C. How'd it go?"

"Heyyy…?" I frown, glancing around. "What are you doing here?" My pulse knocks around in my throat. I told him this morning about my interview, but I doubt he's here, just eagerly waiting to hear if I got the job.

"I, uhh…I remembered you had your interview this afternoon and…" He glances around. "Here." He steps to the door. "Let's get you to the car. I'll drive you to your apartment."

I search his face for clues about why he's really here but

then again, I could use some fresh air since the smell of steak and fries is clinging to me.

I crutch through the door he holds open, keeping my eyes on cars in the parking lot as he falls into step beside me.

"Why'd you really come, Dad?" I stop and so does he. "You could've just called to see how my interview went instead of coming all the way over here."

He hesitates, then lets out a long breath as he shakes his head. When he turns toward me, my body tenses under the weight of what's about to drop.

"I got some news a couple days ago, and I've been trying to figure out the best way to tell you and this isn't it, but it has to be."

"Mei?"

He nods, looking at the cement.

"Is it bad?"

Dad's jaw pulses, and even though a motorcycle screams past and a car alarm wails through the still air, my world is holding its breath.

"Uhhh..." He rubs his forehead, closes his eyes, and swears under his breath. "Can we sit down?" He gestures toward a bench under a tree near the back entrance, and I head toward it. It's bad news. I thought I'd heard the worst. But I should know by now that there could always be worse, and he's about to give it to me.

I stop at the bench, my legs tingling as I turn to face him. "Just tell me." My heart beats out the words. "Please." My eyes are so focused on his face, they burn. "You found Mei, didn't you?"

He swallows and glances around the parking lot, his V-neck doing nothing to hide his heartbeat bouncing in his neck. "I found out that her cousin, Chaz—the one who worked for Nick—is dead." Dad nods, like he's relieved to get the words out as my brain tries to make sense of it. "His body was found in Jamaica. He was shot in the head and there's a homicide investigation underway. Not in my jurisdiction, so I don't know more than that."

My muscles are so tense, I can almost feel them fraying. Mei never really talked about Chaz, but I knew enough to know he was connected to Nick, and that he tried to help Mei in L.A., just not much more than that. "What does he have to do with Mei?" I whisper like the whole world can hear us.

Dad runs his hand through his hair and looks past me, nods, then meets my eyes. "The last traces they found on him were in Newburgh. The day Mei went missing."

My throat closes and I grip my crutches tighter, but can't look at him when I ask, "Did he take her? Is that what you're saying?"

"No." He shakes his head. "We can't assume anything. But I asked some questions and wish I hadn't."

My whole body throbs. "Why?"

He squints into the sun, his jaw pulsing as he slides his eyes to mine, his face pale. "Because I found a death certificate for Mei Li."

CHAPTER 4

EARLY MAY

Three months doesn't seem very long when I compare it to things like how long Marcus and I dated or how long we lived in Vegas. That all went way too fast, but waiting for Detective Chang's clearance to go home is like being tied down and gagged with a front row seat to watch the life I love crumble with no way to fix it. Marcus and I built it for nine months, and it's disappearing faster every day. Marcus has no idea that I'm in Taiwan, trying to get back to the U.S. and to keep him safe, I've followed the rules. If he found out where I was, he'd be on the first plane here despite the huge target on his back. I just wish he knew why I had to do this and that I'm planning on going back to him and our life. But as soon as I wish it, I imagine Chaz's body washed up on a Jamaican beach and the image turns to Marcus's. That's where I always stop wishing and wait some more. I'm doing this for him. And for me. For us, eventually. Hopefully.

Detective Chang has come to the monastery every day to give me updates and food from the outside world. When he dropped me off here, I asked him if he would check the San Francisco news every day for anything that could be linked to Nick. I haven't told Detective Chang who I'm really worried about, but he keeps watching and reporting without asking questions. Today, like every day, Detective Chang had no updates and left a half hour ago.

Wu-Yao, the head of the order, asked if I could help in the gift shop today so I trek from one side of the grounds to the other, because staying busy helps keep my mind off things I can't control. Like the small aches and pains of pregnancy. I'm lucky I haven't been sick, but I haven't felt great, either. I'm sure stress and uncertainty aren't good for the baby, but there's only one way to rid myself of those and nothing's happened with Nick yet.

Still…day after day, night after night, I barely breathe as I wait, afraid any extra movement in the air will disrupt the flow of time. Also, breathing too deeply hurts the bruised, bleeding spots inside me that miss Marcus's smile, and his laugh. The way he rakes his hand through his hair and how he sees all of me with one look. I miss talking to him for hours about our days, our future, or nothing at all. I miss his kiss and his touch, both of which immediately ignite my body. I shouldn't dwell on how he made me come alive, but the longer I'm away from him, the more those thoughts are the only thing keeping me alive.

"Lost?" a nun calls to me in perfect English from across the courtyard, and it startles me. She's coming from the temple, her robes swishing around her, her eyes intent on my face as she approaches. They're gentle but piercing enough to break through the darkness around me. I've seen her a few times but never spoken to her in the three months I've been here.

She reaches out and touches my stomach and I flinch, then inhale sharply when her fingertips relieve pressure that's been building since Indiana. With her other hand, she touches my temple, her eyes holding me in place.

"So much sadness for someone so young, and there is more to come. More that will hurt and heal at the same time."

She searches my face before pulling a small stone from her pocket, pressing it into my palm. "But He is waiting. He will help you." She nods once, then turns and shuffles away, my pain trailing behind her.

I open my hand and my breathing sputters to a stop, my other hand rubbing my burning chest. It isn't just a stone—it's an intricate carving of Buddha's face. Clenching it in my palm, I hurry across the temple grounds and onto the path toward the gift shop, my mind replaying the night so long ago on my fire escape, my Buddha statue, and blue eyes in the dark.

I stop halfway up the stretching flight of stairs to catch my breath, my body heavy and sluggish. The walk was longer than I remember, but I take a deep breath and continue up the steps. When I reach the entrance, a sharp pain tears through my stomach and I clutch it, protectively. My hands press against the spot like that will stop the pain, but it only intensifies and moves to my shoulder as a cry escapes my mouth.

Fear crashes into me and I drop to the ground, landing hard on my knees. Tears stream down my cheeks as sweat beads on my forehead, my body damp and clammy as it surrenders to the pain controlling it.

The gift shop door rings sharply off key and blurred voices blend, urgent and pleading as the world tilts and my body is ripped in two.

———

I'm still angry at the dim light weaving through my open window. I want to fall back to sleep and never wake up.

A tendril of heat wraps around my bare ankles; it's almost audible in the silent room in the silent monastery in the silent afternoon when all the monks and nuns are silent in their meditation. I'm alone for the first time in a week and the extra space pulls at me. Detective Chang just left and memories are seeping into my room, filling his spot in the empty chair beside my bed. Memories of waking up in a hospital, hearing a word in Mandarin I'd never heard before. Asking for someone to translate before its meaning landed, crushing me: *miscarriage*. Feeling my soul wilt. The doctor explaining that my pregnancy wasn't real. *Ectopic*. Not a baby. Being told my chances of getting pregnant again are low because they had to remove pieces of me. If I do get pregnant, I'll be at high risk for more miscarriages.

The one thing that tied me to Marcus from so far away never really existed. If I ever make my way back to him, will he want me, in all my fragmented pieces? Marcus said he wanted at least two kids so no one was an only child like we both were. But now, if I ever get back to him and he forgives me, I might not be able to have one. Our life might look too different from the one he wants.

When I returned to the monastery, I pasted a smile on my face, trying to reassure everyone I was okay. But it grew weary and wobbly and fell off a few days ago and went wherever the other discarded pieces of me went. I can't even pretend around Detective Chang who still visits daily. He's never asked about my pregnancy, even though I'm sure the doctor told him what happened. He just asks if I'm okay and the truth is, I don't know what I am except very, very alone and hopeless.

I push myself off the bed and shuffle to the bathroom, my body achy, heavy, sore even while it tries to hold up my exhausted thoughts and lethargic soul. It's as if someone reached inside me and ripped out all that was living.

Standing in front of the mirror, I force my eyes to look at myself and when I do, a stranger stares back: smudged eyes, sallow skin draped over jutting cheekbones. My eyes drop to tweezers glinting from the pedestal sink and my hand stalls as I visually outline the sharp edges.

Picking it up, I run my thumb along the sharp points,

press harder, feel something rush around my cold, hard insides. My breathing picks up, and I twist my forearm, then hold the tweezers steady as I drag it up the pale skin, lightly at first, just enough to feel a hint of pain. It whispers through me, flowing around my hard, empty places. I dig harder, closing my eyes when the pain surges like warm water that sweeps away bits of old pain, leaving a new one I can control.

CHAPTER 5

EARLY MAY

have a stop to make even though I'm already late for work. The way my stomach is churning, I'll be hugging the restaurant toilet most of the night, anyway. My body's still not used to the idea that Mei's really gone, and I'll never see her again. Such an easy thing to say until it's said about someone I love. Then it's so heavy and dark that every time it plows through my brain, it smashes my world all over again, sending burning hot splinters through me. For the thousandth time since Dad gave me the news, I send up a prayer that this is all just some huge mistake. *Even if she doesn't wanna be with me, please God, let her be alive. It all hurts but it's better than picturing her dead.*

Before my common sense can take over, I slip through the sliding doors of the corner market, desperate for Aisle 4. Mei's scent hung in the steam from my morning shower, and I couldn't shake it, no matter how violently it shook me, even after three months of living without her. I even glanced over my shoulder just to double check she hadn't snuck in without me noticing. Hoping she had, even if it was her ghost. I'll take Mei in ghost form any day over nothing. But she wasn't there, and she'll never be there again. Like…no chance, ever.

My hand goes to my chest to hold me together as I walk faster, scanning shelves for the smell of every morning with Mei. I squat, scan the shampoo bottles, and snatch the glossy blue one. I'm so pathetic, but I gotta have her somehow even if I'll never have her again. The small, tattered shred of hope I'd held onto that she'd change her mind and show up dissolved the day Dad told me she had, too. So now all I have is her smell, the notes she wrote me, the memories of her laugh. Videos and pictures too painful to pull up on my phone. And so much anger. If she hadn't left, she'd still be alive. Even if she didn't wanna be with me anymore, she'd still be somewhere instead of nowhere for no reason, or at least no reason she wanted to tell me.

I set the shampoo bottle on the checkout counter, embarrassed, like it's a box of tampons, then pay the cashier and sprint out the doors toward the restaurant. I hope Audrey doesn't show up tonight like she did last night and ask a million questions about how I'm doing, because I don't wanna talk about it. I can't. Just wanna move on, stupid choice by stupid choice.

Bag in hand, I limp-jog four blocks, grimacing since my leg isn't ready. When I get to the restaurant, I detour to the men's room and lock myself in a stall. I have exactly six minutes to melt down before pretending I'm fine for the rest of the night.

Flipping open the shampoo bottle lid, I breathe deeply, slumping against the wall like a junkie. I close my eyes... remember the first time I smelled this: Mei fresh from the shower in our tiny Seattle cottage. But it wasn't until our first official night together on San Juan Island that I became intimately acquainted with it.

The memory draws blood and I snap the lid shut, my breath snagging on the jagged edges of my heart while I trace the 6-21 still on my wrist with my fingertip. The day will come and go this year without the one who made it the best day of my life.

I stare at it, make myself a promise: when I get back to my apartment tonight, I'll scrub the date until it's gone—until I bleed it off. Tavah asked me a couple nights ago what it means, and while I never thought the girl who sat next to me in high school chemistry would be next to me almost every day since I moved into Johnny's, I want her here. Just don't wanna tell her what 6-21 means, so the other night when she'd picked up my arm during a movie marathon and read the numbers and words written on it—new and old—then asked what they all meant, I'd changed the subject. Not only do I not want to talk about it, but Lin's eyes were lasers on me from across the room, like I was doing something wrong. She doesn't know I'm not because she doesn't know about Mei, and I can't talk to her about it. I haven't even told Johnny. I don't want it to be true and if I tell other people, it will be.

I drop the shampoo bottle in the garbage on my way out of the bathroom and don't look back. She won't be anywhere ever again and even if she were alive, she didn't wanna be with me. Gone, dead…it all feels the same.

CHAPTER 6

MID-MAY

The air is heavy this morning, pressing me into my bed, pushing against my lungs. Suffocating me. Or maybe it's the weight of my heart as it struggles to keep beating when all I want is for it to stop.

I spin my infinity ring around my finger. It's getting looser every day, but I won't take it off yet; I still have a shredded ribbon of hope that I'll get back to Marcus and he'll forgive me even though I can't see how. We've had no contact for over three months. I can't imagine what he's thinking. I try not to because how can he not hate me? He has every right. Still, I'll only take off my ring when all hope has dissolved, which might be soon if I stay in this quiet monastery much longer. This place is taking its toll on my body, which is used to laughter, movement, fear, and Marcus's whirling mind and endless energy. It's excruciating to go from running to standing still.

To keep my mind off Marcus and the distance growing between us, I've been helping here as much as I can. But lately, nothing seems to work, and I slip further into my tortured mind.

When I drop into bed each night, I reach for him, one

hand smoothing the empty space beside me while the other holds our Buddha against my heart. In the shower, I close my eyes and imagine him there, like he was every day for nine months. I imagine what he'd say, how he'd smile at me, and how it would feel to be tucked against him, solid and warm.

This morning, the usual suffocation shoves me out of bed before the sun touches the horizon. I breathe deeply to keep the ache in my chest from spreading throughout my body, which is wrapped in Marcus's hoodie. I took it with me when I left Indiana, and I've curled up inside it every night since. It doesn't smell like him anymore, but it holds life in it—the one left behind. The only one I want. And the one we created together inside me. The beautiful life that was supposed to be part me, part Marcus, and tied us together until it didn't.

I swap the hoodie for a brown robe, pull my hair into a loose bun, and slip out of my room, heading to the courtyard where I can walk among a thousand Buddha statues and tell them things I don't want anyone living to know. But as I reach the courtyard, rain slashes at the pavement and a punishing wind whips the trees, snatching my daily walk from me.

I hurry back to my room, slowing when I pass the meditation chapel. Nuns sit cross-legged on mats, hands on their knees, palms turned toward the heavens. When I first arrived at the monastery, I asked Wu-Yao about what the shaved heads and plain brown robes represented. I'd always been taught our hair holds energy and symbolizes prosperity and luck. She told me nuns and monks shave all their hair off and wear simple robes to strip themselves of vanity and their pasts so they can fully dedicate their lives to Buddha.

I've wondered hundreds of times how people let go of their pasts. It sounds so easy but feels impossible, like it's laced through my DNA and will rip me apart if I try to unlace it. But these women have done it. Their silent meditation is not to merely peacefully coexist, but to reach higher, to find and experience something more.

The problem is, I've already had something more.

My throat tightens and tears fill my eyes, so I rush back to my room to come undone alone. I close the door behind me and darkness greets me once again, wraps itself back around me, secures itself with sharp, piercing claws.

After my miscarriage, darkness and I spent a lot of time together. It got so heavy, I wondered sometimes if it had grown into me. Other times, I wished it would smother me. When the doctor dismissed the pregnancy as if it was nothing, a deep, echoing loneliness seeped into my soul. That "nothing" was the only thing tethering me to Marcus and yet, the truth is, medically, it was nothing.

In the bathroom, I step into the square of light coming through a skylight far above my head. I look up at it, will the light to soak into me and push out the thick coils of darkness. But the silence roars, and I turn my focus to the mirror and the flat, two-dimensional stranger staring back at me. The joy that used to light her eyes is worn and faded.

Reaching back, I undo my bun, and my hair spills over my shoulders. I shiver when self-loathing crawls through me, slithering and cold. I hate that I'm here. I hate that I chose this over including Marcus in my decision to come here or that I didn't think we could do this together. What did my decision fix? It only cost me everything, killed the life I loved, killed the possibility of a future with Marcus, killed my cousin. For what? So darkness could drain a little more of my energy and hope every day? Fill me with sharp, jagged torment and aggressive, bubbling self-hatred.

My breathing quickens as anger flares through me, lighting up reality. The path back to Marcus has crumbled. But what does it matter? I can't go back and don't want to move forward like this. Maybe I should rid myself of the past and the future. If I give them up, will the present be the only place for my mind to land? Like the nuns, will letting go feel like a release?

Dropping my robe, I stare at my naked, sunken body that used to be so alive and warm, then bend and pull out the scissors I took from the front desk two days ago. Sliding my hair between the blades, I close my eyes and cut. I open my hand, watch the strands fall to my feet. The scissors are dull and my hand aches as I hold them as close to my scalp as possible, hacking, chopping, until there's nothing but patchy, black fuzz. My heart thumps against my chest as I stare in the mirror at a reflection that leaves no trace of the old me.

Baldness accentuates the cheekbones jutting from my expressionless face, the dark smudges under my eyes, colorless skin clinging to my ribs. There's no hiding my pain because there's nowhere for it to hide.

I grab the hand mirror and turn to inspect the back of my head. My tattoo reflects, murky but bold:

張
美
麗

My eyes skim the characters of my name and my mind flits to the beautiful letters Marcus once wrote beneath them. They're gone now, faded into the past with him because that's what he is: my past.

My hands tremble and I drop the hand mirror. It shatters into pieces, pointed and sharp like the pain ripping through me. I flinch at the sound and my infinity ring falling off my finger, clinking against the tile before skidding under the cabinet. Panic shoots through me, and I drop to the ground, feeling around for the cold metal, glass shards slicing into my hands and knees.

I can't find it and hysteria chokes me. The pain from the glass bites at my palms but does nothing to dull the shards of loss slashing at my soul. It's gone. He's gone. Everything I have ever loved is gone. I take a piece of glass in each hand, squeeze my fists until dark red dots drip on the floor, smear my vision.

Anguish burns through me, destructive and infectious. "It's lost, Marcus. It's all I had left and I lost it," I whisper, squeezing my eyes shut, trying to hear his voice. But there's no reply. There never will be. He's not here. He doesn't even know where 'here' is. I'm not even all here. And now, neither is my ring.

I scrape the jagged glass along my thigh and when I don't feel anything, I press harder. I just want to release the darkness inside me, just a little. I want it to drag the loneliness with it. But all that will be left is echoing emptiness. It's too much and not enough.

With a trembling hand, I carve into my arm, leaving lines of fire and blood. Light and darkness clash, then weave together. Flash. Fade. Burn.

My name floats on the air but I don't want it to pull me from this spiral, so I cower from it. Maybe this is what it feels like to let go. Maybe this is devotion. Enlightenment.

Light bursts into the room but does nothing to sweep away the darkness trapped inside me. A warm hand touches my shoulder, lifts my blood-soaked hands. A flicker of movement. Softness covers me. I'm rising.

———

My eyes flutter when light streams across my eyelids, urging them open. It warms me and the few spots of light flickering inside me reach toward it, gathering it closer. I'm wrapped in a down blanket, the pillow I'm lying on so soft it creates a cocoon around my head. My hands are bandaged along with my arm, and when I try to swallow, my throat burns.

Where am I, and how did I get here?

My mind flicks through scenes of broken glass and hair falling to the ground. Cold tile, a hollow laugh. I sit up, my eyes sweeping the window across from the bed, closet door open, nothing inside it mine, none of it from the monastery.

My head snaps toward a quiet snore coming from beside the bed and Detective Chang's head rests against the wall, eyes closed. As my focus stops swimming, my mind replays the bright light in the bathroom, a voice, footsteps, a warm chest. I remember my robe slipping over me, then someone carrying me, laying me in the backseat of a car.

Now, as I stare at the ceiling, all I feel is the weight of fear. I'm afraid of what happened…where my mind went. I'm afraid of what I did to myself and what more I could have done. I'm afraid of the darkness left inside me.

"Hey," Detective Chang says, and I drag my focus toward him. He rubs his eyes, ruffles his messy hair. "Sorry. I didn't mean to fall asleep."

I give him a weak smile and turn my attention back to the ceiling. "How long have I been asleep?"

"Almost a full day. I checked on you every ten minutes through the night but must have sat down for a second too long." He leans in, touching my bandaged arm gently. "I'm so glad you're awake. You had me worried."

"I didn't mean for you—for anyone—to…see that." I talk to the ceiling, my voice crackly. "I don't know how you knew. I'm not sure what happened."

"I was already at the monastery. Wu-Yao called me. She was concerned." He sets the words free over me, lets them hover before he goes on. "She says you haven't been eating. Also, that you walk around in a daze. She doesn't think the monastery is the right environment for you, and after finding you yesterday morning, I agree. So I brought you here."

"Is this your apartment?"

He nods. "Yeah. And just so you know, my Nai-Nai also lives here so, nothing to worry about. No shady intentions."

I let the information sink in, then nod. "Thank you." I owe him more than those two words, but the list is too long and keeps growing.

"You'll like my Nai-Nai. As grandmothers go, she's the best of the best. But it's your choice. I just think a change of scenery will be good. And someone to force-feed you so we don't end up like this again." He sweeps his hand over me.

A flicker of light pulses inside me and I see Guo Mama's face, lit up, urging me forward, smoothing the sharp edges of my fear. "You've done so much already and—"

"Mei Li." He breathes my name as he scoots closer to the bed, elbows on his knees, hands clasped. "I want you to stay here. You don't have anyone, but now you have me. And my Nai-Nai."

I blink back tears that spring from the truth in his words. I let go of my someone the moment I left Indiana and since then, he's slipped further away. But now I have Detective Chang. I have his Nai-Nai.

I nod, still working to hold back emotion that could unravel me completely. Again. "Okay," I finally say.

"Also," he says, reaching into his pants pocket, "I found this on the floor." He pulls out my infinity ring that is now on a metal chain. It dangles above my chest. "Looks like it doesn't fit you anymore. My Nai-Nai had a chain, so now you can wear the ring around your neck to keep it safe. Until it fits your finger again."

I clutch it in my hand, hold it to my heart. My eyes fill with tears and meet his as I say, "Thank you, Detective Chang. For everything."

"Please, Mei Li. Call me Leo."

CHAPTER 7

MID-MAY

empty my pockets onto the coffee table that doubles as my nightstand. It's 11:30PM and the apartment's surprisingly quiet, which is nice because the restaurant wasn't. It's exhausting work. My mind goes to Mei and the years she worked in a restaurant, but then I grit my teeth to grind the thought to dust before it goes deeper and messes with the ball of hurt scabbing over in my chest. I've gritted my teeth at least 100 times today. Reminded myself she's really gone, though sometimes, I swear she's right beside me. Today was one of those sometimes.

I drop to the couch, lean forward, rifle through the nice pile of cash, pick out a phone number written on the back of a receipt, another on a gum wrapper: *Call me—Liz. Let's get together this weekend—Ushi.*

Nope—no Asian girls. I had one once, the best one, and now I don't. I crumple both numbers, toss them across the room. Dad hasn't gotten any more information about Mei's death so all I have is open-ended questions for God and inner tidal waves of grief He hasn't stopped, no matter how many times I've asked Him to.

I flop back against the couch and pull my phone from my

pocket, smiling at Tavah's name on the screen: Big T. She pretends she hates the nickname I gave her, but uses it to sign off so...

I take a deep breath, let it out slowly as I scroll through her messages. Five nice, long texts from her while I was at work.

Since Dad told me about Mei, I haven't been right and honestly, I'm not sure I ever will be again but being around Tavah helps. It's been almost a year since I decided to run away with Mei. One year since I thought I knew what I was doing. A year since I gave up everything because I couldn't imagine living without her. And now I don't have to imagine.

I close my eyes, lean my head back and stare at the ceiling. Why did she walk away and leave me with nothing but a one-sentence goodbye that turned into bottomless pain? If she'd known she'd die, would she have stayed or was being with me that awful? And how did it end for her? I see Chaz on a beach with a hole in his head and grimace at the thought of Mei, cold and still...wherever her life ended. I've wondered a million times if it was Nick. Or was it one of his guys? It all goes back to him somehow, I know it. And if she'd just talked to me and we'd worked out whatever was bothering her, she'd be alive. We'd be—

I slam every mental brake. I've spiraled too many times and discovered there's no end to it, only more pain.

I click my phone back to life and stare into the screen's glow. Tavah asked me last week if I'm afraid hanging out with her so much is gonna mess me up, like I'd once told her all girls do. Before I'd run away with Mei and experienced it firsthand. I'd told her there was no way she could possibly mess me up more than I already was. She'd played with my sleeve and said, "I don't usually like messes but if they're like you, then...I could get very into them."

We were sitting so close on the couch that she laid her head on my shoulder. I'd let her. I liked it. I like her, even though I'm not sure how reliable my feelings are or ever will be. But I might be okay letting Tavah have whatever fragments are left. I don't know. Maybe. What else am I gonna do with them?

Clicking on Tavah's name, I sink into a screen full of her texts.

> Big T: Should be asleep but I simply can't. Is your shift over yet? I mean, yeah, I won't see you tonight, but sleeping is such a waste of time. You could always stop by after work and climb in through my window… hint hint.

I smile. I'd crawled through her window last week when all her roommates were home and I wanted to avoid the whole scene, especially Lin who now officially lives there. Last time we were in the same room together she got in my face about why I'm spending so much time with someone who's not Mei, and I walked away from her because I'm not gonna tell her Mei's dead. And I don't want her big mouth telling Tavah about Mei before I do, so now I avoid her and her judgy, clueless eyes that burn holes through me.

I scroll to the next message.

8:09 P.M.

> Big T: Hey. Ignore that girl winking at you from the next table over. I know there's a girl winking at you. Yes, I'm positive—look around. Yep, that one. See? Told you. I know how these things work. Especially when you're dressed in that white shirt and tie. Wowza. But ignore her. She just wants your body.

10:04 P.M.

> Big T: A conversation in our apartment:
>
> Alli: If this were ancient times, I'd be wearing a golden gown right now and have man servants waving me with palm fronds.
>
> Dez: If this were ancient times, you'd also be bleeding on a rag.
>
> You were smart to stay away from girls for so long, but I'm glad you allowed an exception.

Didn't think I'd ever need an exception. Didn't think there'd ever be anyone but Mei. I clench my jaw and scroll to the next text, which makes me smile and shake my head. Girl is crazy. And I like letting her frolic through my mind and my life. She's a very enthusiastic frolicker. She makes me feel good. And that's gotta mean something since I've felt only numb for the last few months.

If things were how they used to be, I'd be smiling at Mei's texts, then coming home to her every night instead of a bachelor pad with a snoring Johnny in the other room. It should be Mei curled up beside me instead of the pillow I clutch to suffocate the pain leaking from my heart. I should be whispering to Mei, touching Mei. But I'm not and she's not and it's all just not. I gotta get on with life. I shouldn't feel bad about it. I didn't choose any of this. So here comes Marcus, version 3.0. Third time's a charm, so I hear.

I got my acceptance to summer term last week and can't wait for the semester to start. Being at school again might be the final nail in my own, old me coffin. The old version of myself basically died when I found out she had so it's time to bury it all. Kenna offered up her therapist if I was interested, but it won't change a thing when the one thing you want to change you can't.

I drop my phone and head for the fridge, running my hands down my face. I'm here, in this life. It's not Stanford, but I'm officially a Berkeley student next week, and I'm making great money at work. Spending my extra time with Johnny and his roommates and…a lot of time with Tavah.

I'm hitting the gym five times a week. My leg's getting stronger. Haven't touched a soccer ball and don't think I ever will again, but everything else around me seems like the impossible is happening: life's moving on and I'm surviving without Mei.

With Tavah.

But I shouldn't. Should I?

I still haven't told her I was married. Haven't told her why I'm not anymore. I gotta figure out how and when to tell her. But what will she think? Mei and I were together for nine months. Tavah and I have been hanging out for about a month—a lot less history to run from if she doesn't like mine.

My phone screen lights up with a call and my eyes snap to it while I hold my breath. It's just Dad and I swear under my breath because I hate myself for being idiotic enough to hope that one of these times, it's gonna be Mei, calling to tell me there's been some horrible mistake and that she's actually alive and wants our life back. It's never her. It never will be. It's just Dad, calling to check on me, but I don't wanna be checked on right now. No one can change this situation. I can't go back in time and clarify to Mei that when I said I was done, I didn't mean with her or us; I meant I was done with cheap, sleazy places and running and hiding. I was never done with her and I never will be, no matter how things did or didn't end. The only time I feel any relief is when I push her from my mind and do whatever makes me happy. Like hang with Tavah. She makes me happy. But right now, she isn't here and I'm, once again, suffocating in Mei's absence.

I blink into the dark kitchen, rubbing the back of my neck, letting my head fall. *Why'd you do it? Why'd you leave and put a target on your back?*

Closing my eyes, I let her face float through my mind, leaning my head back against the refrigerator door, imploding in the silence.

Were you too scared to tell me to my face I wasn't enough for you? That there was something so much better? Were you too afraid to hurt me in real time? You messed me up in the worst way, just like I always knew you would.

My head drops, exhausted, defeated, but I push away from the refrigerator, yanking at my belt as I shed my clothes on my way to the couch.

I can't stay angry and sad because you left and now you're gone forever. I've gotta make a new life without you.

My phone buzzes again, and Tavah's face beams up at me so full of light and life it pulls me out of the hole I was digging for myself.

I answer and before I can say anything she blurts, "Did you get it?" Her excitement bursts through the speaker.

"Did I get what…?"

"The box!"

"Box…?"

"The one on your table. Are you home yet?"

"Just got here." I sit up straighter, glance over my shoulder, over the back of the couch. "Oh. Yeah. There's a box on the table. That from you?" I stand and walk toward it, cradling the phone between my shoulder and ear as I pick up the box. What is it?"

"Open it!" she squeals. "I've been waiting all night."

Tearing off the purple kitten wrapping paper, I lift the lid and a smile tugs at my cheeks as I read: CONGRATULATIONS FOR GETTING INTO COLLEGE, BIG BOY!

———

Tavah's roommate lets me into their apartment on her way out, and I settle onto the couch, prop my Adidas on the coffee table. Probably should've changed my shirt after work since it smells like steak, but Tavah will forgive me. She's the easiest, lightest thing in my life right now.

When she finally walks into the apartment, she throws her keys on the counter, then stops. "Marcus?" Her eyes spark, her smile throwing beams of light at me. "I thought you were having dinner with your dad and Kenna tonight. Not that I'm complaining…" She drops her bag and plops down beside me on the couch, nudging my arm.

I smile down at her, searching her face. "I postponed." I don't tell her why because then I'll have to tell her about Mei, and I can't. Not yet.

"Places to be?" she asks, smoothing her hair as she smiles at me.

"Yep. Like right here, waiting for you to get home from a grueling day of Spanish tutoring."

"Me encanta esta idea…" She wiggles her eyebrows. "But how exactly did you get in?"

I mimic climbing, then breaking a window. "Easy."

Tavah smiles and rolls her eyes. "Did Alli try to undress you when you broke in?"

"Not this time. I'm very grateful she was late for work."

"Me, too." Tavah holds my gaze. "She's spoken her intentions, but I think she's too scared of me to try anything."

"Is it your intimidating size?" I squeeze her bicep and she laughs.

"I can't think of anything else it would be."

"I can." I stretch my arm along the back of the couch and turn into her. "I might have confessed that you forced me to play Scrabble for five hours last Sunday. She looked horrified."

"Oh, trust me—so did you." Tavah laughs at the ceiling.

"Or it could be that crazy glint in your eyes." I point,

leaning toward her. "It's making me second-guess my breaking and entering…"

"If Alli touches you, you'll definitely see my crazy."

"Then I hope she does. I'd love to see this crazy I've heard so much about. Maybe I should come around more often." I curl my toes in my shoes and smile, leaning my elbow on the back of the couch, resting my head in my hand.

"Maybe you should." Her smile ricochets off every shiny surface before splashing over me, making me shiver.

"Maybe I will." This is me, moving on. Or saying things that sound like I'm moving on.

"Yeah?" Her eyes roam my face.

"Yeah."

Her cheeks flush as a slow grin spreads across her face. "I guess wishes really do come true."

I glance at the ceiling, then back at her. "Be careful what you wish for." Because some wishes will never come true.

"I'm a very responsible wisher," she says, straightening. "Sometimes, I just skip the wish and make things happen."

"So, like, a proactive wisher?"

"Exactly like that. Remember lunch yesterday?"

"Uhh, yeah…think I can remember that far back." And also, how I couldn't stop staring when she smiled at me from across the table or how we'd leaned in to talk to each other and how my body responded to hers after being numb for months. "What about it?"

"Just thinking I could do that every day if you're available." Her voice is quiet and wispy, and I shift on the couch, looking down at her hand before catching her eye again.

"I'm in. Don't waste a wish on that."

Her fingers play with her necklace as we stare at each other. She's not Mei. She's nothing like her. Does that make it okay to like her? How long should I wait before I let myself feel things again?

Tavah's bright and beautiful. When I walk her to class or

work, I feel jealous when other guys check her out, but jealousy feels infinitely better than the other emotions I've experienced the last few months.

She smiles at me and points to my eyes. "There's something different in there tonight."

I wonder if she can read what's in my eyes; if so, we're on a new level, effective immediately. I want her to. I want anyone to understand me like Mei did. There are no distractions, no interruptions. I could tell her everything that led me to Berkeley and everything that's happened since. I swallow, study her face.

Or…I could keep it to myself for now so she doesn't freak when she finds out what a wreck my life is. If things get serious, I'll tell her. Maybe it isn't something she needs to know. I don't know what's happened in her most recent past. We're not on that level yet.

I can't right now. It's just not time yet. Besides, not sure it's possible to trade my Mei darkness for Tavah's light.

Tavah reaches over, plays with the hair at my neck, smiles. Like a searchlight. "What are you thinking right now?"

She can't read my thoughts so I should just tell her. Tell her. Tell her. Tell her.

I talk to our legs. "That…I'm…just glad you're around." I glance at her again, then play with the cushions. "Glad I decided to move into Johnny's and glad I was there that day you showed up."

"Yeah?" Her voice is higher, like it might be laced with a squeal.

"Yeah." I nod, meeting her eyes. "Really glad."

CHAPTER 8
MID-MAY

The kitchen table is loaded with food, and I've been up since 5AM making it that way. If I keep going, it'll sag in the middle from fruit and pastries, breakfast sandwiches and scallion pancakes. Chang Mama's been helping me between naps and even correcting some of my "American" habits, but she always does it with a laugh.

I like her; she's like Guo Mama, but even more mystical. She's been saying things in riddles in her thick Taiwanese Hokkien. My Nai-Nai used to talk to me in Taiwanese, and it always sounded like she was yelling even though I never saw her angry. So, when Chang Mama speaks in Taiwanese, it's like Nai-Nai is speaking through her, and I pretend it's true.

She's been telling me stories of Leo's childhood and how she practically raised him. As if hearing my thoughts, he breezes through the kitchen door, then stops, scanning the feast on the table, the crowded counters, Chang Mama, me.

"Did you turn my apartment into a restaurant?"

"Are you sad about it?"

He grins and holds up a hand. "If this is what happens every time I pull a graveyard, I'll pick up a few more."

I smile at the sizzling oil in the pan. "Your Nai-Nai is

helping me unlearn bad American cooking habits." I grab the spatula and move the scallion pancake to a plate then turn off the stove.

He leans back against the counter next to me, crossing his arms. "That doesn't surprise me. She's not shy about her opinions." He glances at her and Chang Mama rattles off a scolding in Taiwanese. She tsks her tongue but smiles at him before grabbing a plate of cut mangos and setting it on the table.

"Sit down and eat." I gesture to the waiting table setting and empty chair.

Leo shakes his head. "Mm-mm. The only way I eat breakfast is with company."

I haven't had an appetite since arriving in Taiwan, but if I don't sit and eat, he won't let it go. So I slide into the chair across from him as Chang Mama announces she has to get to the park for her exercise class and shuffles out the door.

"How was working all night long while everyone else slept?" I scoop a few mangos onto my plate to avoid thinking about what my mornings used to look like and who used to sit across from me after his graveyard shift, hair messy, eyes tired.

"Productive." Leo takes a bite of a breakfast sandwich and raises his eyebrows, nodding. "This is incredible." He continues to nod as he chews and swallows.

"How often do you work graveyards?"

He licks his lips. "Never. Unless I have to. And I had to." He takes another huge bite, talks around it. "Stake out."

"Oooh." I glance at him, popping a papaya chunk into my mouth. "Did you catch the bad guys?"

"Yep. They're officially booked and will spend lots of quality time behind bars." He downs a pancake in two bites. "Seriously Mei Li. How did you learn to cook like this, American or not?"

I smile. "My not-father owned a restaurant in San Francisco. I learned a lot in that kitchen. Then I took a culinary class. It just comes naturally to me. Probably the same way you are with your job. I'd love to own my own restaurant someday. Like a small café. One that isn't fronting a trafficking ring." I stop, press my lips together, pick at my sandwich. Leo pulls long-hidden sentiments out of me. Normally, I would hate it, but since he also knows all about my family's criminal history, it feels like a burden I share with him instead of carrying it alone. But talking drags up emotions and my head's already too crowded, my chest chronically tight.

Leo doesn't push further. Instead, he leans back, wipes his mouth before throwing the napkin on the table in surrender. "So, after catching the bad guys, I had this idea…"

He waits for me to ask for details but when I don't, continues.

"Why don't you spend the day with me where the bad guys don't like to go? I'd love to take you to one of my favorite places. If you're up for it."

———

Leo rented two bikes and we rode along the seashore, the warm sun beating against my skin. When he noticed I was tired, he found a shady, out of the way spot on the beach for us to relax. Right here, on this side of the world, I feel safe. It's been a long time since I've felt that way, and I breathe in the salty air and close my eyes as the breeze whispers across my face.

Sitting on the blanket Leo laid out, I stare out at the ocean that seems endless, but I know the truth: nothing lasts forever. Everything has its end. The water that looks so carefree now has slammed into sand and rocks, over and over again. It's changed direction and moved wherever the current takes it. I wonder where my side of the ocean meets Marcus's. And was the collision just as passionate as ours was? When the two oceans finally recede into themselves, do they feel the same loss that's been my steady companion since the current changed my course?

I glance at Leo where he sits next to me on the blanket, lost in his own thoughts I can't even begin to guess like I could Marcus's. "What are you thinking?" I ask.

He shakes his head and clears his throat. "Nothing. Just… glad you came today. This is one of my favorite places."

"What is this place, exactly? It's like a mixture of adorable beach town and artists paradise wrapped in old Taiwanese charm."

"Qijin Island."

"Do you bring all the women you save here?" I nudge his shoulder with mine.

"Only saved one, so…yes. Every time." He smiles at the blanket, his arms draped over his knees. "Coming here is supposed to give you good luck."

"Luck has never been on my side."

He picks up a smooth stone and tosses it into the lapping waves. "From what I know of you, it seems you've been very lucky."

"You don't know me very well."

He looks out over the ocean, avoiding eye contact. "What should I know?"

I stare at the waves, letting thoughts crash through my mind. There's just so many of them.

"Because," he says, pulling me from my thoughts, "if we're going to be friends, it would be great to know something about you."

"I think you've got plenty of friends."

"Can someone have too many friends?"

I shake my head and allow a weak smile despite the tugging in my chest.

"But actually, you're right—I already have too many friends. Guess I just want to see what it's like to spend time with a miserable, mysterious woman who wants to cook herself into oblivion to ignore whatever's going on in her head and make me gain 50 pounds. So, I become miserable, too, and then lose all my many, many friends."

"Then today really is your lucky day."

He laughs, deep and warm. "Guess so—first bad guys, then miserable girls. Think I get a medal for this day."

"You're forgetting breakfast." I smile at the ocean, the sun soaking into my skin and warming my whole body.

He turns toward me, his eyes serious. "Listen, Mei Li. For real. I need you to know something." Leo puts his palm on his chest and leans in. "There is absolutely no way I could ever forget the breakfast. And to repay you, I think it only fair I take you to dinner."

CHAPTER 9

LATE MAY

My shirt smells like Tavah after our lingering goodbye hug which could've turned into way more if Mei hadn't squeezed herself between us. It's like she was between us on the train ride home from the concert tonight, then standing and watching us in Tavah's living room until I lost the nerve to kiss her and left. The whole night I had kept Tavah close, flirted, talked so she wouldn't suspect anything, but I'm pretty sure she could tell I was off; she kept giving me sideways glances and playing with her hair.

I sigh and push away from the door I've been backed against, replaying the night. My ears are ringing from concert noise and my head is fuzzy and stretched, but all I know is that I'm sleeping in this shirt so I can smell Tavah all night. And maybe, if I'm lucky, I'll wake up with amnesia and won't remember Mei.

I walk toward the bathroom to get ready for bed, but my phone lights up and I glance at it, ready for whatever Tavah's text is gonna say. But it's my photo app, throwing its daily notification across my screen and in my face. It's decided that right now is the perfect time for a collage reel of Mei and me.

I curl my fingers, forbidding them to touch the screen, but my pointer finger goes rogue and swipes the notification. And just like that, with one picture, I'm back in Mei-Land. It's of us on our honeymoon like my phone is playing a cruel joke on me. Mei lying on her stomach, grinning at the camera. I can feel her skin on my fingertips and—no. Nope. Not doing this.

Still, I scroll through hundreds of videos—Mei running down the beach, smiling at me over her shoulder. Me, chasing her around a Redwood tree pretending to be Sasquatch. Videos of her doing her hair and makeup. Us, kissing and doing other stuff. I tap the screen so hard, I expect cracks.

The next video is an interview I filmed at the top of the Space Needle, asking her where she thought we'd be in ten years. She'd been very specific. She'd lied. There's one of her running from an aggressive duck at a pond near our apartment in Indiana, another of her sitting across from me, eating breakfast, her hair the closest thing to an Afro a Chinese girl could get.

The mini-series of her making dinner in only my button-up shirt, her hair piled on her head. I'd called it *'Makin' it with Mei'* and done step by step commentary while she'd laughed.

I hold my breath as I swipe through videos of her laughter and her random questions and reactions to everything that happened during our nine months together.

I swallow, breathing heavily like someone's holding me at gun point. I've been there and it's equally frightening because this was my life and I loved it.

I bend over, hands on my knees, eyes squeezed shut. I just need to hear her voice.

I click out of the photo app and into my voicemail and push play on the message she left the night of my last graveyard shift in Seattle. "I wish you were here with me instead of in a stupid warehouse full of stupid boxes so I thought I'd tell you what we'd be doing if you were home." I grip the phone, picturing the smile that laces her words. "So close your eyes…are you closing them? I'll know if you're peeking…"

I end the torture. I don't need to hear it again; I have it memorized. She'd gone on for two more minutes, detailing what a typical night had looked like for us. I swipe at my face and straighten, clutch my chest, and let misery crash over me until I bolt for the bathroom and drop to my knees in front of the toilet, puking up emotion.

Yanking on the shower, I crank the heat and step in, letting the steady stream burn stripes into my skin. I grimace, then turn the water hotter. I will scrub her off my skin, layer by layer. Steam her out of me.

I scrub every inch of my body, furious and desperate. The heat in the bathroom is suffocating and my head's fuzzy, but I blink it away, determined to finish the job. Weak and shaky, I shut off the water and step out of the shower, fumbling through Johnny's cabinets. He has hair clippers here somewhere.

The cool metal is a relief, and I grip the clippers in my hand, set to work on my hair. I have to get rid of anything Mei touched. Anything that existed while she existed.

When I'm done, I don't recognize myself. My hair's been shaggy and wayward as long as I can remember. Mei said she likes it that way. She's gone, and so is the guy she knew. Here's the new version—the one who will live without her. New hair will grow, never knowing what it's like to have her fingers run through it.

———

When I open the apartment door, I unbutton my shirt as I step inside but stop when I see Johnny and Lin sitting on the couch playing a video game. Immediate exit strategies flash through my head because I hate seeing them together.

"Sup, Miller?" He doesn't take his eyes off the screen.

"Hey." Guess I'm gonna skip doing homework here and go straight to Tavah's to avoid Lin. Feels like Mei sent a spy to watch my every move and Lin does a great job of it; she's a human microscope with a really big mouth that doesn't actually know what it's saying.

I put my backpack on the table, rifle through it and pull out the wad of cash from tips I need to deposit. Everything in my backpack smells like grilled onions and I go to the kitchen for the Febreze.

"May I have a word, sir?"

My head snaps up from where I'm bent to pull the spray bottle from under the sink. Lin leans against the counter, arms folded. Her blue eye makeup makes her eyes look like a stuffed animal, but I know she's not that innocent and cuddly.

"Uhh, sure...what's up?" I focus on the bottle as I walk toward my backpack.

"In private," she says, following me.

I glance over my shoulder, hesitate, then set the bottle on the table. "Okay...like, outside or...?"

"Sure. Yeah." She points toward the door, then walks, and I follow her, tossing a glance at Johnny who's yelling at the TV.

When the apartment door closes, she steps across the hall, leans against the wall, crosses her arms again and pins me with her glare. "I know what you're doing with Tavah. And I also know what you used to do with Mei Li. Those two things don't work together."

I stare at her, then visually sweep the hallway. Someone burned dinner and there's a haze drifting along the ceiling. "Uhh...okay...not sure it's any of your—"

"I was at your wedding. You can pretend you aren't married, but Johnny knows the truth, and you definitely know. I only hope with all my soul that you haven't done all the things with Tavah you did with Mei Li, if you know what I mean."

I squint at the dingy carpet, tilting my head because her words tip me off balance. Maybe I should just tell her about Mei. Rip off the band-aid so we can both be raw and bleeding. At least I wouldn't be the only one feeling this way. But I can't say it out loud. To anyone but especially to Lin. "I get you're Mei's best friend, but I don't really want or need to have this conversation with you."

She plays with her earring, and I hold my breath, afraid she's gonna drop information that will end me.

"I might be the only one at this point holding onto hope that she'll be back, but I'm still her best friend and feel like it's my duty to stick up for her."

She doesn't know there's no point in hoping. I could tell her now and save her the extra dose of pain when she finds out.

"She loves you. I don't know why she left or where she went, but I'm sure she had a reason."

I turn to open the door, but she steps toward me.

"I haven't said what I need to say."

I stare down at her and her eyes falter for a second before meeting mine again. I haven't told her what I need to tell her, either. I can't. Feels like I'm making it all up so I can move on with my life. And I wish I was.

"I get you want to move on. I get you're hurt. I am, too. I don't know why she cut us both out of her life, but this isn't the first time she's done this to me. Remember how she dated you secretly and didn't tell me for weeks? Or how she'd spend all her extra time with you when it used to be me? Or what about the months of silence while you two went wher-ever you went? She had a good reason for leaving me then, and I know she has one now. I wish she'd tell us what it is but, in the meantime, I need you to know that if you don't tell

Tavah you're married, I will. Tavah's become a really good friend of mine, and she deserves to know."

I close my eyes, swear under my breath, look down the hall over Lin's head as her threat crawls up me. "You don't even know half of what happened with Mei so don't make any of this messier than it already is."

I turn the doorknob and walk through the door as she calls, "Tell her or I will."

A scream is gathering in my chest the longer I sit in Leo's apartment. I want it to drown the voices in my head and the things they whisper. Like that I'd be better off not existing or that all the darkness I feel would vanish if I would just sink into it and let it consume me. Kitchen knives and scissors constantly glint in my peripheral vision. I thought these ideas would go away if I stayed at Leo's, but they've stretched out, settled in, and grown louder, bolder, more persistent. They've become plans.

I grab the magazine on Leo's coffee table and flip through it, frantic for another image to drop into my head and shove out the dark ones.

Leo's apartment was a sanctuary while I was healing. I'd done a pretty good job of not thinking and keeping my eyes wide open since I no longer see Marcus's smile when I close them. I've kept busy with cooking, cleaning, and talking with Chang Mama, who has become my Taiwanese Guo Mama. But today, she's helping a friend, and I've already cooked, cleaned, and paced and it's not enough; fear and worst-case scenarios crowd my head, spill over into the room.

I take a deep, shaky breath, let it out. The magazine is a

smear of color, and I wish that the colors would arrange into the scenery of my old life. I'd give anything if they'd settle into snow falling outside our Indiana apartment window or Marcus and I lying together with Charlie purring beside us. But I'm still in Leo's apartment, clutching this magazine so desperately I've crinkled the pages, the words and pictures a squirming mass, twisting around itself.

My eyes linger on the scars on my wrists, still raised and puffy as a constant reminder of how close I came to not being in this apartment or anywhere. I blink, swallow, shift in my chair and concentrate harder as I flip the pages until I stop on a picture of a monkey perched on a boardwalk, an apple in its mouth and a human-sized backpack in its hands. I mentally translate the caption: "Do not feed the monkeys."

The article features a place nicknamed Monkey Mountain and outlines a full day of activities and hiking. I have a full day. I have endless, empty days.

I grab the extra phone Leo's letting me borrow and call his cell number. He answers on the second ring. "You okay?"

"What are you doing right now?" I pin the phone between my ear and shoulder as I skim pictures of monkeys.

"Snowboarding, obviously." His voice smiles at me and I smile back.

"Makes sense since there's snow everywhere." I glance out the window at the steamy sunlight melting over the tops of buildings, picturing him in his office across the city. He's probably leaned back in his chair, his hand resting on the back of his head like it does when he's relaxed.

"Indeed. What are you doing right now, besides making snow angels?" he asks.

"Thinking."

"About...?"

"Monkeys."

Leo's deep laugh vibrates against my ear. "You will never

believe this, but I also was just thinking about monkeys. Just now, before you called."

My smile stretches my face, stiff from being tense for weeks. "Then that's perfect. You'll know exactly where I could find some."

"As a matter of fact, I know just the place. And I happen to personally know the only tour guide you can trust. Unfortunately...he's snowboarding right now so..."

"So maybe when it stops snowing, you can ask the number-one tour guide if he's available?"

A smile lifts his voice. "Actually, I think I feel a warm front moving in. I'll tell him and he'll be at the apartment in thirty minutes."

———

"His bare bum is on my lap. And it's warm. Way too warm and squishy," I shriek. After hiking up a thousand wooden steps surrounded by tall, lanky trees, we finally made it to the top of the trail. On the way up, the monkeys were cute; we passed mama monkeys with adorable babies holding onto them and giant monkeys perched on tree limbs, far enough away they didn't seem menacing. None of them acted scared of us, so I wasn't scared of them. Until three minutes ago when I sat on this bench to catch my breath, and this monkey plopped down on my lap. He's staring at my face and obviously doesn't understand personal space. I wonder if this is the worst idea I've ever had, but at least I'm filling my head and time with these things so I don't think about others.

Leo is turned toward me on the bench, laughing and holding up his hands like he's helpless and I want to punch him.

"If you get him off me, I'll give you whatever you want. I promise."

He laughs more, wipes his eyes, then composes himself

and gently nudges my stubborn companion off my lap. The monkey scurries away and I stand, brushing off my leggings.

"That was terrifying." I pick off stubbly hairs and shudder. "And so gross."

"I don't know what the big deal is. All you had to say was, 'shoo.'" Leo shrugs and I punch him.

He dodges my fist the second time, smiling down at me. "You ready to go back the thousands of steps we just climbed? Or we can stay up here with the monkeys who quite possibly think you're either their mother or...something else..."

"See you at the car!" I call over my shoulder as I hurry down the steps, his laughter trailing me.

Leo catches up and we walk side by side in silence, concentrating so we don't trip and roll down the mountain. He's completely comfortable with silence. There wasn't much of it with Marcus and it's usually my enemy, but with Leo, silence is reassuring and safe. As long as he's next to me. When he's not, the voices, thoughts, and memories overtake me, paralyze my reasoning until I'm afraid of what I might do to myself again. But it's like fear and panic don't dare come around him.

When we make it back to his car, Leo opens the passenger door for me, and I slide inside. I sip my water bottle, as he rounds the car to the driver's side, but he stops at his door and pulls his phone from his pocket, glancing at the screen, then answering.

I can barely hear the inflection in his voice, but his words are clipped, serious. He turns into Detective Chang before my eyes, and I wonder what the person on the other end is saying. I need to open my door and let in air, but don't dare, in case the call is confidential.

Leo shakes his head at the ground, his fingers pinching the bridge of his nose as he listens to whatever the other person is saying. He fires back a response, pauses, and listens again until he slaps his palm against the car roof, leaning against the driver's side door and talking over the car.

I tense, focusing on the car parked in front of us, until Leo straightens, jabs at the screen, and shoves his phone in his pocket. He turns his back to the car, waiting a few thumping heartbeats before sliding into the driver's seat.

"Everything okay?" I ask, my words crackly and dry.

"Yeah." He swallows, and his jaw pulses as he puts the car in reverse.

"You sure? You kind of don't seem okay."

He pauses, then throws the car in park and turns toward me in his seat. "I just found out Nick Chao is in Taiwan."

My stomach lurches so violently, I put a hand over it. "Like where exactly?"

"He was flagged in Taipei three days ago, but we lost his trail. Now he could be anywhere." He runs his hand through his hair and down his face. "My guys have been following leads, and every single one has ended with nothing. Now we've got to watch the whole island."

I glance at my trembling hands clasped so tightly in my lap they ache.

"There is one lead that could be promising. But I'm not sure I want to follow it."

My eyes snap to his. "Why not?"

He taps the steering wheel, looking out the windshield as he talks. "Because it involves you."

"What do you mean? How?"

"I mean…I've been avoiding asking you this for weeks, but this might be our only shot at finding Nick and putting him away for good."

"Whatever it is, I'll do it. I want him behind bars more than anyone." Hope flickers before the dread on Leo's face snatches it.

He shakes his head. "Mr. Zhang told us he knows how to find him, and he'll give us the information on one condition."

Leo closes his eyes, and I'm not sure I want him to say anything else. But he continues, ready or not. "If you'll go see him in prison."

Blood drains from my face, and I turn forward in my seat like the windshield will help me understand what exactly Leo is saying.

"The problem is, you're supposed to be dead."

I snap my head toward him. "What?"

He nods, his eyes skittering from me to the window behind me, out the windshield, back to me. "When we put you in hiding, we created a fake death certificate for Mei Li Zhang so we could work our case without Nick looking for you. The hit on you would go away and you would be safe."

My mouth goes dry and my breath lodges in my throat when I try to swallow this news. Dead. Not alive. Non-existent. "Why didn't you tell me?"

His eyes are intent on mine. "I didn't think it was necessary. It would have only been a matter of time before Nick showed up on our radar again. And once we caught him, the death certificate could be deleted from all our systems." He shakes his head at his lap. "I'm so sorry I didn't tell you. We thought it would be over by now."

"So that's why you haven't been worried about me going places with you?" I search his face. "Because, legally, I don't exist."

He swallows and nods. "Yes. Except, when I went to see Mr. Zhang and showed him your death certificate, he didn't believe it was real. He told me I better figure out how to bring you back to life if I want information, because his conditions were that he'll give us what we want for one conversation with you."

EARLY JUNE

My first week of classes felt like a fresh start and so does the person waiting for me on the other side of campus.

Tavah texted the secret meeting location during class, and my focus bolted toward it. Berkeley has crazy good energy and the classes I'm taking are making me use parts of my brain that have been dormant for months. And Tavah? She's consuming my life, making me feel things that have been just as dormant since Mei left.

I run my fingers through my hair, and there's so much less of it. Maybe a little less of the old me, too. When I showed up at Tavah's with my new haircut, she'd smiled, then told me she loved it because she can see my eyes better now. I smile just thinking about her hands in my hair. Or maybe from thinking about how her eyes sparkle when we're close. Or her quirky, brilliant brain. Or that I never, ever have to guess what she's thinking or feeling; she just tells me. If only I were that brave. I'm too afraid to admit to myself how I'm feeling because I don't know what any of this means or if it's okay to feel things for someone who isn't Mei. The more of Tavah's warmth I soak in, the more it burns out the cold, stale stuff. I think less about Mei and want Tavah more every time we're together—every time I read one of her texts or hear her voice or see her smile at me. I don't stop myself from thinking about kissing her. Going full Tavah might fill all my dark holes.

My phone buzzes and I pull it from my pocket, reading as I walk.

> Tavah: Remember a year ago, on Stanford's soccer field? When I interrupted your alone time and told you things I never should have told you? And—AND—do you remember how I said I'd work on getting over you? I changed my mind when you opened Johnny's apartment door four months ago. Just thought you should know.

I smile and take longer strides to get to her faster, take a shortcut, break into a jog. I round the corner of the building, our meeting place within sight at the end of the walkway but stop when I see her standing on the steps, talking to some guy who's so obviously into her. He's too close and leaning in too much not to be interested.

Fear pours into my chest, and it goes cold. I can't lose Tavah to this guy. Or any guy.

I veer off the sidewalk, take another path so I can get closer without her seeing me.

"What do you think?" The guy squints in the afternoon sun and shrugs. "You up for it? I've wanted to ask you out for awhile, and now I've got a pretty good reason."

Whoa. My body tenses. Maybe I'm not officially her boyfriend but this guy most definitely wants to take the title. No way that's happening.

She glances around, smooths her hair. "Ummm…here's the thing, Andrew…" She puts her hand on his arm. "I would have loved to a few months ago but…I'm…"

I hold my breath, and she scans the air behind the guy, a

smile slipping onto her face. "I'm kind of dating someone. It's new, but I want to see where it goes, so I'm sorry, but I just want to be honest with you and with him."

Yesss. Title's all mine. I round the building, stride across the grass toward her, gripping my backpack strap like it's a brake, but my brain tells my legs to not stop until my mouth is on hers.

Tavah glances around and sees me, her eyes widening, her smile stretching toward me. Andrew follows her focus, and when she turns toward me, my smile breaks loose.

"Hey, gorgeous," I say, sliding one hand around her waist, the other resting on her hip, pulling her body against mine before my lips find hers.

Tavah tenses, then sinks into me and slides her arms around my neck. The heat from her body makes me light-headed, and I hold her so tightly, our stomachs move against each other as we breathe.

She runs her fingers up the back of my neck, into my short hair, and she presses closer. Our lips explore each other, my teeth lightly grazing hers as I hold her neck with both hands, my thumb caressing her jawline. Adrenaline and hormones pour through me, running loose. She tastes better than I imagined and my body, which I thought had shut down, has definitely not.

I surface when Andrew slips past us. Guess he knows who Tavah's dating. Guess I do too. If it feels this good to kiss her, imagine how good it'll feel to—

A memory of Mei tangled in sheets covered in sharpie messages bursts into my thoughts. My stomach twists, and panic surges up my throat, comes out as words when I pull away. "I'm so sorry, Tavah," I blurt, my face hot, body suddenly ice cold. "That was…I'm so, *so* sorry. Seriously— that was not how it was supposed to happen." I swallow and step back, shove my hands in my pockets.

But the apology isn't really meant for Tavah—it's meant for Mei.

"That was terrible timing," I say, talking to the cement steps and squeezing my eyes closed. I swallow crackling guilt and embarrassment that fizzes into nausea. "You deserve better."

Tavah's hand slides to the side of my neck. "Marcus, no way. That was—"

"No." I shake my head. "That was stupid. I gotta go. I—" Panicked, I look around, half expecting to see Mei, but it's only me, standing in a quicksand pit of emotions. "I'm sorry, Tavah," I say, turning so I can break into a run. "Call you later."

———

I have thirty minutes to get home, get changed for work, and mentally beat myself bloody for kissing Tavah then running. She should go out with Andrew and forget about me. I should tell her why she should forget about me, but I'm pretty sure she knows now just how messed up I am.

I cut through the train station, but someone calls my name, and I glance over my shoulder, scanning the crowd. It wasn't Tavah's voice, but I don't see anyone I recognize, so I keep walking, dodging people stepping off the train until I hear my name again and, this time, the voice sounds a whole lot like Audrey.

I turn toward her as she darts around a group of students and walks up to me. Her green stilettos scare me, but not as much as the intensity in her eyes that's about to explode all over me, and I'm barely holding it together as it is.

I scan the arrival board like it will tell me why she came all the way over here but snap my eyes to her when she stops in front of me, her face flushed.

"Hey…?" I grip my backpack straps and glance around before looking back at her. "What are you doing here?"

"I talked to Ray last night."

"Okay…" I search her face. "Is he alright? I was just texting him a few hours ago and he seemed fine…?"

"Yeah. He's fine." She swallows and nods. "He's fine, but he told me something that kept me up all night, and I picked up my phone a hundred times to call you but decided this is an in-person conversation."

"Am I in trouble for bailing on lunch yesterday?"

"No, Marcus." She rests her hand on the side of my arm. "Of course not. Definitely not."

I glance around the train station, scratch my neck. "Why did you come all the way over here? Aren't you supposed to be at work right now?"

"I couldn't concentrate on work."

I don't respond because I have to grit my teeth when waves of nausea from what just happened with Tavah combine with straight-up terror about whatever Drey's about to launch at me.

"Ray told me about Mei Li."

Her words slam against my brain and spin it until I have to close my eyes because now my chest is splitting open again. I swear under my breath.

"I'm so sorry, Marcus." She wraps me in a hug before I can step back and run from her compassion that does nothing but pick at the oozing Mei scab.

She squeezes tighter, and I stiffen. I wish Dad hadn't told her, and then I'm glad he did and feel bad I didn't. I just don't wanna talk about it right now when I've got newer problems I just created by kissing Tavah.

Audrey pulls away, tears quivering in the corners of her eyes, and I look away, over her head at people rushing toward or away from the trains squealing into the station.

"I had no idea, Marcus, and I'm so sorry if you didn't feel like you could tell me."

"I haven't told anyone, Drey." My voice squeezes through my tight throat. "Only Dad knows. He's the one who told me."

"No one knows? Not Johnny? Or Tavah?"

I shake my head. "No. I don't wanna talk about it. I can't."

She blinks at me, her shoulders sagging. "How are you handling this, then? I mean…this is life's hardest stuff. I was headed to your apartment because I just wanted you to know that I'm here for you. You can talk about anything, anytime. Call me at 3 in the morning, I don't care. Just don't do this alone. Please."

"There's nothing to do, Drey. She's gone and I can't change it."

"Yes, there is. Grieving is emotional torture when you go it alone, so I'm mostly here to tell you that I'll grieve with you. What happened is awful."

I shake my head and laugh once. "If only I knew what happened."

She watches me. "I know you're devastated and confused and probably angry, Marky, so—"

"How do you know anything about what I'm feeling?"

She straightens, her jaw set as she shifts from compassion to indignation. "Because I've lost someone close to me, too. My best friend? High school? Yeah, I get this whole loss thing. And I know you and know you never do anything halfway. Including feeling things. So I'm here to prove that I'm here for you, and you can be as mad at me as you want. Sometimes it just feels good to be mad, but when you're ready to talk, I'm here. Anytime. You can tell me anything. Everything you wish you could tell her but can't. You can throw it all at me."

I release a frustrated sigh. "I'm not mad at you, Drey." I shake my head. "I'm just…" Swallowing, I rake my hand through what's left of my hair, my eyes scanning the station.

"I'm mad at myself. I don't know." I talk to my feet now. "I don't know what I am right now except so messed up."

"Yeah. Makes sense." She nods and shifts her bag on her shoulder. "Wanna go grab some food and talk?"

I shake my head. "Can't."

"Because you don't want to talk about this or because you actually can't?"

"Because I have work in twenty minutes."

Now she glances around the station, nods. "Okay, then, ummm…will you call me later? I'd like to hear things from you instead of Ray. And I want to help you through this so we can have the old Marcus back."

I close my eyes. "Yeah, I want the old me back, too, Drey, but that's never gonna happen, because he's gone, too. So this is what's left. Not awesome, I get it, but I can't change what happened no matter how much I wish I could."

Audrey presses her lips together and reaches for my hand. "Sorry to upset you. Just wanted you to know that I'm here for you."

I wish it was Mei telling me she was sorry she upset me, and that she's here, but Audrey's words smother the small fire that blazes every time I have to talk about Mei, and I nod too many times. "I know. It means a lot that you came all the way over here. And I'll call you later. Promise."

"And maybe lunch this week? Now that you don't have to hide from me?"

I give a weak laugh because hauling laughter up through Mei hurt feels like manual labor. "Yeah. Lunch on you sounds great."

"Name the place and time, and I'll be there. With tissues."

CHAPTER 12
EARLY JUNE

When I think about how I want to spend my day, this is far from it. Yet, despite trying to outrun this moment, here I am. The last resort. There really is no other way to get the information to find Nick and take him down. All other leads are dead as am I, apparently, and I'm left with no other option but to trade my pride and bottled-up pain for a face-to-face with the man who sold me to a criminal.

It's only ten minutes of my life, but what we could get in return could change my future. Better yet, it could give me one. I'll talk to the man who did a terrible job of pretending to be my father and get the information about Nick's location. Simple. And when Nick's behind bars, and I have my passport and Visa, I'll allow myself to hope that Marcus will someday forgive me.

I close my eyes. I'm not sure which will be harder: getting information about Nick or getting Marcus's forgiveness.

Leo pulls the car up to the gate. He's been quiet the whole ride here, which isn't unusual, but it's left too much time to think and rehearse my next, dreaded steps. I grabbed Leo's hand on the drive here, to transfer some of his calm to me. He keeps squeezing my hand, reassuring me that I can do this while my insides churn in an internal typhoon.

Leo rolls down his window, shows his badge to the officer who says something into his handheld radio, and a few seconds later, the gates squeal open. There's no turning back now.

I'm not going to pretend it's going to be a warm greeting or a pleasant conversation; months ago, when I called the police and spilled everything about Nick, I put 'Mr. Zhang' here. He'll try and get back at me somehow.

"This will all be over in no time," Leo says, gently responding to my thoughts. "And if at any moment you want to leave, we leave, with or without information."

Nodding, I breathe through the fear that's coiled in my legs, ready to lend them energy if I run. *You can do this*, I tell myself on repeat as Leo pulls to a stop. He doesn't turn off the engine, doesn't get out. His eyes are fixed ahead as if he might just put the car in reverse and back out the way we came.

"Mei, I am so—"

"This is my choice." My words come out more assured than I feel, and Leo turns to face me as I continue. "I have every reason to not be here right now, except one. This could be what brings Nick down and my ticket home. I have to do this."

Leo nods and shuts off the car, and then we're getting out, walking through gates and security turnstiles. We pass guards with weapons strapped across their chests, then through more bars meant to keep the monsters inside so the rest of us are safe, but I'm choosing to walk right in and face one of the worst.

A guard speaks to Leo in Mandarin, but I hear only my heart beating. After a thorough security search, we follow the guard until he stops in front of another heavy, steel door. I take a deep breath, because once this door opens, I'll be on the other side of it until I have the information I need to get home.

My stomach clenches so violently, I might throw up, and I take an unsteady step back. Leo grabs my hand, keeping me steady, then turns me to face him. "One word and this is over."

I nod, and the door grinds open. I'm ushered into a large, open room filled with small, square tables. Halfway across it, a man sits at one of the tables, his hands secured by handcuffs to a metal pipe bolted to the floor. I almost don't recognize him. It's like he's aged twenty years since I last saw him—the night he watched as Chaz led me to a car, and he and Xander drove me to the airport and walked me onto a plane that would take me to L.A. and Nick's attack. He let it all happen, so I'm going to let all of this happen to him without guilt.

His skin is pale, and when I approach the table, his eyes lock on mine, a smile twitching on his lips. He may not look the same, but the cold smile and indifference is all his.

"Mei Li," he says, his voice deep, rough. "It's good to see you. Alive." His laugh is guttural, full of deep darkness.

I step closer, then slide onto the small bench bolted to the table across from him. I lean back, keeping as much distance between us as possible.

"What? Not even a smile for your baba?" He laughs weakly. "After all you've done to me, I should at least get that."

"You are not my baba." My voice is hard and hollow. "You deserve nothing from me or anyone else."

"We'll see."

I can't tell if his words are threatening, but I don't care—I just want this to be over, so I straighten. "Why did you want to see me?"

"Would you believe I missed you?"

"No."

He leans in, resting his elbows on the table, cuffed wrists

clinking, but before he can say anything else, I set my jaw and ask again, "Why am I here?"

His eyes trap mine. "Because you took a lot from me. My life in San Francisco, my business, my wife." His words are a growl. "One minute I am on top of the world, and the next…" He tries to raise his shackled hands, but the chains pull them back down.

"I didn't make the choices that brought you here. That was all you."

"Yes, well, you and I know my being here was a combination of others' decisions, and I'm paying the price for them." He tilts his head and clenches his fists still in restraints. "Why is that?"

"Maybe you should ask Nick. He seems to get out of every bad thing he's ever done." I stare at him. "But maybe you should also be more careful about who you associate with."

He clenches his jaw, his feelings about Nick hardening as he speaks. "He made me his fall guy," he spits. "We were both in jail, sharing the blame. And then he was out, and I was out of the country."

"How did he get out?"

"Find the owner of the diamonds, and you'll have your answer."

I shake my head. "What is that supposed to mean?"

He sneers at me, blinks, his arm muscles rigid as they protest against the handcuffs. "While I am not your real father, I raised you smarter than that."

I clench my jaw and wait, hoping information will slip out on the edge of his cutting words.

"Nick is owned by men far more powerful than I am. Far more powerful and in much higher places, I assure you. The diamonds trace back to them, and Nick will do anything to save himself. Even if that means making sure you're really dead."

"How high up is his involvement?" I ask, but he just

stares, so I veer the conversation toward my other questions. "You got me here, and while I've thoroughly enjoyed this little chat, you promised information." He's silent too long for my limited patience so I push the conversation. "I should have known you wouldn't—"

"Here." He opens his fist to reveal a crumpled slip of paper, and I glance at him, then the paper before snatching it, like his fist will close and trap me. I unfold the paper, my eyes scanning a phone number.

"Who said I never followed through on a promise?"

I stand and look over my shoulder for Leo, ready to leave.

"I'm not doing it for you." He shakes his head at the table. "You were always worthless to me, just like your mama." He slowly raises his head, his eyes hard. "And one day, when I am out, I will find you both and make you regret the day you ruined my life."

My back tenses, my throat swells, but I swallow as I stare into his darkness. "Then I'll make sure you never get out of here."

CHAPTER 13

EARLY JUNE

put all my instruments and bins inside my lab locker, then wash my hands before grabbing my phone from my backpack and dropping into a chair. I haven't seen or talked to Tavah for a couple days. Since the incident on the steps. We've texted a little, but I've pretended to be crazy busy with work and labs because I don't know how to say what I need to say. My last text to her said I wanted to talk to her in person, and I'm hoping by the time that happens, I'll be able to explain why I was so weird about the kiss. I'm so messed up, and I'm messing her up too. I wasn't planning on kissing her like that. But man...I did. For awhile. And it was so good. Then I ran. Classic. Guess Mei and I have that in common.

I've wrestled Mei thoughts every night and every night, I've shoved them behind a steel door in my head, bolted it before replaying the five-minute Tavah kiss. She's...decisive with her mouth. She knows what she wants, and she knows how to get me to give it to her. I wanna do it again. A lot. But I have to tell her everything about who I am and why I'm here and where I've been. It's part of me now, and being honest with her is the right move, just not sure how.

I click on my phone to a screen covered in Tavah, just like my mind has been.

> Tavah: I have to know if that kiss was so bad that you had to run away? You've been too quiet and conveniently too busy to talk. Is everything okay and by everything I mean are we okay?

My stomach twists, wishing it could run away from the messed-up owner of its body who's hurting Tavah. Our kiss was definitely not bad. Been thinking about it nonstop.

> Tavah: Call me please? Not sure if I should be offended or worried. I'm currently both. It's a terrible combination. I feel stupid but I don't know why.

I close my eyes, mad at myself that she thinks this has anything to do with her instead of being all my problem.

> Tavah: We should talk Marcus. I'm trying not to be a weird-insecure girl, but it's kind of happening since you haven't been acting normal since we kissed. I didn't expect it to happen right then, but I definitely didn't expect the silence afterward, either, so call me, okay?

I swallow and clench my phone, screen face-down on my thigh. I know what I need to say, but I keep creating bigger problems because I can't control my emotions. Wonder what my life would look like if I figured out how to do that. I'd be at Stanford. Never would've left with Mei. Never would've dated her, fallen completely in love with her.

I settle back in the chair, stare at the gray lockers, clench my jaw. Think about the Tavah kiss again. That was me, diving headfirst into her, but I'm not who she thinks I am.

Crazy thing is, kissing Tavah made it feel like I could be anything she wants me to be. Like we cliff-jumped into pure electricity.

I close my eyes, replay the moment until Mei slips in and crushes all of it. I turn my phone over, stare at the screen again before rolling my neck and dialing Tavah's number.

The other end rustles and she whispers, "Hold on." A few seconds later, a door shuts and the background noise fades. "Marcus." She breathes my name in relief. "I've been dying to hear your voice." The edge of her words are ragged, like she's been saying them over and over in her head, and I hate myself a little more

I swallow. "Sorry, T. I've been in the lab working on a huge project and…I wasn't sure how to say sorry again for kissing you like that."

"You're sorry? Umm, okay. I mean, I was a little… *surprised*, yeah, but…" Her pause stretches through the phone. "I'm not sorry. Sorry alludes to regret so…do you regret it? Because if you do, then—"

"No!" The word bursts out of me. That's not the issue. It's the guilt that pushed and shoved its way between us. "No. Definitely not. It was just…not how I would've kissed you for the first time, and I was afraid I scared you. Or embarrassed you."

"So…that's not what being scared or embarrassed feels like in my experience. But your distance definitely scared me." She pauses and her phone rustles before she continues. "I mean, yeah, I wasn't completely sure about our status before that, but I have a pretty good idea now. At least I think so? I just need to hear it from you, I think. Because if I'm right, I'd say…our first kiss had zero elements of wrong. It was pretty perfect, actually. 12 out of 10. Would've broken the scale if you'd stuck around. But I don't want to talk about this over the phone. Are you still in the lab?"

"Yeah."

"Headed your way. Not even dead people can keep me away from you."

I forget how to breathe as I stare at the polished cement floor between my shoes and almost choke when I inhale. She has no idea that a dead person is keeping me from her, and it's not my sixty-three-year-old stroke victim on the lab table. I can't tell her about Mei. But I have to. I want to be next to Tavah, kissing her, reassuring her and myself. Mei's never, ever coming back, so why does she keep slipping between us? Why do I let her? If I had taken the Tavah road after prom and not gone to Guo's shop and found Mei, my life would be straightforward and easy. Tavah and I would be spending days at school and nights all over each other. There wouldn't be a past between us.

"You still there?" Tavah asks, pulling me back to the conversation.

"Yeah. Still here." I sit up straight in the chair, stand.

"You should know that I'm so serious about you that I'm skipping out on the very relevant topic of medieval land ownership in class, so I'll have to study later since I definitely need to know that."

"Add that to my list of things I'm sorry about."

"The only thing you should be sorry about is making me worry for the last three days. And costing me a pretty hot Friday night date with Andrew. Who was probably even more surprised than I was."

"Still sorry but not to Andrew." A smile breaks through the storm in my head. "My Friday night plans can beat up his any day."

"Do those Friday night plans include me?"

"Only you." *Please go away like you wanted to, Mei.*

"Your lips kind of told me that, but I didn't want to assume. But I'll clear my schedule. How about some pre-Friday plans, though? Like tonight?"

I smile at the floor, take a deep breath, then glance up and nod to a guy as he walks into the lab. "I'll have to tear myself away from this sixty-three-year-old stroke victim I've been spending my days with. But she didn't even offer to buy me dinner or breakfast, so…"

"May she rest in peace."

I stretch, then walk toward the lab to clear the last of my assignment. "You here yet?"

"Almost. I'm walking fast."

"I like fast-walking girls."

"I'd love to hear more about what you like about them."

"I only like the fastest."

"Oh! Perfect. I'm the fastest, and I like tall, hot guys who hang out with dead ladies by day and fast-walking girls by night."

"There's one tall, mildly decent looking, messed up guy that likes that fast-walking girl. Maybe more than likes." I almost choke on the dust from the words screeching out of me. No. I can't say that. I don't even think I have enough left in me to love someone again. That was too much. Too far, too fast. But was it? Past or not, I want Tavah. Are there rules about timelines after your wife leaves and dies? Because I know how to love someone and given enough time, I could love someone again. Right now, I want it to be Tavah.

When I push through the lab doors, warm sun streams down on me. But there's something even brighter headed my way, grinning and glowing. She jogs the rest of the way to me, her bag bouncing against her hip.

She stops when we're toe to toe. "Did you mean what you just said?" Her eyes are searching, wide, all-seeing,

I did mean it. I'm falling hard for Tavah. I know what it feels like and recently, I lost my grip on whatever I was clinging to. I'm free-falling toward her and can't crawl back up the slide, because there's too much trailing me; it's all gonna plow into her. I'm gonna hurt her.

"Yeah. I meant it, even if nothing with you is happening

like I want it to. Words just come out of my mouth, and I do things I—"

Her lips are on mine, her hand sliding around the back of my neck, steady, confident, holding us together. She's beautiful. Our days together are easy and rooted, bright. I'm not afraid when I'm with her. Everything flows. I don't have to wonder what she thinks or feels. She's a surge of energy every single time I'm with her.

My hands pull her closer, and I deepen the kiss. She dives with me as we explore new levels of each other, making my head fuzzy with the depth or altitude or wherever we are. My hand drifts to her lower back, holds her close.

"I've completely fallen in love with you," she breathes, her eyes closed, our noses resting against each other. "It was the easiest thing I've ever done."

We stand beside the door, holding each other, the air relaxing around us from the currents we just sent through it. Realization trickles through my chest and my hands flex, but I'm so tired of being desperate and afraid just because Mei left me with a gaping hole full of guilt and unanswered questions.

I pull Tavah even closer. I could've lost her because I was letting Mei interfere. It's not gonna happen again.

Tavah's mouth is on my ear. "I want to continue this riveting conversation our lips just had, but it'll have to be tonight, because I have to get back to Medieval land owner-ship. But before I go…" She pulls back, her smile washing my world in light. "I have something for you. I was going to give it to you later but can't wait." She steps back and reaches into her bag, pulling out an envelope. She holds it toward me, grinning.

I search her face as I take it, then lift the flap, pull out a birthday card, glancing at her before I open it.

Marcus + Tavah (and friends) + weekend in Vegas = happy birthday to me

"Are you serious?" I ask, still staring at the card.

She nods. "So serious. I'm giving myself the weekend with you and friends in Vegas for my birthday. I mean…if you're okay with that. But…" She smiles at the sky before meeting my eyes again. "You should probably be okay with it because that's what I asked my parents for my birthday. My dad gave me a bunch of frequent flyer miles and hotel points so all you have to do is come and make all my birthday wishes come true. And maybe kiss me a few more times."

I nod slowly.

She tilts her head. "I'm sensing hesitation…"

"No—sounds awesome, actually. There's just…no way my birthday gift for you could ever compete."

"You missed the part where I said *you* are my birthday gift." She wiggles her eyebrows. She loves making me uncomfortable. Every time I get uncomfortable, I spill a little more and she's learning a lot about me. Except for the thing she needs to know. But now I have a deadline to say goodbye to Mei for good.

CHAPTER 14

EARLY JUNE

Leo opens the door to his apartment for me and waits for me to walk through. We didn't speak on the way home from the prison. He knew I needed time to process what happened. But the truth is, my mind is still there—at the table bolted to the cold tile floor, across from the man chained to it because he can't be trusted with people. I wish there was a way for them to chain his mouth shut.

"I need some time." I say, the weight of today growing heavier.

"Of course," Leo says. "For what it's worth, I think you are the bravest person I've ever met."

"You obviously haven't met many people." I give him the biggest smile I can muster, which isn't much, then head to my room.

Behind my closed door, I pull the slip of paper from my pocket and hide it under my clothes in the bottom dresser drawer. Then I crawl in bed, pull the comforter over me, and try not to replay every moment at the prison, but fail miserably.

During our conversation, the fire in my chest that grew cold in the monastery blazed to life, sizzling through my veins. Even now, I'm still overheated and lethargic. When the comforter grows too warm, I throw it off, roll to my back, and stare at the ceiling. Shadows cross it like storm clouds then disappear as the day gives in to night.

I need Marcus. I want to tell him I was strong and that I left the words spoken in the dingy prison gasping for air instead of bringing them with me. Marcus would tell me with his words and arms that he's proud of me. And they would somehow heal me.

If only it were the truth.

In reality, the entire conversation shook me. I didn't think it was possible to be more afraid of the man than I already am. But I found out today, it is very possible. And while he's still in prison and hopefully will be for a very long time, his threat follows me.

Emotions hang like chains, swaying back and forth between relief and pain, weighing down my thoughts and pulling out carefully stowed memories.

When I was six years old, he bought me a used bike. It hadn't even been my birthday. He didn't give gifts, nor did he pay much attention to me, so it was a day I would never forget.

"Here you go, Xiao Jie. Don't let anyone steal it," he'd said before walking away.

It wasn't shiny and the tires were flat, but it was mine. I had been too afraid he would take it away if I told him I couldn't ride it, so I pretended I could and walked it to the store, to school, and the park, locking it up so no one would steal it. Not that anyone would have wanted it, but it was the only thing he'd ever given me.

But then, one day, he told me to deliver something to one of his co-workers. I didn't want to go. I was scared as it was in a rough part of San Francisco, but he told me, "I gave you a bike and now you must do something for me."

So I did. To this day I don't know what was in the package, but I learned that when it came to him, there were always conditions. I never touched that bike again, but weekly, I was forced to deliver his packages. His conditions were even worse for Mama. I'd watched from the crack in the door as he'd yelled at her for being gone too long running errands. He'd hit her, and fear had become part of me in that moment. Mama had done nothing to protect herself, only apologized and told him that she would never do it again. Then he'd slammed the door, locking her in the room with him. I didn't fully understand then, but after Nick, I know how he must have forced her to prove she was sorry. I had treated her so badly. I should have been more understanding. Instead, I'd blamed her for all my problems when she was drowning in her own. I'd made everything worse for her. It's what I do with the people I love the most, my own, personal tradition.

My finger traces scars, and I wish Leo hadn't shown up at the monastery. Then all of this nightmare would have just disappeared. According to him, I'm legally dead. If only it were my reality. Then all of this crushing weight would go away, and I would be finally free. No more running, no more hiding, no more pretending…no more me.

CHAPTER 15

MID-JUNE

Tavah and I are curled together in the corner of our train seat on the way to dinner at The Clubhouse, and I couldn't care less who just watched us kiss for a solid ten minutes. We only stopped because the train pulled into another station and people needed seats. Otherwise, we'd still be all over each other.

Instead, she's snuggled into my side, her legs draped over mine while she reads the Sharpie messages on my arm and adds a new one, blowing on it when she finishes. Chills scatter through me, and I smile down at her when she looks up at me, our faces inches apart.

She straightens and kisses me, long and slow, her hands in my hair. "You can read it now," she says against my lips.

If we had this train to ourselves, I'd be in so much trouble right now.

I glance at my arm where she's drawn a line of symbols.

"I'll tell you what it means when you tell me what this one means." Her fingers drift along my arm over the words "lava lamp."

I smirk at her. "I'm offended you don't remember."

Her eyes widen. "Is that…?"

I nod and smile. "It's that."

She throws her head back and laughs, and I laugh into her neck before pulling back. "So tell me what these symbols mean." I hold up my arm.

"Nope."

"You made the deal."

"Changed my mind," she says through a smile as she traces the other messages with her fingertip.

I pull her closer until the side of her head rests against my forehead. "Remember how you used to write 6-21 on your arm? What did that mean? Tell me that and I'll decode my message."

A knot of burning hot pain curls in my throat, throws up smoke and sparks. I blink a few times like I can release some of it through my eyes, then clear my throat. "Uh, it's just...it was a big day for me."

"How come?"

I spread my grimace into a wobbly smile. "Give me clues about your message and I'll talk."

"Is it a good big day or a bad big day?"

I stare at my arm and Tavah's fingers resting on it. "It was...a day."

"What's that supposed to mean?" She twists in my lap to fully face me. "It's happening again in four days so you should probably tell me."

Three days and eighteen hours, actually. One year ago...

Relief washes over my panic when our stop is announced, and I straighten in my seat until she has to put her feet on the floor. "This is us."

When I stand and grab the post to steady myself, she pokes me in the chest. "I will find out your secret behind 6-21, Marcus Miller."

I scan the train above her head, gather myself, then smile down at her. "You will. Maybe you'll even get lucky, and I'll tell you just because I can't resist you."

———

An hour ago, Tavah and I strolled into The Clubhouse together for the second time since prom—the same night my life took a sharp right turn into a canyon, flew off the edge, and exploded on the rocks. Somehow, I managed to crawl out of the wreckage and Tavah was here.

I chug my Dr Pepper while Dad chats Tavah up from the other side of the table. He likes her. And I like that he likes her, because I'm so into her. Liking her is one of the easiest things I've done.

I lean back in my chair while Tavah describes for Kenna how her roommate leaves remnants of her face mask all over the shower walls. It's nasty and Kenna's reaction is perfect, so I smile and scoot my plate away, hoping no one notices that I hardly ate. After the 6-21 conversation, hunger stayed on the train and is probably in Oakland by now.

Dad laughs his full belly laugh at something Tavah says, and I love it. He's resting his elbow on the table and playing off Tavah's jokes, jabbing the air with his fork. His Southern manners only slip with the people he likes. I could get so, so used to this. That's why I gotta tell Tavah about who I've been for the past year. And why 6-21 matters. Why, in three and a half days, I hope I fall asleep and don't wake up until 6-22.

I snap my focus back to Tavah and how much I love the way she takes control of the conversation and asks Dad and Kenna a thousand questions. I've learned things about Kenna I didn't know. Like that she lived in Finland for a year and a half, is super religious but not in a weird way, and is obsessed with storms. She even talked Dad into going on some storm chasing tour in Oklahoma next spring. I also learned that Tavah has been stung by bees nine times, is fluent in ASL because her grandmother is deaf, and is currently studying Transcendentalism just for fun.

Kenna says something that makes Dad laugh hard, and he

leans over and kisses her. I swear if they do that one more time tonight, I'm gonna throw a meatball at Dad's face. Then again, maybe I should just lean over and kiss Tavah and see how Dad reacts. He never saw me with Mei and never will now. Maybe I should let him see how comfortable Tavah's and my mouth have gotten with each other, even if I never thought I'd kiss anyone but Mei.

My thoughts land back in the room when Tavah leans closer, smiling as she whispers, "I don't think your dad hates girls." She tilts her head toward him and Kenna, keeping her eyes on mine as she grins.

"Gross," I say as I stand and take Tavah's plate, but she's on her feet, grabbing it. "I can clear my own plate, thank you very much. You do this enough at work. Plus, I'm not tipping you."

I don't let go so we play tug of war with the plate while Dad and Kenna laugh at us. If I pull it closer, Tavah will come with it and...

I tug and she collides with me. When she laughs, I lean down and kiss her. Come at me, 6-21.

Judging by the most amazing pink spreading across her cheeks when I pull away, she doesn't wanna make out in front of Dad and Kenna. Even if her matching pink lips are inches away, slightly parted, glossy, ready to help me forget.

"Good thing I'm not making another motorcycle bet with you, yeah, M.C.?" Dad calls from the kitchen, and I tense, hoping he'll stop there but knowing he won't.

"All we gotta do is get it out of Lex's garage and it's all yours again. Maybe take it back to Berkeley with you. You like motorcycles, Tavah?"

"No. It's all yours." I talk loud and fast like my words can run over Dad's as I shoot lasers into him with my eyes.

"What motorcycle?" Tavah asks, but I yank the plate from her hands.

"Gotta do dishes. I'm so good at them. Let me show off a little."

"I sometimes imagine you washing dishes," she says, wiggling her eyebrows, then grabbing her glass, throwing me a look over her shoulder on her way to the kitchen. That one look launches a firecracker inside my chest and sets fires all the way down. If I'd already told her everything and Dad and Kenna weren't here—and we weren't standing in the same spot Mei and I had our first kiss—I'd grab Tavah and set this thing between us in flames. Instead, I focus really hard on clearing the table before stepping to the sink next to Dad.

"What was that look for?" he asks as he scrubs a pan.

I stare into the sink, my face hot.

"You haven't told her?"

I shake my head once before loading the last few dishes in the dishwasher. "No."

Dad sighs, then grabs a towel. "Can we talk for a minute? On the fire escape?" He glances at Kenna and Tavah, who are pushing chairs under the table.

I avoid his eyes, swallow. Here come the questions. I was wondering if they were invited to dinner. "Sure." I put away the last pan before following him through the living room and out the window onto the fire escape while Tavah and Kenna get out dessert. This conversation will destroy any sliver of appetite I have. Think I might throw up instead.

I turn my back to the street, leaning against the railing so my eyes don't stroll toward Mei's old window. Dad backs against the brick wall across the fire escape from me.

"Why haven't you told her yet, son?"

I shrug, gripping the railing and looking down at the street below. "Not sure how."

Dad nods, his jaw pulsing. "I get it, it's a lot."

"Yeah. And I'm not exactly in the mood to lose another girl."

He watches me. "I'd never tell you what to do but you two seem—"

"Can we not have this conversation right now?"

He stares at his feet now, nods. "Yeah, just…wondering where your head's at right now."

"Barely above water. But it's a nice change from drowning."

He watches my face again, then scans the street behind me and lets out a long breath. "I'm actually really glad to hear that because I've been worried about you. Audrey said she talked to you a few days ago. She's worried, too. We all are. You getting enough sleep? You and Tavah aren't—"

"No, Dad. No—we haven't done anything."

He looks at his feet again and crosses his arms on his chest. "As hard as all of this is for you, I'm just selfishly glad you and I are in a good place, honestly. It's nice. More than I hoped for a few months ago, that's for sure."

Now I stare at my feet. This isn't exactly where I thought I'd be a few months ago, either, but here I am, and it definitely feels better than where I've been.

"So, M.C., Tavah's not really why I brought you out here."

"Okay…" I watch him carefully, looking for signs of good or bad news.

"I've got something I need to tell you, but I'm not really sure how to say it. It's kind of funny—I talk about hard things all day at work, but, when it comes to you, I freeze."

"If this is about me telling Tavah everything, I promise I'm going to. Probably on the train ride home."

He shakes his head. "No. I got some news a couple days ago and it doesn't really change anything, but I wanted to tell you anyway. In person. And privately."

My throat goes dry, my legs stiffen, and I search Dad's face. He's chewing the inside of his lip and not meeting my eyes. Blood free-falls to my toes, and my feet throb while I wait for him to explode my life again with whatever words come out of his mouth. But what could possibly be worse than what's already happened? "They found her. Her body." The words scrape up my throat, leave it raw.

"No—sorry, M.C. No..." He holds out his hand like I might fall forward. "Sorry to lead you to that thought." He rubs his chin, swallows, watches me, but I can't respond because my toes are gripping the metal landing, my hands holding the railing behind me so tightly, I'm gonna break it and plummet to my own death.

"I got a little more information about where she went after she left your apartment in Indiana."

My blood slowly pulls itself up through my body and I swallow, take a shaky breath. "Okay."

"An Uber driver took her to the airport. I contacted the driver, and he confirmed she was alone. It appears she wasn't taken by force."

The news drops like a boulder on the fire escape, rumbling all around me, then through me, threatening to snap this thing off the building. I close my eyes, breathe through my nose, let the aftershocks settle. "So it was her choice to leave me," I say to my feet. "Not Nick. Or Chaz forcing her to go."

"No, they weren't with her, but it's not smart to assume motivation. Not until we have hard evidence. Right now everything we have is circumstantial. There's no airline records, no transactions, no passport hits, nothing. Just this new information that she took an Uber to the airport alone. It doesn't tell us much, but I told you I would tell you everything I find out. I've requested footage from their security cameras. However, since this isn't an official investigation, it'll take time. But I'll keep looking so we can at least give you some kind of closure."

"Don't," I blurt, the pain chasing the words up my throat. "There's no point."

"I'm sorry, Marcus. I know it's not what you wanted to

hear. I went back and forth about telling you but ultimately thought you should know."

I force myself to nod, then grit my teeth as everything hardens inside me and drops into a dark hole. Shoving down my emotions, I slide back through the window into The Clubhouse and plaster a smile on my face so Tavah has no clue I just found out that Mei definitely chose to leave me. Then again, who cares—she's gone and Dad's never gonna pull me aside to tell me she's coming back. She's dead, and I'll never know why or how she left me and this planet for good.

If Marcus and I were together right now, we would be celebrating our one-year anniversary. I would be telling him how much I love him and showing him in all his favorite ways. If we were together right now, everything would feel right. If I could just call him, I could repair some of my damage. I could apologize and explain. I could replace the fading memories of him with reality. I need truth to cut through this confusion. If I could just hear his voice, I wouldn't feel so completely alone. And if he could just hear mine, he would know how much I miss him and how much I wish I had never left. He would hear how sorry I am and that I still love him with all my damaged soul.

But it might not be enough for him.

These thoughts have been pulsing through my mind all day today. I glance at the phone on the counter—the untraceable one Leo leaves for emergencies. I imagine picking it up, calling Marcus, changing my direction toward him instead of further away from him.

I jerk my eyes away. It's been too long. There's too much time and distance between us. I don't even know where he is or what he's doing. Maybe I don't even really know him anymore.

Still…

If I can go to the prison and face the man who handed me over to a criminal, I can face someone who always kept me safe. Marcus saw the worst of me, and he stayed. He got hurt and he stayed. He gave up everything for me. If I can't face him, why did I ever make him give up everything? I owe him an explanation and apology, no matter if he wants to hear it or not.

I pick up the phone, pull up the world clock, look at the locations. It's 6 PM yesterday in California. I can't imagine where else he'd be. I'm certain he didn't stay in Indiana after he came home from the hospital to an empty apartment. Maybe he's back at Stanford, living his real dream. I want to picture him there, smiling and laughing and happy. I close my eyes, lay the phone face-down on my chest, let silence drift over me. I was so lost in my thoughts this morning, I didn't even hear Leo leave for work. He's predictable almost to the second so he's been gone for at least twenty minutes. Chang Mama is on a retreat with her sister and I'm here, alone. With a phone. And zero self-control.

I stare at the outline of my legs under the light blanket as I lay on the couch, imagining how they used to be tangled in Marcus's every morning. I give in to the pull of memories and slide backwards into inside jokes, Marcus smiling at me from across our tiny table in Indiana, piggyback rides on our walks home, and his face so close to mine as we talked in the dark, his eyes electric. When my chest tightens, I breathe out slowly, steady myself even though I'm lying down. But no oxygen can dilute pain this heavy.

My hand trembles and I drop the phone on the coffee table, then sit up. I grip the edge of the couch, touch the floor with the tip of my toes. I could dial his number with my eyes closed; my fingers know exactly which buttons to push to hurl me across the ocean to Marcus. But what if he hangs up when he hears my voice? What if he's changed his number, and I can't reach him?

I wouldn't blame him. This seemingly important trip to Taiwan was never meant to last this long and hasn't done what it was supposed to do. It's done the opposite. Five months is half the time Marcus and I were on the run and double the time we dated before leaving San Francisco together. Five times the number of months we were in Seattle.

So much can happen in five months.

In five months, I can carry around a child that's only theoretical, then lose it. I can uncover secrets about my past, talk to the man I despise and fear, and be on the verge of losing my mind and myself. But in five months of losing things, I somehow haven't completely lost hope; it's still there, barely hanging on just beneath the grimy layer of fear that coats everything these days.

My hand shakes as I grab the phone and quickly push each number I remember by heart. I swallow, then hold my breath.

The other end rings. Again. Three times.

I inhale or risk passing out. I lose track of the rings, hope he doesn't answer, pray he does. My heart flutters, flops, sinks until there's a click and a voice.

"Hello?"

A girl.

I clench the phone, stunned. A girl has his number now.

"Who is it?" A deep, muffled voice asks in the background, and the room fades despite the morning sun streaming through the window, my head fuzzy.

"Spam," the girl says, her voice far away until it comes back through the line. "Beeeeeeep. You've reached Marcus Miller's phone. He's terribly sorry he missed your call but he's busy right now doing something way better than telling you he won't send $10,000 to a Nigerian prince. Thank you most sincerely for calling, though."

The other end clicks, disconnects, leaves me here and the girl with the beautiful voice there with Marcus.

My heart pummels my chest like it's punishing me for making it hurt again and for a new, bigger reason. Words slump in my throat, choking me, and I put my hand around my neck.

I'm here, he's there. With another girl. I was then, she's now. She answers his phone. What else does she do with him?

My stomach lurches as bitter acid works up my throat. No, no, no. It took Marcus and I ten years to talk to each other. It took us three weeks to kiss, a month to have our first fight. It took us two weeks to get back together after we broke up. Seconds, maybe a full minute, to decide we couldn't live without each other.

Five months. I've lost everything and she's answering his phone.

What happened after one month of them being together? Two? What will happen in another week of being away from our life together? Was he always looking for a way out so he could move toward someone else? Someone less like me?

I made it so easy for him.

CHAPTER 17

LATE JUNE

"You guys, we should give Tavah and Marcus the bedroom," Alli says, laughing as we stand in the middle of the penthouse suite, everyone staring out the wall of floor-to-ceiling windows. This hotel room reminds me way too much of a similar one I stayed in last fall with a very different girl in a very different life. The phone call from Taiwan four days ago didn't help things either. How is it possible that it came on the day that would have been Mei's and my one-year anniversary?

To shove away memories and questions, I laugh loudly at Alli's comment. "Good one. Thanks for always looking out for us." I glance at Tavah who's playing with her hair while she blushes, overly interested in something outside the window twenty-six stories below.

"People, people, people," Johnny claps his hand on my shoulder. "Let me tell you how it's gonna be. We're all gonna experience life from the 26th floor together. In the living room. No sleeping allowed. Or anything related to it."

I leave the group and follow Johnny into the bedroom. "Thanks man."

"I got you," he says, punching my arm. "Although...I

would add that I'm fully supportive of you getting with Tavah. You got no motorcycle to worry about now, if you catch me."

I help him lift the mattress and carry it into the living area, dropping it in front of the windows as an extra lounge spot for watching the Bellagio fountains far below. I keep my eyes off those windows, though, because just beyond them, up The Strip, are memories I can't handle right now or ever again.

Tavah and the girls pile onto the mattress and start a dance party. She catches my eye and smiles, and I smile back, watching her before rubbing my neck and flopping into a nearby chair. No clue what she thought about Alli's comment. I've been avoiding the "next step" conversation, scared of what that means to her. If she wants to go there and I don't, I could lose her. If she's freaked out that I waited so long to tell her I'm a twenty-year-old widower, I could lose her. I wanted to do everything perfectly with Mei, and I have the same problem with Tavah. Problem is, perfection was impossible then and it's even more impossible now.

Even if I can't bring myself to regret marrying Mei, I regret letting her hold me hostage in my new life without her. I can't go back, and I can't move forward; I'm just stuck until I decide to let her go. Which means telling Tavah about her.

In the meantime, I'm almost done moving a year's-worth of pictures from my phone to the cloud where they can float around without me seeing them. Or Tavah, if she ever goes through my phone. Which she so easily could have when she answered the call from Taiwan on Monday. Of course my spam calls are now coming from Taiwan, of all the places in the world.

I aim my phone camera at Tavah as she dances, snapping a photo when she runs her fingers through her hair, doing her best to be seductive until she laughs. I snap another one, her head thrown back, smile beaming off every shiny surface. They've got nothing on her.

Lin shoots me a look and her warning pulses across the room and lodges in my mind like a flaming arrow. I clench my phone tighter, watching Tavah while my brain rehearses how and when I'm gonna tell her the truth. I definitely don't wanna do it during her birthday weekend, so I'm gonna have to endure Lin's evil eye and my pounding guilt a little longer.

———

"Let's walk back to the hotel," Tavah says, slipping her arm through mine as we walk out of the show she's been dying to see. I'd been extra charming at work to bring in the tips so I could afford tickets for her birthday present. She'd once told me she would love to be a fire dancer. and she lit up tonight when there was a stage full of them.

We push open the outside doors and step onto the side-walk, my nerves humming under my skin. Walking back to the hotel means plenty of time to spend in my past and risk spilling my guts or puking.

"This has been the most perfect night of my life," she says, smiling up at me.

"Your life?" I ask, shaking off nerves and pushing them away with a smile. "A little fire, some aerial acrobatics, and that's it—perfection?"

She squeezes my arm and leans into me. "You left out the most important part. You, all to myself."

I have been all Tavah's tonight. Somewhere between her whispering, 'Thank you for the best birthday ever' as she snuggled up to me during the show and her fingers laced through mine all night, I forgot I was in Vegas. Until I walked outside and saw The Palazzo.

Now I remember.

We have to pass it to get back to our hotel, and I have to keep my focus on Tavah and off the memories leaping from the windows of room 1824.

"You sure you wanna walk?" My throat's tight as I scan the blur of passing taxis. "It's a long way back."

"Walking equals more time alone with you, so…yeah I do. In fact, could you walk a little slower maybe?"

I just need to get past The Palazzo, then I'll walk however she wants me to walk. But right now, all I wanna do is run.

"It's my birthday and that's what I want—you and me. Walking slowly. Alone."

"Your birthday's not until Monday, so technically, I don't have to give you anything yet." And you won't want what I'll eventually give you, birthday or not…

She stops walking and turns me to face her. "You okay?"

I close my eyes, breathing deeply, inhaling the night air, greasy with fried food and exhaust, cheap perfume and cigarette smoke. When Tavah's hands go to my chest, I cover them with mine and exhale, adding my guilt and anxiety to the haze above The Strip. I'm gonna leave it there. "Yeah. So, so good." I pull her into a hug as people jostle around us on the crowded sidewalk. I'm not gonna waste another second thinking about Mei or what I need to tell Tavah. I'm just gonna be here with her.

"Miller?"

I let go of Tavah and glance over my shoulder, my eyes landing on Patrick, the guy I'd worked valet with at The Palazzo. My heart trips over itself, stops, restarts, and pounds so hard it shakes my whole body.

"Hey, man! Thought that was you. What is up?" He opens his arms, and we give each other a quick, back-slapping hug.

His eyes flick from me to Tavah and back. "It's been awhile, yeah?"

I swallow panic. "Yeah. It's definitely been awhile. What's new with you?" I shouldn't ask questions—don't want this conversation to go too long or too deep or I'll have to answer more questions from Tavah than I'm ready to answer. I glance at the girls clustered beside Patrick, talking and pointing at something across the street. "Looks like you've got a party following you." I smile and slide my arm around Tavah's waist, holding her tightly against my side. "By the way… Tavah, this is Patrick."

She smiles and waves. "Hey, Patrick. How do you and Marcus know each other?"

"What?" Patrick says through a smile, throwing his thumb over his shoulder. "Miller didn't tell you about the good times working valet at The Palazzo?" He backhands my chest, and I return the favor. "We drove cars and got paid for it. Might have taken a few for a joy ride." He eyes me and blood drains from my face when I catch his reference to the night he picked up Mei and drove her to The Palazzo for me.

"Yeah, Patrick made sure I didn't get into too much trouble," I say, then glance at the group of girls. "But we'll let you get back to your chaperoning before you lose a few. It was great running into you, man."

"You, too. Still got the same number? Texted you a few times, and you didn't respond so I figured you changed it."

"Yeah, sorry man. No—same number, just forgot to respond. I was moving."

"It's all good." He glances at Tavah, then back at me before turning toward the group of girls. "Guess I better head. Great to see you, though." He gives me another back-slapping hug, then waves goodbye as he walks in the opposite direction.

I slide my arm around Tavah's shoulders and continue our walk, our hips bumping against each other, bracing for the question I know she'll ask.

"When did you live in Vegas?" Tavah asks, looking up at me as we veer around a group of men gathered around a topless flamingo girl.

I talk into the air ahead of us. "Last summer." The words trickle between us, test the stability of the moment, but more words want out, sick of being recycled in my head for the last few months. "Know that thing I said I needed to tell you?"

"Is it going to interfere with my most perfect night?"

"It's just something you should know about me before we go any further with this relationship." I test her reaction.

"Is it bad?" she asks, tilting her head up and toward me, her eyes wide.

I shrug, jittery. "Depends."

She stops walking, puts her hand on my chest. "Were you, like, an exotic male dancer or something? I mean, you could be, but I hope I'm so very wrong with that guess…"

I laugh at the sky. "Uh, no. Not a male dancer. I've got no moves."

She smirks. "Guess it depends on who's watching." She wiggles her eyebrows, then waits for my answer. "So why did you live here? I'm dying to know now."

I take a deep, dramatic breath. "I…ummm…"

"Hurry!" she shrieks. "Get it over with!"

A group of older women cackle as they pass, bumping me from behind, the noise and movement sweeping away any chance of me dropping the bomb here. "I was a sky-diving Elvis impersonator."

Her eyebrows jump. "Are you serious?"

"No," I laugh. "Not even close. But…yeah, I lived here and…" Do I tell her the rest? The biggest part? "Worked valet the summer after high school."

"And…?" she prompts.

"And I also…like Lionel Richie," I blurt, scrunching my face like I'm ready for her explosive reaction. "A lot. And it tends to be a dealbreaker for most girls. Not sexy at all."

She bursts out laughing and we cross the street in the middle of a group of Asian tourists. "Oh yeah?" She wraps my arm around her shoulder again, and we keep walking, her hip bumping against mine. "That's nothing. Sometimes I cry during Disney songs."

"Please." I roll my eyes, relieved by the conversational detour. "I've spent hours trying to put my fist in my mouth."

"I iron when I'm stressed. Sheets included."

I look down and meet her eyes, hold them while people swerve around us. "I dry heave at the sight of egg yolk."

She laughs. "I have a lucky rock."

"I've always wondered what it would be like to wrestle an octopus."

"I just so happen to have eight arms." Her cheek twitches like she's fighting a smile, but she holds my eyes, face serious even as neon reflects off it. "Wanna wrestle?"

Her lotion or perfume or shampoo floats past my nose, beckoning me. "As enticing as your eight arms are, you should know I'm adamantly opposed to changing the status of planets once established."

"Well, I'm passionately opposed to the exploitation of lionesses. Hope that's not a deal breaker."

"You're so weird," I whisper through a smile. We're so close, she's blurry and my lips are buzzing. "You win," I say against her ear as we weave around a street performer.

She smiles into the night, then stops and turns into me, stretching up to kiss me in the middle of the crowded sidewalk. The questions about Patrick or my time in Vegas are trampled under hundreds of feet passing us, so I give into her, and when we break apart, I brush away hair on her forehead, our eyes holding onto each other. With a sigh, I grab her hand and start walking again, and she snuggles into me.

Even with the lights of The Strip blinking and circling, Tavah's easily the brightest spot in Vegas. If I focus on her, I'll make it through this night. If I don't, I'll look behind me. If I do that, I'll see Mei through an eighteenth-story window, my arms wrapped around her from behind, I'll hear her heartbeat, feel her skin. I'm afraid I'll hear the words she whispered that night because she promised and there's no way she can keep it now. 6-21 came and went, just like any other day.

And every year will from now on. She's gone and she's not coming back. Someday—very soon—I'm gonna have to say it out loud and make it real.

My arm tightens around Tavah. Forget promises. Forget Lin and her threats. Mei and I have spent 149 nights apart now with thousands more to come. So I'll make a new promise—one I can control: for every Mei-less night, I'll take one back with Tavah. Starting tonight.

CHAPTER 18
LATE JUNE

The girl's voice has been on repeat in my head for almost a week now, and I can't get it out. She sounds beautiful, happy, whole, and I imagine the face that belongs to the voice, settling on flawless pale skin, long, soft hair, and a bright smile that bathes Marcus's world in light. She isn't held hostage by ghosts from her past and she isn't holding him hostage in a life he doesn't want.

He doesn't have to save her.

I stare into the bathroom mirror, run my hand over my short hair, prickly against my fingertips and try to see the real Mei—the Mei Marcus used to love. But apparently, she's dead. Marcus, however, is very much alive and not only is his heart beating, but it's beating for someone else.

Does she know about me? Does she even care that he's married? Has he even told her? I might only be dead on paper, but Marcus doesn't know that. How long did it take him to move on?

I close my eyes and grip the edge of the counter with both hands. It isn't his fault—or hers. I did this to myself. I should never have listened to Chaz—I could've found another way to navigate my problems. With Marcus beside me. Or at the very least, I could've told him what I had to do and given him the choice to come with me or stay. We could have done this together, as a team. It might have torn us apart anyway, but at least I would've given him the choice. I was trying to protect him but ruined everything in the process.

In fact, if I would've listened to myself in the very beginning and left him alone, he wouldn't be on one side of the world starting a new life and I wouldn't be on the other, wanting to end mine. I never should have gone to his apartment that first time. I had no business falling in love with him; someone like Marcus was never meant for someone like me. No matter how many times I felt him watching me as I walked across the room or did a simple thing like tie my shoe or read a book. He always said the way I moved drove him wild. Even when I put on my makeup, he'd often stop and watch me in the mirror. I didn't imagine that look on his face—it was real. I felt how he felt about me, physically and emotionally. I've felt it thousands of times.

I'd asked him one morning why he looked at me like that and he'd said, "Because every time I look at you, I remember how crazy lucky I am, and I like being lucky."

I remember turning back to my mascara and laughing. "You might change your mind in fifty years when I'm old and saggy and in a wheelchair."

He'd wrapped his arms around my waist from behind and rested his chin on my head, his body curved around mine. "If you think a few wrinkles are gonna scare me away, you've got the wrong guy. I'll take you any way I can get you. Besides, never done it in a wheelchair," he'd said, kissing my neck.

I hadn't finished my makeup that day.

The purple spots under my eyes are growing darker, more permanent. *You'll take me any way you can get me? What about now, Marcus? How long did it take you to fall out of love with me and into it with someone else? Were you relieved when I left? Did you feel liberated? Do you laugh into her neck like you used to laugh into mine? Do you kiss her like you used to kiss me? Have you felt the fever of her skin on yours? Has she found that spot that drove you crazy every time I kissed it?*

Jealousy rages at the thought of him with someone else, and I want to rip the mirror off the wall, throw it to the ground, watch it shatter into a million pieces so my heart isn't the only splintered thing.

Instead, I open the drawer and pull out Leo's electric razor as tears roll down my cheeks. I choke down sobs as I move it over my scalp, feathery clumps drifting to the floor. It's grown a couple of inches since the monastery, but I don't want anything new. My hands shake, unfamiliar with letting go when they've been clenched too tightly, holding on for too long.

If I could just forget like he did.

Forget his touch and warmth.

Forget the laughter.

Forget the days we had nothing to do but be wrapped around each other.

Forget—

"Mei Li?" Leo knocks on the door, and I breathe through the pain, focus on masking my voice.

I shut off the razor and stare at myself in the mirror. "Yeah?"

"Are you okay?"

I shake my head, unable—unwilling—to tell him any of this. "Yes."

"You sure?" His voice hovers just beyond the door.

I wipe my cheeks and push the pain away, my heart hardening. Just as my death certificate states, Mei Li doesn't exist anymore, and my past can die with me.

An idea flares in my head. "Actually…could I get a ride to the monastery?"

———

I pull Buddha from my satchel and stare at him one last time. This is it. This is how I finish it and move on. Today I will bury Buddha with my past and the memories that belong to it. Hundreds of them. They don't matter anymore, anyway.

Rummaging through my bag, I find the box that used to hold my personal belongings at the monastery and fill it with my written memories I attached to Sharpies back when I was living at the monastery, then set Buddha on top.

I will bury him with what's left of my heart, then grow a new one in a new life. If I don't, I'll be stuck in this agony forever. I'll only see Marcus's smile, hear his laughter and his voice, and that will only lead to hearing her voice and remind me of my biggest regret.

I grab the box and wrap it in tape, layer upon layer, mesmerized by the motion of closing this part of my life forever. I don't stop until the tape runs out and my chest hurts because I've been holding my breath.

On the drive to the monastery, Leo's eyes repeatedly land on me, then skitter away, but I don't care because I can't. All of my feelings have torn away from me, too wrapped in Marcus.

Leo doesn't ask questions. He doesn't ask why I shaved my head again, or why I want to go back to the monastery, or what the box on my lap holds. Sometimes I wonder if he doesn't ask questions because he already knows the answer. Or maybe he doesn't care. But he gets quiet when anything about my past comes up and he watches my face too closely.

When he pulls up to the gates, he shuts off the car and stays in his seat, glancing at me. "Do you want me to go with you or stay?" His eyes jump from my face to the box on my lap, then back to my face, which he's studying again, looking for clues.

I shake my head. "I'll be right back."

Pushing down emotions, I get out of the car, gripping the box as I walk through the gates. I nod and bow to nuns as I pass, headed toward the Garden of the Buddhas where I spent so many mornings talking to Marcus in my head. Those mornings kept me alive, but like everything else in my life, they're in the past.

I stop in front of my favorite Buddha in the garden—the one that seems to stare into my soul. I lift my eyes to his before kneeling in the soft dirt at his base and digging a hole with my hands.

CHAPTER 19

LATE JUNE

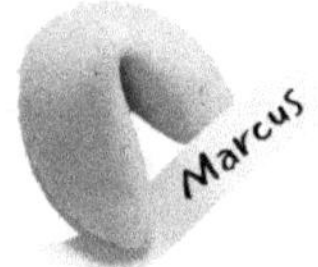

t's 3AM and everyone is either at the pool or somewhere on The Strip, but Tavah and I are sitting on the mattress, watching the Bellagio fountains.

"There must be something really good going on in that head of yours right now," she whispers, looking up at me from where she's curled into my side, her smile reflecting among the bright city lights.

I wind my arm around her, pull her even closer. "Just enjoying the moment."

She plays with one of my shirt buttons, directing a question to it. "Do you remember when I told you it wouldn't be hard for me to fall in love with you?"

I swallow and my eyes scan the glittery nightscape outside the window. "Yeah."

"It wasn't."

My gaze wanders to her face. She's holding her breath and so am I because I know where moments like these lead. I promised myself I'd take it slow, but right now, with her looking like that and me feeling like this, slow doesn't seem possible.

I pull her onto my lap, my mouth hungry against hers.

She matches my intensity, her hands running up my chest. "I've been waiting for this all day," she breathes.

My hands press into her lower back, pulling her even closer, her hair a curtain around us as she deepens the kiss.

I know this heat. I know this urgency. I know exactly where this is going if I don't stop it. She has the potential to wear me down or completely wear me out. And I like it, want more of it.

My mouth moves down to her neck, and she throws her head back so I can kiss her throat, make my way around her jaw.

Gasping, she presses her chest against mine. Tavah's a good girl, but the way she's moving has nothing to do with good girl, and it's only making me want more of her.

"Marcus," she whispers, straightening in my lap as she kisses my forehead down to my closed eyes.

I swear under my breath, taking her jaw between my fingers, bring her mouth to mine.

She laughs against my lips, her hands on either side of my neck, her mouth wandering.

I sink back into the mattress, breathless, my body humming and ready to take off when she yanks my shirt loose and slips her hands under it, running them up my bare chest and setting me on fire.

Her shirt rides up, and I grip her bare waist, rolling her onto her back before diving into her. When I kiss her neck, she whimpers and her hand flies to her mouth, eyes wide as she laughs, and I rest my forehead against hers, smiling. "Guess you liked that?"

"I like everything you do."

This girl is ready to combust, and I can only imagine the intensity.

But I can't go there until—

She whispers my name again, and I lose it, my mouth on hers, coaxing her head off the mattress until she arches into me. I slide my hand up her back to her neck, holding her as I kiss her deeper, trying to reach the depth I crave.

The depth I found in Mei.

Like the flash of a thousand cameras, memories of kissing Mei assault me. Our first kiss, my knuckles white from gripping the counter, the heat that made us delirious. The mirrored elevator in Indiana where there were dozens of kissing Marcuses and Meis. The way she stood on tiptoe, stretching her body against mine. The rhythm we always found and the times we kissed so slowly, it left us disoriented when we finally came up for air. The ravenous times, trying to breathe but needing each other more than oxygen. The deep, warm purple when my body ached to show all of hers how much I loved her.

All the nights I had.

My breath catches like someone punched me in the gut, and I exhale too sharply, my stomach clenching. I grab Tavah's face between my hands and scramble to my knees. *I'm so sorry*, I say with my eyes, but hers are closed, and she smiles as she sinks into the mattress.

"Whoa," she groans, "I knew you were good, but that was...*wow*..."

No. Not wow.

I'm paralyzed by guilt. But where's it coming from? I need to run. Beg forgiveness from Mei's memory or whatever part of her is still with me. Beg forgiveness from Tavah for the things I haven't told her. Things she needs to know before anything like this happens again.

"I'm not good," I choke. "I'm not treating you right, I'm not..." I trail off, trying to catch my breath, fear smothering my confession.

"Stop, Marcus." She wraps her arms around my neck and pulls me down to kiss her. "You have no idea how good you are," she says as she looks into my eyes.

I lace my fingers through hers and pull her up until we're

wrapped around each other, slumped together. I smooth her hair, her back, bury my face in her neck so she can't see mine. I should move. I should run. But I don't. Because it feels too good to hold her. It's easier to fall apart with someone than alone.

————

"What's wrong?" Tavah's crackly voice makes me jump as she slides the balcony door closed quietly behind her and stands against the railing beside me. The sun hasn't come up yet, but I'm waiting for it to end this eternal night, like I do most nights.

"Did I do something wrong...?"

I shake my head, clear my throat, and shove away my thoughts. "No. Definitely not." I swallow. She did everything too right. "I'm fine, just thinking."

"Mmm," she says, skeptical, slipping her arm through mine and leaning into me. "I'm not sure who told you that you're a good liar, but they lied."

I'm supposed to smile. And her sleepy voice and crazy hair—which is mostly my fault—are pretty irresistible, so I try. But it's more of a grimace as I grip the railing, trying to breathe through the pain of the confession pushing its way upward.

"It's definitely not you, Tavah. It's not. It's me."

This is her birthday weekend. I'm really gonna do this now? Ruin our relationship with a few stupid words to describe my stupid past? Tell her that my heart still belongs to someone else and even though that someone is dead, the biggest piece of me will always belong to her?

I want to feel lucky that Tavah chose me to shower with affection. I want to want her and know it's okay to want her like I do.

But Mei won't let me.

"Still sticking to the story that you're okay?"

I glance at her and the world crumbles around me, her smirk so innocent and completely adoring. "Uhh…know what? No, actually." I rock back on my heels, stare at the cement beneath my bare feet. "I'm not okay. This place is kinda painful."

She frowns.

"Vegas," I say, not meeting her eyes, but letting mine roam up The Strip to The Palazzo. She waits for an explanation, and I grip the railing tighter, begging it for support. "It holds some pretty…" I can't think of the word. Can't bring myself to say bad because my memories of Mei in Vegas are some of my best.

My chest tightens and I swallow, breathing in deeply. "There are just a lot of memories here." My heart is thumping so hard in my throat. "I shouldn't have come here because my head goes back to last summer and it just…I'm not really all here and it's not fair to you."

She looks down, embarrassed. "Marcus, you don't need to talk about it if you don't—"

"Tavah, I was married," I blurt before I talk myself out of saying it. I can't stand here and watch her blame herself for the awkwardness and my need for space and privacy. I squeeze my eyes shut as I go on. "On graduation day, when I should've been walking across the stage, I was driving to Seattle and…a month later, I got married. And then we lived here for a few months, then Indiana, and then…she left. I had no clue where she went, she was just gone."

Tavah's mouth opens and her eyes widen, like what I said hurt going in. But then she closes her mouth, her hand over it as she studies her feet.

I stare into the murky morning. "That's why, when you saw me for the first time at Johnny's I was wrecked. I didn't have answers. Never got closure and had no idea what I was supposed to do. And I know I should've told you everything from the beginning—I know that. But I didn't, so I have no right to be falling in love with you, because I can't be what I want to be with you. I'm messed up and there's no way I expect you to ever forgive me for what I've done to you."

Turning my back, I grip the railing again, disgusted with myself. The silence is too loud, drowning out everything but how pathetic I sound. I can't imagine what she must be thinking, and when I try, it's too much, so I bolt past her, but she steps between me and the door, her hand landing firmly on my chest.

"Why didn't you tell me?" Her eyes are intent, her jaw set.

Here it all comes—the emotions, the memories. The reasons. They're sprouting from the place I've shoved them and I'm erupting. "Because I knew the second you saw how freaking messed up I am, you'd leave." I close my eyes and concentrate on remaining standing. I put my hand over my mouth because if I start talking, I'll puke or let everything out in one painful rush and die from the pain. The knot inside will tear its way out of me and bring everything I've held in with it.

But if I'm honest with myself, I'm equally afraid to lose the emotions that keep me tied to Mei. No matter how masochistic, I'm not ready to let go of it. Pain is all I have left of Mei, and I wanna keep it all to myself.

"Who was she? And why did she leave you?"

My mouth is so dry, my hands shaking, so I put them on my hips. Talk to the cement balcony. "She was…someone I thought I could save." No. She was someone I wanted to save because I loved her, wanted to be with her, be married to her, never be apart from her for the rest of my life. And I still want all of that—everything we had. But I can't. So I do what I always do when emotions rise too high. I slip past Tavah with a choked, "I'm so sorry," and leave her standing on the balcony with unanswered questions and a broken heart. Just like Mei did to me.

"Something's different about you." Leo suppresses a smile, tapping his nose, then sipping his milk tea, the black boba pearls sliding up his thick straw. "I just can't put my finger on it."

I shrug, letting silence be my answer as I take a drag of my own tea, sucking up a few boba, chewing.

I never told Leo about calling Marcus. I deleted the evidence and decided it was time to delete Marcus as well. If I had to choose between calling him and finding out he's with someone new or visiting Not-Baba in prison all day every day for ten years, I'd choose prison.

Marcus and I are officially over and buried, just like our Buddha and my memories.

I'd covered his box in a layer of dirt, then symbolically thrown all my emotions in the hole with it and added more dirt until there was nothing but a darker brown spot in the garden. That girl's voice was like a shove from behind for me to move on. Since then, every time Marcus thoughts intrude, I remember her voice. But today, the thoughts have been relentless, so I decided to reinvent myself and become unrecognizable. Last time I needed a change, I got a tattoo, so after Leo left for work this morning, I left, too. I didn't have a plan, just knew that I needed to do something other than sit in the dumpster fire I built all on my own with hasty decisions and stupidity.

It didn't take long to find that something drastic.

"I think," Leo says, setting down his tea, "and I could be wrong, but did you always have that nose ring and I missed it?"

I reach up, rub the tiny jewel on the side of my nose which is still a little puffy and tender from the piercing. "I needed something to offset my baldness. It was either this or a facial tattoo. Should I have gotten the tattoo?"

Leo laughs and leans back, folding his arms across his chest. "You should have done both, obviously."

I give him a short laugh. "It's never too late, I guess. And I have the perfect one in mind. I'm thinking a dragon right here." I tap my cheek and he laughs. What he doesn't know is I got a tattoo on my side as well as a nose ring—a cherry blossom branch whose blossoms have blown off the branch and are transforming into birds along my ribcage, wings spread as they leave their past behind them. I'm trying to do the same: break free, fly away, and transform. I just don't know where or into what yet.

Leo shakes his head. "Maybe the nose ring was the only choice after all. It's actually growing on me. Kinda like your company."

I drop my eyes to my cup while charged silence swoops in to fill the space between us like it always does when Leo says things he shouldn't. I've recently noticed it happening a lot. Like the other day when he told me he liked the ring of blue that outlines my brown eyes. He promptly left the room, saying something about work. Or when he grabbed my hand at the top of Monkey Mountain, then dropped it and took a step backward, putting space between us. Or last night when he told me he was glad I'd fallen into his life as he said good night and closed his door with a glance my way.

Has he always said things like that, and I've been too preoccupied with getting back to my old life to notice? Or has he noticed I'm not always glancing over my shoulder anymore?

"So…Mei Li." Leo stands, grabbing both empty cups. "I have this…thing." He walks to the garbage, tosses them into it.

Subject changed.

I swallow and straighten in my chair, watching him as he walks back to our table. "Thing?"

"A dinner party thing. For work."

"Are you asking my permission to go and extend your curfew?" I smile at him, and he grins, then rubs his jaw.

"More like…I was wondering if I have your permission to take you as my date since you still owe me from saving you from the monkey." He leans his hip against the counter. "If you come, I'll consider your debt paid in full. Until the next time I save you from another man-eating creature."

I tilt my head and smile, throwing up a shield against the spark in his eyes that finds its way to the bottom of my stomach. "You just want to prove to your coworkers that your outlandish stories about a Buddhist nun dropout are actually true."

Leo's smile falters and he drops his eyes before lifting them to mine again. "I wouldn't want them to question whether I can be trusted with the truth, no matter how crazy." He holds up a hand. "I want to prove that you really are as unbelievable as I've told them."

Heat flares in my cheeks, and I squirm. "Is this you flattering me so I'll go with you? Or is this flirting?" If I keep talking, the guilt over going on a date with someone who's not Marcus will surely exit my body. Then again, why should

I feel guilty? If Marcus can move on and have a girlfriend, I can go on one date with the second-best guy I've ever met.

"Definitely flirting, though it's hard to tell since I'm a little rusty, but I hope your avoidance is a yes?" His shoulders rise with his eyebrows.

"What, exactly, do you think I'm avoiding?"

"Do you want my full list, or should I just start with one thing?" His smile spreads, and my neck grows hot.

"Let's just start with one thing. I'd love to hear your detective analysis."

He pins me with his eyes. "Fine. I'll start with the biggest thing: feelings."

"I don't like feelings."

"First honest thing you've said in weeks." He lowers himself into the chair across from me. "Come with me. I promise it will be worth it. Maybe not my company since you already know what to expect with that, but I hear the food is going to be incredible."

I take a deep breath, then blow it out as an exaggerated sigh. "Fine. I'll go. For the food."

"Yeah?"

"Sure. Yes. Let's go make a spectacle of ourselves."

Leo's grin widens. "My reputation cannot thank you enough. Everyone will believe me now."

"So when is this 'thing,' anyway?"

He rubs the back of his head. "Short notice, I know, but it's tomorrow night. It's black tie. You can borrow one of mine."

I frown and Leo smirks.

"I'll take care of the dress unless you have something in your suitcase from the monastery prom."

CHAPTER 21

EARLY JULY

Tossing my phone on the ground beside the couch, I flop back and rub my eyes. I've drafted at least 50 texts to Tavah. Haven't sent one. I've started to call her probably 30 times but shut off my phone before I hit the button. I have no right to call or text or ever speak to her again. All I deserve is to lie here in the dark and let consequences hit me like torpedoes. This is what happens when a guy doesn't tell the girl he's in love with that he was once in love with someone else enough to run away and marry her, leaving everything and everyone else behind. This is what happens when a girl can't trust a guy.

And I haven't even told her the whole story yet. I might never get the chance. Also deserved.

But I can't take the Tavah silence or Mei's ghost anymore. Since I left Tavah in Vegas, I've seen four sunrises from this couch, and I'm so done with it. Once it's not 2 AM, I'll go to Tavah's, apologize again. See how angry she is so maybe her fire will burn her designated part of my heart to ash.

I've considered my feelings and options and rewound the balcony moment a thousand times. There aren't enough "so's" in any language to add to "I'm sorry" that would even touch my stupidity and guilt. If Mei came back from the dead and said the same thing with all the added "so's," it wouldn't be enough.

My phone vibrates into the carpet, and I reach down, pick it up, squint at the screen as I tilt it toward me. Tavah. My heart stutters, and I sit up as my thumb slides.

"Hey," I rush in a raspy whisper.

Her voice is shaky and hushed when it reaches me. "Can we talk?"

I swivel my legs until my feet land on the carpet, lean on my knees. Squeeze my eyes shut. "Yes. Please. Tavah, I'm so—"

"I'm sitting on my bathroom counter in the dark so I don't wake up Alli, but my heart hurts so bad, I think I might be dying. So before I do, I have to get these words out of me."

"Tavah, I..."

"Just let me get them out," she says, and I go silent as she continues.

"I feel so stupid for still wanting you. I'm a lot of things but was never desperate until I found out you're still in love with someone else who also happens to be your wife and Lin's best friend."

I swallow. Drag in air as my chest crumples under the weight of her accusation. Responses fly around my head, crash against my skull, but Tavah sees through me. "Lin told you?"

"No, Johnny did. After you ran out, he and Lin came back and heard me sobbing in the bathroom. We talked for hours until I was done talking about you. Lin explained why she hadn't told me, and I understand why she didn't say anything What I don't understand is why you didn't and why you left your best friend to do the dirty work." Her voice is hard now, her lump of emotion turned to stone.

"Because I'm selfish and terrified."

"Yeah, I got that."

"But I'll tell you everything—the whole story. Anything you wanna know. If you want. And if you don't, I get it."

"I don't want to hear it." Her words cut through the line. "But I have no choice if I want to understand why you lied to me and who you really are. And for some stupid reason, I want both of those things. No, actually, it's not some stupid reason, it's because I'm so sick of imagining you with someone else even if she was officially and legally your someone else. I just need to hear the reality of it."

"She's not mine anymore. She didn't want to be and now she'll never be."

"Did she file for divorce?"

"No."

"Then you're still married."

"No. I'm not." I close my eyes, hang my head, run my hand through my hair. "That's the thing I—"

"Which is it, Marcus? You're either married or you're not."

"Can we talk in person, maybe?" I stare at my feet as my heart thumps. I will tell her everything. Every detail.

"Be there in fifteen."

———

When I open the door twenty minutes later, her swollen eyes skitter across my face, get stuck in my facial hair, move to my eyes in the yellow lights next to the apartment door.

"Hey."

The car key in her hand jingles as she shakes it, her hands jittery, hair limp, and sweatshirt inside out. She steps past me into the apartment, backs against the wall, her eyes never leaving mine.

I shut the door, shove my hands in my pockets. "Tavah, I know sorry isn't enough but I'm—"

"No more apologies. It's too late and doesn't fix anything, so just talk. From the beginning."

I swallow. "How about I start from the end?" I say to my feet, dropping the question in the dark cavern between us.

"What do you mean?"

"I mean…" I take a deep breath, let it out. "I don't know where she went or why she left and I'm not married because—"

"You mean Mei Li? Just say her name."

The sharpness of Mei's name coming from Tavah slices me and I sway, then dig my toes into the carpet. "Yeah. Mei."

"She's a real person between us so let's just treat her like a real person."

I almost choke but swallow hard instead. "That's the thing, Tavah. She's not between us. Mei left, and I'll never know why and can't ask her because she's dead."

The word shatters the dark, a white-hot blast of pain leveling the sharp edges and drop-offs inside me, leaving a wasteland of dust and nothing.

Tavah's wide eyes reflect the devastation, and her hand shoots out, grabbing my arm like she thinks I might dissolve, too. "Marcus, are you serious?"

Her words echo in my head, any reaction delayed by waves of destruction still rolling at me.

"Johnny and Lin said nothing about her being—"

"They don't know." I can't look at her but can feel the rumble between us.

"You haven't told them? Lin's her best friend."

"I haven't said it out loud to anyone."

She closes her eyes, trapping whatever light was in the room behind her eyelids.

"I should've told everyone sooner, I know. But if I said it out loud, then it would be real, and I wasn't ready for that kind of reality." I shake my head and it moves enough air in the room to take the message to her. "I'll tell them. In a few hours. So, don't mention it to either of them, okay?"

Tavah lets out a shaky breath, blinks at the carpet. "Who

are you?" she whispers, her eyes rising to mine in the darkness.

"I'll tell you. If you still wanna know."

"I'm not sure I do right now." She nods and swipes her eyes, blinking at the ceiling. "I think…" She pauses, wipes her eyes again, then brushes her hands over her pants. "I think I need time to think."

"Okay," I choke out. "Yeah." Ice clogs my veins, and I take a few steps away from her as she walks out the door and closes it behind her.

CHAPTER 22
EARLY JULY

The dress Leo bought for me is straight off a 1950s model. Deep blue satin covered in lace drapes my entire body. The high neckline sweeps across my collar bone held up by delicate straps. The last time I wore a fancy dress for a black-tie event and what happened afterward was one of the worst nights of my life. But I'm not with Nick, I'm with Leo and his eyes won't creep along every curve like Nick's did. I'm not sure what Leo's eyes will do or where they'll go first because this dress hugs my waist before flowing into an A-line with a petticoat underneath, stopping just below my knees. The good news is, it will do a better job of taking attention from my bald head than my nose ring ever could. It's backless and the tops of pink blossoms-turned-birds peek from the edge of the fabric at my side.

When I walk into the living room, Leo stands from where he's sitting on the sofa, his eyes wide. "Wow. Mei Li. You look…" He clears his throat and smiles. "Yeah. I have great taste in dresses."

"And I have great taste in dates." His hair is smoothed back, and the shadow of a beard draws attention to his jawline. He's wearing a tailored black suit and silver tie.

He slides his arm through mine and escorts me out of the apartment. I haven't worn heels since before Marcus. There wasn't room in my duffel bag for heels when we ran.

I tense my toes in the stilettos, ground myself in this moment. I'm going to enjoy every minute of these heels because I don't have to run tonight. I can stand still. I can stand beside Leo.

Outside, his car is waiting at the curb, and he opens the passenger door, then helps me into the seat. But before he shuts my door, his eyes meet mine and an unexpected rush of heat flares through me. I press my back into the seat and stare straight ahead as he drives.

There is something positive and true about Leo Chang—something I've been missing and something I want to hold on to. He makes me feel important and safe. And beautiful. I haven't felt any of those things in so long, it draws me to him. I have to move away from Marcus, anyway, so why not move closer to Leo?

When we pull up to the curb, he gives his keys to the valet and strides to my door, opening it for me. I slip my fingers between his and don't let go after he helps me out of the car or when we walk into the ballroom. I have to let go of a lot of other things, but not his hand.

Leo leans into me as we weave through the crowd, his mouth almost touching my ear, sending ripples through my stomach. "Thanks for coming tonight."

This. That voice and this connection and borrowed confidence. This is how I move on.

Leo straightens as a woman approaches in a black satin gown. "You actually brought a date, Chang," she says in perfect English.

My cheeks flush and I look up at a smiling Leo.

"Yes, I actually did. Ana, this is Mei Li." He shifts toward me. "Ana is one of our senior officers."

"Nice to meet you," I say through a bright smile, shaking her hand.

"When Leo mentioned he was bringing a date, we all made bets about whether he actually would. I'm happy to see you here, though my wallet is not."

"Your fault for betting against me, I guess," Leo says through a smile, and Ana shrugs, laughing before turning to talk to someone walking past her.

Leo leans into my ear. "I'm going to get a drink. Do you want anything?"

"Whatever you're having is fine."

I watch him as he greets people along his way to the bar, feeling suddenly empty without him.

Ana steps next to me again, her eyes following mine toward Leo. "He must really like you," she says as she steps beside me, pulling my attention from emotions that are way too close to the surface. She's closer to Leo's age and beautiful, and I wonder if he's ever taken her out or flirted with anyone at work like he flirts with me. She seems to know him well.

"Oh, no—we're just friends." I wave my hand and smile.

She raises her eyebrows and smirks. "Leo never brings a date to any party. That's why I betted against him."

I glance at her, then at the ground, her words lodging somewhere in my head. I haven't let myself consider what he might really be feeling about me. I've noticed his flirting, but Leo knows how to flirt, which, I figure means he does it a lot. I don't think I'm special. If he hadn't saved me, he wouldn't give me two seconds of attention. He feels protective. We've been through a lot together.

I watch as he strides back toward me, a wine glass in each hand, and my mouth goes dry as something deep inside squirms. Marcus never drank. I've always avoided it because Nick was drunk a lot, but tonight, I thank Leo and ignore all internal protests, taking a long sip, then grimacing. The new me tries new things even though, apparently, she doesn't like wine. But she's got no other reason to stop.

The liquid slides down my throat, and I follow Leo from person to person and, soon enough, I'm replacing one glass of wine with another, and my cluttered mind with an empty, sloshy one.

———

"Thank you for inviting me tonight," I say to Leo as we walk down the hallway to his apartment door. My arm is wrapped around his for balance but also because I haven't felt this light since…who cares since when.

Leo fishes his key from his pocket and opens the door for me. "It would have been a boring night without you. Turns out, you are very decent company." He locks the door behind us, kicks off his shoes, and drapes his suit coat and tie over the armchair, then drops to the couch. "How did you wear those heels all night?"

I bend to take off my heels but sway and reach for the wall, a bubble of laughter breaking from me. When I finally get them off, I set them in the shoe bin and walk toward him.

He smiles, shakes his head. "You're going to fall and break your neck. Or wake my Nai-Nai."

"Oh. Sorry," I whisper loudly, then smile and slide onto his lap. "You can just kiss me to keep me quiet."

You're married, Mei Li.

I close my eyes.

Really? Because last I checked, my husband forgot so why can't I? Besides, Mei Li no longer exists, so her marriage doesn't either.

Leo's hands circle my waist, his eyes searching my face. "I noticed the new tattoo, by the way. A little curious about what the rest of it looks like." His hand glides along my bare back, goosebumps rising.

"As they say in your business, I could show you, but then I'll have to kill you."

"I wouldn't want that," he whispers, his eyes on mine.

"What do you want?"

"I really want to kiss you," he says, reaching to cup my face, his hand warm against my skin before his fingertip traces a line down my cheek, over my chin. "But I won't unless you want me to."

I slip my hands through his hair and his run down my arms before inching around my back to pull me closer.

"I want you to," I whisper, my voice muffled and unfamiliar because the words are meant for someone else.

No.

That someone is not my someone anymore.

I press closer to Leo, and he stills, holds up his hands. "We can't do this, Mei Li. I'm sorry. You're drunk and I'm losing control."

"And?" I don't wait for him to respond but kiss him slowly, and from the way he's breathing, I know his resistance is crumbling. I smile against his lips. "You've been flirting with me."

He closes his eyes. "I have."

"Does it mean anything?"

He nods, and I run my hands through his hair again.

"What does it mean?" I ask, breathless.

"It means..." He kisses my neck down to my shoulder. The straps of my dress slip off as his hands slide to my lower back, pressing me closer, setting me on fire.

I undo his top button, then the next and he closes his eyes when his shirt slides off, leaving only a white tank top.

His grip on my waist tightens, and I move to his mouth, but Leo's hands tense, his body stills before he slides me off his lap and onto the couch. Standing, he takes a few steps away. "I can't do this. No matter how much I want to."

His rejection churns in my stomach, mixing with embarrassment and shame. As much as I want to forget my life and leap into his, he's right. I'm the one who's been wrong, not just tonight but for days and weeks and months. I'm a mess and can't get a grip on the ups and downs, the hope and despair, the pain of loving and losing and the fear of what lies in my future now that my past is no longer an option. My will to forget surrenders to guilt and I bend over, heaving the contents of the night and all my shame onto the rug.

CHAPTER 23
EARLY JULY

The cement curb outside the restaurant is warm even through my work pants and harder than the conversation I'm about to have with Lin and Johnny. My hands shake as I hold my phone to distract myself by reading an assignment. I've read the same sentence at least twelve times and still have no idea what it's saying, because I've got other topics blocking entry to my brain. If Lin and Johnny ever get here, I'll tell them what I need to tell them so I can get to The Clubhouse before midnight. No way am I going back to the apartment to wrestle myself now that Mei's ghost and Tavah have both gone quiet. I told Tavah I'd give her time because it's all I can give her.

I swear to myself and click off my phone, grip it in one shaking hand between my bent knees and stare at a beetle navigating the cracked asphalt. It takes me back to the day in Seattle when I got a phone call from Stanford and watched an ant attempt to cross a cement table. That was a lifetime ago as a different version of myself in a different universe. I couldn't be further from that life. Or any life that feels like a real one.

"Miller, you look kinda pathetic sitting on the curb behind a restaurant. It's a new look, though."

I stand, brush off my butt, haul my backpack onto my shoulder, and watch Johnny and Lin cross the parking lot toward me. I lift a hand, wave, drop it.

Lin avoids my eyes, and it's a relief. Maybe we can have this whole conversation without looking at each other. She wanted me to tell Tavah, I told her. Little does she know, I'm about to wreck her world, too. It's what I do best these days.

Johnny punches me in the stomach in greeting, and I smack his hand away, my aim unsteady and sluggish because all my energy's going toward keeping words I need to say near an exit instead of locking them in my vault again.

"Sup, Miller? Why the mysterious meeting?"

Lin pretends to pick at a thread on her shirt, and all I can think is how she's been friends with both of the girls I've been with, and right now, she knows more about Tavah than I do.

"How's Tavah?" I ask, and Lin's head snaps up, her eyes landing hard on mine.

"She's…not herself, as you can imagine."

"Yeah."

"No. You have no idea what you've put her through," she says, hands on her hips as she stares me down. "Think of the worst, then think of the worst of that."

"Lin, dude…" Johnny looks down at her. "Easy, killer."

"It's okay." I shake my head. "I deserve it."

"I'll forgive you someday," Lin says. "When Tavah's not crying eighteen hours a day and after we find Mei, and I see that she's happy. Then we'll talk forgiveness."

I nudge the asphalt with my shoe. "One of those things is never going to happen."

"What do you mean? Which one?"

"The Mei one."

"Oh, she'll come back," Lin says, hands on her hips again. "Just probably not to you."

"No, I'm telling you she's not coming back." My heart is

beating out of my chest when what it needs to do is stop altogether.

"And you know this how?"

"Because she's dead." The words taste like metal. Rusty, corroded metal.

Lin blinks at me, her hand freezing where her fingers are playing with her hair. "What?" She narrows her eyes. "Did you just say she's dead?"

"Miller, what are you doing, man?" Johnny warns.

I let out a shaky breath and hopefully send some of the pain out with it. "It's true." My voice shakes, and I nod to the ground, trying to hold back the emotions pushing their way out of me. "My dad told awhile ago, and I didn't tell anyone because I didn't want to believe it and thought if I never said it out loud, it wouldn't be true."

Lin's eyes widen, and she shakes her head. "You're lying, just like you've been lying about everything else."

I kick the asphalt with the toe of my shoe, fighting back tears. "I wish more than anything I was."

Lin turns to Johnny. "He's lying right? Tell me he's lying like he always does."

He wraps her in his arms, shakes his head, glances at me but looks away. "This is the first I'm hearing of it, but I don't think he is."

"How?" she cries into Johnny's shoulder. "What happened to her?"

"I don't know," I answer. "My dad has been trying to find out. All he knows is that her cousin was murdered and there's a death certificate for Mei."

Johnny pulls her closer, leans over her protectively as she sobs into his shirt.

"I'm so sorry, Lin. I'm sorry about Mei, and I'm sorry I didn't tell you sooner."

Anger sloshes inside me as I stand alone, watching Johnny with Lin. He was never this sad for me when Mei left; he was relieved. He let me move in, yeah, but he acted like I was finally doing what any normal person should do, even if it's not what I wanted. Lin was just her best friend; I was married to Mei.

"Why didn't you tell me, Miller?" Johnny asks, his eyes holding onto mine and not letting go. "It didn't have to be like this."

"How could you have changed anything?" I shake my head, laugh once. "She's gone and she's not coming back, and while you're happy to hear that, I'm not. I never will be, but the only thing to do is for me to get over it, let her go like you told me to when we broke up the first time. But this time, I can't just go to Guo's and fix it. I won't ever find her or know if she's happy and safe somewhere in the world. Because she's not in the world anymore even though she used to be the only thing in mine. She left, she died, she's gone. Like… forever. And I'll still love her, no matter how hard I try not to. If you've got some way to magically fix that, let's talk. If not, don't tell me I did everything wrong." My voice breaks, so I walk away, across the parking lot, a burning knot writhing in my throat. But Johnny's there, wrapping me in his arms, and I tense, then sag into him, shaking as the wave of tears crashes inside me, pulling up pain and hurling it against my insides until some of my tears mix with Lin's on Johnny's shirt, others falling to the asphalt.

"So sorry, man," he whispers, his voice choked as he squeezes me tighter. "I'm so sorry." He swears. "Just let it out, dude. I'm here for you. Don't hold back."

CHAPTER 24

EARLY JULY

Hazy morning light floods the room, and I shift on the bed, rubbing my forehead, my eyes. It's not just the room that's hazy; everything is blurry and distorted, but I can't figure out why this morning is any different from the string of others before it.

I blink my sore, heavy eyes and focus on a spot on the ceiling as the throb in my skull beats backward to last night. My sluggish body suggests it was not a dream.

Closing my eyes, I press my hand to my head where fuzzy memories bob to the surface, then float in embarrassment.

I try to remember the after part of what happened in the living room. How did I end up in my bed, wearing Leo's pajamas when last I remember, I was in a dress, ready to drop it?

My face burns and my chest is cold as I remember how strongly I came on to him last night. Who was that girl? Where did her confidence come from? Was that confidence or desperation?

My neck aches as I recall how I must have looked to him— young, sloppy, and clueless. I don't blame him for stopping me. I would have done the same if I were in his place. I should have stopped myself. But it felt too good to be wanted.

Three knocks rattle the door, and I panic, adjusting the pajama top hanging from me.

"Yeah?" The word scratches my dry throat, and I clear it.

"Brought you some breakfast," Leo says from the other side of the door.

Heat flares up my neck. I can't face him. I should have pretended to be asleep. And stay that way until he forgets that I'm living here.

"Can I come in?"

"Yes," is all I manage to squeeze through my throat as my hands fuss with his pajamas, making sure no skin is showing. If only I'd cared this much last night. I will never drink another drop of alcohol again.

The door eases open and Leo steps in, holding a tray. "Hope I didn't wake you."

"No. Nope." I avoid his eyes and stand, but my head spins so I perch on the edge of the mattress, gripping it to stay upright. "I woke up a few minutes ago," I say to the floor, rubbing my head, my very bad choice still clinging to every movement.

He sets the tray on the nightstand, and I watch the orange juice sway in the glass. "Thank you."

"Yeah, definitely. You're probably starving after..." He pats his stomach and smiles.

I close my eyes. "I'm so sorry, Leo. I'll clean your rug."

"Already done."

I cover my face. "I'm so embarrassed." I hope he knows I mean for everything, because I can't say it out loud.

"No apologies. I should have stopped you at one glass. Or offered you water instead." He shoves his hands in his pockets and smiles, his eyes skittish.

I groan to my lap. "I thought alcohol was supposed to

make people forget but I remember every humiliating thing about last night."

He smiles at the floor, then rubs the back of his head. "Trust me—I do, too."

I meet his eyes. "I'm so sorry, I—"

"Don't apologize. Please. I was very much aware of what I was doing, and it took all my willpower to stop things before…" He mimics vomiting, and I cover my face.

"Don't say it. Please. I'm so embarrassed. And so disgusting."

"Not gonna lie—cleaning up your vomit wasn't my favorite thing but also not going to lie, you weren't disgusting me before that."

I curl my toes into the rug, my eyes burning a hole into the floral pattern.

"But I think you should avoid alcohol in the future."

"That was my first and last. And…about the other…stuff." I swallow. "You've always been so respectful and thoughtful, and I took advantage of that. I was selfish and wrong and I just…I can't lose you over this." I look at my feet as the real fear emerges.

He hesitates, clears his throat, leans back against the wall and crosses his arm over his chest. "Don't get me wrong—I'm pretty sure I'll never stop thinking about last night, but I should have stopped it earlier. I was weak, and I liked it because I like you." He shrugs, talks to the floor. "But I didn't bring you here to seduce you. If all we ever are is friends, I'm okay with that. Kind of." He smiles, his eyes sparking. "But I swear I'll never push you to be anything more. And you will never lose me." He hesitates, then adds, "I should also tell you that I obviously had a lot of alone time last night to think and…I've tried so hard to give you space and not ask too many personal questions. I know there are things you don't want me to know, but last night left me confused and…" He swallows. "I know it wasn't right, I just…I had to know."

I meet his eyes. "Know what?"

"Who you really are. So I went looking. And I found you."

I look around the room then back at him. "Was I missing?"

"Yeah. It seems you were."

Panic ices my insides. He knows. Somehow, he found out. Did I say something I don't remember last night? "What did you find?" My words are sharper than necessary, fear chasing them out of me.

"I—"

"If I wanted you to know any more about me, I would have told you."

He looks away, nods. "I know."

"Then why?"

His eyes scan the floor, his back straight against the wall now, no longer relaxed.

"Tell me."

"Because I was scared." He nods as if to confirm it with himself, then looks at me, his eyes guarded. "Because I don't understand what I'm feeling, and I don't know how to deal with it. And now that I know your story...I still don't know what to do about my feelings. Probably even less now than I did before." He steps out of the room, his footsteps heavy.

I watch as he crosses the hall into his room and seconds later, he's back, holding something toward me.

My eyes lock on the manila envelope in his hand. Hesitantly, I reach for it, then ease open the flap like something's going to jump out at me. I peer inside, slip out the stack of paper and, pressing my lips together, scan the top page. It's a printed copy of a marriage certificate for Peggy and Darius Bromley in the state of Washington on June 21. Signed by Guo, Fen Hua. I flip to the next page, a Standford married student housing application, rental agreements followed by job applications in Vegas and Indiana, a copy of a Berkely student ID with Marcus's picture smiling up at me.

My stomach clenches, and I press my hand over my

mouth as I stare at his picture—short hair, wide smile, dark lashes and darker circles under blue eyes. He's bulkier, his chest and shoulders thicker, like he's been working out. My eyes devour every detail of him, but I don't know this version of Marcus. This is someone else's Marcus.

My heart beats so hard, it threatens to erupt inside me as I pick up the final paper with shaky hands, my world crumbling around me in white paper, black ink. My fake death certificate.

A thought creeps through my mind, and I shove everything back in the envelope to get it out of my sight. "Is it possible that somehow this death certificate could have gotten back to him? Could he think I'm dead?"

Leo pauses, then shakes his head. "I don't...I mean, it's possible, I guess. If someone went digging for information on you. Then yes, they could find it. That's why we did it—

to protect you while we wait for Nick to show his face."

Deep, welling sorrow rises and turns to anger, filling all the empty spaces in my soul. I throw the envelope across the room, eyes on the ceiling as I blink back hot tears.

"I'm sorry, Mei Li," Leo whispers, but I can't respond. I don't know how to respond to this possibility.

When his footsteps move down the hallway, I stare at the floor, tears dripping onto my bare feet. I buried my past a week ago, and I didn't need Leo digging it up and presenting it in an envelope.

Anger boils hotter, and I grab the envelope from the ground and walk out of my room and into the living room where Leo is standing, looking out the window. He glances over his shoulder, then turns to face me when I slap the envelope down on the coffee table.

"This was none of your business." My voice is tight, threatening to snap.

"I never wanted to hurt you, Mei Li. I only wanted to understand you, so last night, after you fell asleep, I went to the office. I found you and then I couldn't stop. I know it was an invasion of your privacy. I was wrong and I am so sorry."

His words singe a path through me, paving the way for hateful words. "Stay out of my life." Turning, I grab the envelope from the table and stride back to my room, slamming the door shut behind me.

CHAPTER 25
EARLY JULY

The view from the fire escape hasn't changed, no matter how much my life has. Guo's shop is still three stories below with a giant window display of Chinese gems this month. And just around the corner, the building where Zhang's used to be and where Dad and I used to be every Tuesday night. The building's still the same, but the inside has changed dramatically from red and black Chinese vibes to a yellow and blue breakfast place. Just above it is Mei's old bedroom window and fire escape where I invited myself up and into her life, because I wanted time with her. I'd gotten my wish, just not as much time as I'd always planned to have with her.

I shift in my creaky lawn chair, the shredded nylon itching the back of my legs near the hem of my shorts. Don't even know how many hours I've spent on this rickety thing, waiting and watching for Mei when I should've been doing biology or chemistry. Can only imagine how stupid my smile was when she appeared on the sidewalk, a burst of light in the otherwise shady Chinatown streets. She didn't even have to notice me or say anything—she always sent a buzz across the street, up the building, and through me like the electrocution I craved.

It's just tourists today, though—a few families wandering in and out of shops, a couple of guys holding hands and carrying matching purple shoulder bags. A group of middle-aged women talking and laughing so loudly, I can hear them over Chinatown traffic and the delivery truck idling at the curb.

When I'd slipped into The Clubhouse two nights ago, it was just past midnight. I'd taken off my shoes and maneuvered around the squeaky floorboards, but Kenna was awake to read my text that told her and Dad I was coming for a few days. She'd waited up and for two hours, I'd dropped the whole story on her. Afterward, I'd curled into a ball in my old bed and cried my way through the new level of loneliness. I'd whispered to Mei's ghost, then to Tavah until the sun rose and I got up and made my bed to trap the emotions inside it.

I've spent hours in my room this weekend, tucked away and protected from the mess I've made of my life. Dad and Kenna have made sure I don't starve but have given me space and are gone all day today at some church party, so I've had plenty of time to think, clean out desk drawers, rifle through my closet and the old pieces of me. I found my shoebox full of Mei's notes and needed fresh air so I slipped onto the fire escape to read every single one.

Now there's a blank sheet of paper on top of the shoebox in my lap, and I'm clicking a pen against the plastic armrest while I think about what to write in my final note to Mei. She'll never get it but maybe she'll read it over my shoulder like she has all my texts to Tavah.

Blinking to focus, I stare at the pen, wondering what will come out of it. What will it help me say? It better have something good because, right now, my head's too full, thoughts pushing against my skull in the form of a headache.

Mei—

The pen sputters, the ink fading to invisible. I rifle through the box for another one, disturbing a few fortune cookie slips floating around inside. I pick up one, flip it over. *You will soon walk a path that feels both unfamiliar and deeply right.* Shaking my head, I crumple it, flip over another. *A forgotten dream will soon resurface.*

If only I could actually forget. Who are these people who forget their dreams? Like my Stanford dream that I gave up for an even bigger dream I also lost. Can't forget either of those even if they've forgotten me. Two for two. Maybe three for three if my Tavah dream ends before it has the chance to get really good.

I lean the chair on its back legs until my phone buzzes, and I slip it out of my pocket to find a text from Audrey.

> Audrey: I hear you're in town and could use some excellent company. How 'bout lunch? 1 PM? My treat. Wisdom is free. :)

I glance at the paper with the faded "Mei" on it. What was I going to say? Maybe it's better to leave things blank, open— unsaid. I've always said too much, then more recently, not enough. My plans have been awful, my ideas nothing but heartache. If I leave this paper blank, fold it, put it some- where, nothing will happen. It'll just be Mei's name on an otherwise blank paper. She'll exist there forever at least.

Folding the note into a star, I put it on top of the others inside the box and close the lid. My phone buzzes again, and I swipe up to tell Audrey I'll meet her at her place in an hour. Except the text isn't from Audrey.

> Tavah: Outside The Clubhouse. Can you talk?

———

Tavah and I talk on the couch until our voices are raspy. Until the spot where our knees touch burns like my throat from too much talking, my heart from too much bleeding, my chest from too much feeling.

Our shoulders touch, both of us surrendering to the couch, gravity, and the weight of the details she asked me to dump on her. Tavah knows everything now—the whole story of Mei and me, beginning to end to present. And she's still here. She didn't even move away from me.

"I know it's all so messed up, and I'm so messed up, but I'm working through all of it." I toss the words out like a grenade.

Her eyes slide to mine and hold them. "Because you feel like I forced you to or because you're ready to?"

"Because I don't want to live in the past anymore. Or hide from it. But also…" I watch my finger trace a pattern on the couch cushion. "I'm not gonna lie and say you're not added motivation to move forward. Because you are. Because I have a lot of feelings that are only for you, and I'm just trying to separate everything." I glance at her, and she looks at her lap, so I duck to catch her eyes. "For the first time since we started dating, I don't know what you're thinking or feeling besides hurt."

She closes her eyes, shakes her head. A tear escapes and rolls down her cheek, and I hate that I caused it. "I'm thinking you're not the Marcus I thought you were."

I nod. "Yeah. I'm not the Marcus I thought I was either."

"I've created a version of you in my head ever since seventh grade. I spent my junior high years waiting for Monday mornings so I could see you again after an eternally long weekend. I studied your yearbook signature for weeks into the summer and talked obsessively about you with my closest friends. I lost my voice cheering for you at games, hoping for one smile or a glance. And now you've told me all of this…really hard stuff…I see you so differently."

My eyes jump around the living room, then land back on hers, my chest tight. "Like how?"

"Like…a guy who gave everything. Like a guy who messed up and who's so hurt and confused and grieving and who maybe I should give up on because he hurt me." Her eyes travel over my face, her hand reaching for my leg. "But…I've also been thinking." She watches her hand. "Just because I haven't done what you've done or experienced what you've experienced, I've made my own mistakes and withheld the truth and needed people's forgiveness more than a few times." She pauses, then takes a deep breath and lets it out slowly before continuing. "I've needed understanding, too."

I shake my head. "You don't have to say those things to make me feel better, Tavah."

"I'm not." She shrugs. "I spread a rumor about one of my friends in eighth grade so my friends wouldn't know I was the one who'd actually said things about a girl I was jealous of. I hurt a lot of people and lost friends. I've hated myself for years over that one. I've lied to my parents before. I've been selfish and afraid of people finding out I wasn't who they thought I was. I've taken credit for things I didn't do, because I was afraid of rejection." She brushes her hair from her face and talks to the empty, quiet room. "I understand intense emotions and what they make us do sometimes because that's what's happening to me with you." She turns her head toward me, her eyes glossy. "Even after Vegas, when I thought you were still married, I knew I couldn't give you up. How pathetic is that? I was willing to be the other woman just to have you. And from the outside looking in, people would call me stupid for being with you. But being on the inside doesn't feel stupid. It feels like…" She looks at the ceiling, sighing the words. "Like I recognize that fear of rejection. And like without you, I might not fully breathe again, no matter how pathetic it sounds. But the thing is, even though this isn't how I pictured my life going, I want it to go this way." She levels her gaze with mine. "If that's what you want."

"What way?" I whisper, my eyes tangling with hers.

"Toward each other." She presses her lips together.

I lean closer, smooth her hair away from her face. "Are you sure? Because I'm not sure what I'd do if I were on your side of this."

"Like if you found out Andrew and I were once married and he'd run away, then died, and I wasn't sure I'd ever be over him?" Her smile is quick, like she's testing it out around me again.

"Yeah. Like that. You're way more understanding than I think I would be."

She looks at the ceiling again and shrugs. "What is there to understand, really? You fell in love, she's gone, now you're grieving her loss with no closure. Who couldn't understand how hard that would be?"

"I was terrified you wouldn't. And would've understood if you didn't."

She curls against me, her hand resting on my stomach. "I'm not going to pretend I don't hate thinking about you being married to Mei Li, but I also can't understand how she could ever have left you. Like, did you two fight a lot or..." She shakes her head, waves a hand. "Never mind. Sorry. It's none of my business." Her fingers trace the pattern on my shirt, and it hurts how much I missed her. "I also get that we can't just turn off our feelings. If it were possible, I would've just turned them off in Vegas and moved on. But...here we are."

We're quiet for a few seconds, the hum of the refrigerator and someone walking in the upstairs apartment the only sounds.

"Marcus?" Her voice is steady but hesitant.

"Yeah?" I wrap my arm tighter around her side.

"I know you're going to eventually move on from everything that happened, with or without me, so I just want you to know that when you're ready, I want it to be with me. If you want that, too."

My eyes roam her face, a trickle of warmth cutting through my icy insides. "You're exactly what I want."

"I know it will take time to let go of Mei Li. So I'll wait until you do. Because I won't share. Only child." She smiles and shrugs.

"From one only child to the other, I'm beyond ready to let her go and move on."

"Because of this?" She sits up and waves her hand between us.

"No." I shake my head. "Because I'm tired of being angry and sad. And those are definitely not the feelings I have when I'm with you."

She stares at our legs and her hand slides to mine, threading our fingers together.

It's my turn to stare at our hands, and while they look so different together than mine and Mei's did, I want something different than I've lived for the last year and a half. I want to live completely unafraid that the girl I want doesn't want me enough. I don't want to worry that she'll leave. I want honesty and stability. I want boring routines and predictable outcomes. I lived in constant fear that Nick would find us or that Mei would leave and both happened, along with the worst possible outcome. But Tavah's still here, on the other side of it all, even after everything she knows about me. If she's not scared away by any of this, there's nothing that will scare her away. I've wasted too much time wishing for Mei to magically reappear when Tavah's been right here in front of me.

"I want you to want me because you want me, not because you feel like I'm conveniently distracting," Tavah says to our hands.

"I've made my decision. I want you and only you. I'm dying to find out what we look like now and in the future. If you wanna go there with me."

Tavah wraps her arms around me, crawls into my lap. "Can't get there fast enough.

CHAPTER 26
EARLY AUGUST

The island is raging, a typhoon howling outside.

I curl up on the sofa, wrap myself in a thick blanket, and close my eyes. I hate storms and I hate being alone in Leo's apartment. I haven't seen him in a couple days. Ever since I freaked out at him, he's been leaving for work before I wake up and coming home long after I'm asleep.

I can't blame him. I was awful to him. He shouldn't have dug around in my past without my consent, but that's not an excuse for how I treated him. I saw my death certificate and Marcus's Berkeley ID and spiraled.

I think about the girl who answered his phone, wonder if she's in his life because I'm supposedly dead. And now I can't take it back, no matter how badly I wish I could. What would I say now anyways? "Surprise! I'm not dead after all." I couldn't. I wouldn't. Not after everything I put him through. He's moved on. I never thought I'd know what was on the other side of us, but now I do and there's no choice but to accept it and let it all be done. I'm so tired of holding back when what I want to do is give in.

The sliding door to the balcony rattles and I glance at it, uneasy as the building sways with the wind. I turn up the TV volume, flip through channels, concentrate on practicing my Mandarin. I've almost distracted myself when thunder cracks, and I flinch, clutching the remote as a memory bursts in my mind:

"Marcus, I'm scared," I whisper and squeeze my eyes shut as I huddle against him in our bed. Wind thrashes against the windows, the apartment creaking in resistance.

"What are you scared of?" Marcus asks, lifting my chin, his eyes searching mine.

I can't say it out loud; it sounds ridiculous, but my physical reaction is making it impossible to hide anything.

"I hate storms," I whisper, clutching his bare stomach when thunder cracks the air.

"That's a shame," he murmurs, his voice playful in the darkness. "I happen to love them because they make you crawl all over me." He wraps me against him, shielding me. "But if you need a distraction, I'm sure I could come up with some…"

Lightning rips open the black sky, and a deafening roar shakes the room. The power flickers, then goes out, and darkness swells around and inside me.

I wish Chang Mama wasn't at her sister's all week. Her steady presence would keep away the fears and memories that are blending, creating a mini-typhoon in my head to rival the one outside. It stirs up more Marcus thoughts, hurling them against my skull, and I clench my jaw before moving aside the blanket and standing, facing the window. Marcus isn't frozen in time. He's not waiting to pick up our life where I left it. He's with someone else in a new life. My worst fear has come true so what could I possibly be afraid of now?

I ball my fists and edge toward the sliding glass door, breathing deeply. I stare through it to the street below, which is just as dark and still as the apartment until lightning slashes the blackness, illuminating shimmering, hateful rivers where streets used to be.

Rain pounds the glass, the storm threatening to break

through it, but I won't give it the chance. I'm tired of waiting for things to happen to me. I'm done fighting the temptations. Grabbing the door handle, I unlock it, and step onto the balcony, closing the door behind me.

Rain pelts me, wind whips my hair, and in seconds, I'm soaked, eyes blurry. Wind hurls thoughts of Marcus with another girl at me, then memories of lying in a puddle of blood at the monastery collide with the moment I said goodbye to Charlie in our Indiana apartment. What has Marcus done with Charlie? Is he still around, letting Marcus's new girlfriend take my place in his life, too?

My final note to Marcus smashes into me, bumps against the mental picture of him lying in a hospital bed. The eternal flight to Taiwan, scanning crowds of unfamiliar faces for Nick's, and the news of Chaz's dead body on a beach slash at me, echoing off the emptiness inside me. The memory of losing the small piece of Marcus I thought I was carrying flies past me, followed by embarrassment from throwing myself at Leo, vomiting on his rug. They slam into me before the wind whisks them away to punish me with the sound of a voice and the beautiful, flowy girl it belongs to. Marcus is kissing her, touching her. Is it the same way he kissed me? And has he given her the parts of himself he promised were only mine forever?

I drop to the cement, blinded by rain and wind, disoriented between then and now, internally bruised and bleeding as the world crashes down on me.

Rain stabs me, something thuds against the building, and I squeeze my eyes shut, wrapping my arms around myself as I shiver. But I don't hide or huddle against the building. I face the reality that's raging around me: I'm not okay. I might never be okay again.

"Mei Li?"

The wind carries my name but whips it away so quickly, I must have imagined it. I turn my face toward the angry sky, knowing it can't hurt me worse than I've already hurt myself.

"What are you doing?" A hand grabs my arm, but it doesn't startle me. I remain still.

"It's not safe out here," the voice calls over the wind. "Come inside!"

I shake my head. "It's not safe anywhere."

Leo squats in front of me, wipes the rain from my face and hair, his eyes following his movements. He squints against the rain, wraps his arms around me, holds me against his chest as he carries me back inside, sliding the door shut behind him. He lowers me to the sofa, grabs my discarded blanket, and pulls it around me.

"I didn't mean to push you away, too." I say through chattering teeth and tears.

"You didn't." He adjusts the blanket, then kneels beside the sofa. "I'm here and I'm not going anywhere." He smooths my hair out of my face. "I'm going to get you some help. Will you let me do that?" He searches my face, pulls the blanket tighter around me.

My body trembles, and I can't find my voice, but my mind reaches out and grabs his words, holding on tightly to them as I nod.

CHAPTER 27
MID-AUGUST

Tavah laughs so hard that the sip of Pelligrino she just took dribbles between the fingers she's holding over her mouth.

I laugh harder and slouch in the corner of our booth at the burger joint we stopped at after the beach. We spent the day learning how to skim board and failing miserably but getting to know the hard sand pretty well. Johnny and the others took off early, and Tavah and I walked up the beach until chafing became a problem for me and shivering overtook her, so we stopped at the first restaurant we saw.

We took some kind of incredible shortcut back to normal even though I thought for sure we were over, but after our talk at The Clubhouse, I didn't want to waste a minute. Since I've been back at Berkeley, I've spent every spare second with her. Made out for, like, two hours yesterday. Didn't even stop when Johnny and the guys walked in on us—I just surfaced long enough to yell for them to get out, but I've got nothin' to hide these days. Tavah and I decided we're both good moving slowly forward. No hurry, no end in sight, just an unlimited number of days together. Since that discussion, we haven't stopped smiling at each other. There's no reason to now that I'm in full Tavah immersion.

She wipes sparkling water off her chin, her face flushed from embarrassment, laughter, and a day in the sun. I lean across the table toward her. "I bet if I made you laugh hard enough, that would come out your nose."

"Please no," she groans, laughing and throwing her napkin down. "It's happened before. It burns."

"Didn't know you were so leaky." I devour some fries, steal a few of hers.

"Didn't know you were so funny. All this time I thought you were nothing but a pretty face."

"Except there was that one time…" I wiggle my eyebrows and squirt more ketchup near the pile of fries between us.

She flings herself back against her seat, hand over her mouth as she laughs, eyes wide, because she knows exactly which time I'm talking about. When she stops laughing, she wipes her eyes and spreads her hand across her stomach. "My aching abs are proof this has been an incredible day." She takes down some fries, then wipes her mouth and crosses her arms on the table and leans toward me. "Can you believe our five-month anniversary is in two weeks? I'm counting from the day we started hanging out."

I gulp some soda. "How do you feel about wasting this much time with one guy?"

"I feel like five months is not nearly enough wasted time with that one guy."

"Approximately how much time do you want with him?"

"All of it," she blurts, nodding. "All the minutes of time."

"You win, then. It's the only thing the Marcus Lottery has to offer. Absolutely no money, but a whole lotta time. You should be more careful what you wish for."

Tavah's green eyes spark as she smiles and studies me, but before I can ask what's on her mind, she tells me. "It's kind of weird, right? That you were married? I mean, I get you thought you had to, but it's a pretty drastic decision for an eighteen-year-old, right? It's so weird to think about. Like you had this whole different life before this one."

I watch my fries, like they're gonna do something extraordinary any minute. "Uh, yeah. Kinda weird, kinda young. Both."

"Would you take it back?

Whoa. She just went for the jugular. There's no excuse or distraction to get me out of this —I have to answer her question. It's not like I haven't thought about it a million times, it's just that I've shoved all million thoughts behind a door and bolted it shut. Besides, depending on the day, the answer changes. No, I wouldn't take it back. Yes? Sometimes. Every time? Never.

I glance at Tavah. "I can't go there, because then I hate that I'm not at Stanford. But then I hate that I think that, because then we wouldn't be together. So it's a pointless, endless sequence of mental cliffs. Plus, I like where I'm at now, sitting across from a gorgeous girl who has a drop of ketchup on her lip."

Tavah swipes at her mouth, then blows me a kiss. "I know how much you like ketchup." She wiggles her shoulders at me, and I lean across the table and kiss her, her lips salty from the ocean and fries.

When we pull apart, she interlaces her fingers with mine, and we hold hands on the table, her green eyes searching my face while her fingertip traces the message she wrote on my arm with Sharpie yesterday. "It's kind of like you're doing life backwards right now, if you think about it."

"What do you mean?" Her touch is sending shivers up, down, and all around me.

"Like…you skipped the whole single life thing and went right to married with responsibilities and loss and now you're back to college and dating."

"They're both stressful." I lean back, my fingers playing with hers.

"How?"

"Because feelings are stressful."

"I love my feelings." She picks up a fry with her free hand and bites it in half, her hair frizzing around her temples, her nose sunburned and shiny. She's gorgeous even after a day of getting pounded by the ocean.

"Don't get me wrong. Feelings can be freaking amazing," I say, smiling at the ceiling. "Especially the right-now kind, looking at your wild hair and sunburned face and the way you handle your fries."

She tilts her head. "How do I handle my fries?"

"You're very decisive about their demise."

"I know what I want."

I pause, wondering what she'd do if she were in my situation. What decisions would she make and how quickly? Would she have moved on faster or slower? Would she have tracked me down immediately and never given up if I were the one who left? I know she would've demanded an explanation. I want one, too, but will never get it.

"What are you thinking…?" She leans farther across the table, and if she leans any closer, I'll see right down her tank top to her very, very small bikini that kept my attention all freaking day. "You're thinking something, I can see it whirling behind your eyes so just say it."

I shake my head, take a long drag on my soda. "Just wondering something."

"Like what? Ask me—you know I'll give you an honest answer. Unless you tell me you're actually still married, and then I'll just leave."

I swear through a smile and shake my head, talk to my soda cup as I rotate it on the table. "Wow. You don't hold back, do you?"

She grimaces. "I went too far on that one. That was insensitive. Sorry, Marcus."

"Nah. It's all good. I mean, I would be. Still married. If she hadn't left and then, you know…left."

She reaches across the table and cups my face with one hand, leans closer and kisses me. "I'm sorry. And I'll never leave you, just so you know."

When we pull apart, I stare into her eyes, which are intensely green when she's serious. I kiss her again, then ease back, playing with my plastic spoon. "What would you do if you were in my position? Like if you were the one who'd gotten married, and your husband took off and was…permanently gone and you never knew why or how?" I glance at her, my legs tense. "What would you have done?"

"Oh." She wipes her mouth, interlaces her fingers along the table's edge, and scans the booth. "Wow. Okay. Umm… that's a huge question. I can kind of see why you hesitated."

"Wish I hadn't asked?"

"No, I just…I'm not sure." She holds my eyes, and I sit up straighter.

"Pretend it was me. Pretend that prom was so unbelievable, we ran away that night. And then a few months later, I ran off to…I don't know…Ecuador or somewhere, but you didn't know that. All you knew was I was gone and then found out weeks later I was dead. No explanation. No goodbye."

The smile slips from her face and she's quiet, her fingers folding her napkin into a tiny square. "First of all…prom *was* unbelievable. Secondly, I love the idea of running away with you." She gives me the side-eye and smiles. "But…in all seriousness, I guess I'd…do the same thing you did." She nods, her eyes clear. "Actually, I probably would've died from heartbreak, but if I narrowly managed to survive all of that, I'd have to move on, because there's really no other choice, no matter how badly I would wish there was. But I wouldn't move on with another guy, because who cares about guys after you?" Her knees bump mine under the table, rest against them. "And while we're on the subject, I'm really glad you decided to give girls another chance. One girl, at least. I personally feel like it was the best choice."

I glance at the table now, avoiding the question in her eyes and bracing myself for whatever she's about to ask.

She tosses the folded napkin aside and leans toward me, her arms folded on the table. "Do you think you'll ever do it again? Get married?" Her eyes rest on my face as she waits, so light even when they're loaded with meaning.

The thought of being with Tavah on a more permanent level has worn a path through my head. But I can't even think about getting married again. Not that I wouldn't commit to her, because I would, it's just…people can walk away from being married.

Instead of answering, I smile and lean in, pointing a fry at her. "Are you proposing to me, T?"

CHAPTER 28

MID-AUGUST

There's finally room inside me to breathe.

The river boat glides down the He River as the hot, hazy day slips into night. From our table for two next to the boat's railing, my eyes skim the dots of light stacked along the shoreline, shimmering on the water.

Leo sits back in his chair across from me, his hair ruffling in the breeze as he sips his soda. Comfortable silence settle between us, silverware clinking against plates and the low murmur of conversation sways around us. The reflection of the city lights rests on his skin until he glows, and I smile to myself. I haven't known very many good men, but there have been two who have made me feel safe and special. And they couldn't be more different.

When Leo found me on his balcony the night of the typhoon and brought me inside, he told me he'd give me space to think. Instead, I'd asked him to stay with me, and the next morning, I'd spilled my soul to him since it was waiting on the surface, stirred up by the storm. I'd told him that every day since I'd left Indiana had felt like I was teetering on the edge of a cliff, staring into the dark nothingness that would eventually swallow me. How it had only gotten worse since my miscarriage. I'd admitted how hard I'd fought every day not to throw myself off that cliff.

He'd listened, and his face had never registered shock or concern. He deals with human stories every day, so I'm not assuming mine is the strangest, but then he'd shared his own.

His mother was pregnant with him when his father decided he didn't want to be a father and left. After she had Leo, his mother had changed and a few months later, she'd taken her life. Chang Mama had raised him, and the question that had always trailed him was whether his mother would still be alive if she'd just told someone how she was feeling and asked for help.

He'd turned to me and said he was here to help me on behalf of his mother.

The same day, I met with a therapist and a doctor and finally, this week, the fog in my head has started to thin. I no longer feel like I'm suffocating in my own thoughts and pain. I realized pretty quickly that my whole life has been a series of me stuffing down emotions I didn't know how to deal with. Lin always tried to get me to talk, but she had her own family issues, and I didn't want to burden her with stuff neither of us could change or fix.

Then I'd met Marcus.

My eyes wander along the skyline as he slides into my thoughts. Usually, when that happens, my first instinct is to distract myself, but tonight I allow him to maneuver through my mind, fill the space that will always be his but hopefully not so painful, given enough time. Having him inside my head should be a shot of energy because that's what he is— adventurous, enthusiastic, hilarious. He dissects every moment and possibility to find the perfect way to accomplish what he wants, and he always succeeds. There isn't a lot anyone could do to slow him down. He's happy most of the time and never accepts no for an answer. Although he uses every moment to his advantage, he also knows exactly when to take things slow. Especially when it comes to me. He's gentle and patient, sometimes shocking, but always bursting with feelings he's never ashamed to show.

He always tried to fix everything by sweeping away the negative emotions, but they always blew right back into my life and are still cluttering my insides. My miscarriage wasn't the beginning of my emotional spiral; it was the drop that had sent ripples through me until I overflowed and almost drowned.

I glance at Leo as he responds to a text, still slung back in his chair, relaxed. He always takes his time and allows me to have as much as I need. He's unassuming and completely content to give people space. He observes every angle and makes sure everyone around him feels important and safe. He's sincere and his honesty bleeds through him. That's why so many trust him. That's why I trust him.

Leo sets his phone on the table and catches my eye, pulling me into the moment with him. "How's your fish?"

I look down at my untouched plate and smile. "I've been too busy enjoying the view, I guess." Blushing, I adjust my napkin on my lap, hoping he doesn't take my comment as flirting. It sounded like it. "Besides, I had a lot of dumplings."

He glances out over the water again, nods, then smiles. "Sadly, I'm disappointed because my dinner doesn't even come close to what I've gotten used to having every night at home." He sighs through a smile. "I think you've officially ruined me."

I laugh, meeting his eyes, which shine in the light reflecting off the water. "Thank you, but I'm fine letting someone else cook tonight, especially if we get to be out here with that view." I tilt my head toward the skyline. "It's beautiful. And it's finally starting to cool down outside, so there's no danger of melting. So thanks for tonight."

"Think of it as a celebration. For your new healing endeavors." He smiles and plays with the fork lying beside his plate. "You seem lighter the last few days." He looks at me for an answer and I nod.

"Yeah. I do feel lighter." Folding my napkin, I lay it beside my plate. "I have a lot more to work on, but it's been so helpful. So thank you for that as well."

"What do you think has made the most difference, if you don't mind me asking."

I slide my eyes to the cityscape, talk to the lights. "I think…I realized I don't know who I am. I'm not sure I ever have. I think I relied on others to tell me what to do and be. Guess it's time to discover myself. As stupid as that sounds."

"Not stupid." Leo leans toward me, folding his arms on the table. "I know things haven't been great since you came to Taiwan, but…" He talks to his plate. "I just want you to know that you're one of the bravest people I've ever met even if you don't think so."

I smile and roll my eyes. "You must not know many people, then."

"I have hundreds of friends, remember?"

I take a sip of my water, smiling against the rim.

"But seriously." He leans back, crossing his arms on his chest. "You've taught me something. Which is really hard to do since my knowledge is already so vast."

Laughing, I set my glass down. "Obviously. So what did I manage to teach you?"

"That life doesn't wait around. It just keeps going, and it's up to us to either ride along or watch it pass."

"Ooh. That is very profound of me. Too bad I haven't learned that lesson for myself, because I've definitely let life pass right by me. I've even let it punch me in the face a few times as it passed."

"Do I really need to remind you that you hopped a plane here and brought incriminating evidence to take down a notorious and very international criminal?" He tilts his head, raises his eyebrows. "Plus, it seems like you've been more confident and self-aware lately."

"Guess I'm growing up before your eyes." I take another sip of water as an unexpected wave of emotion rises from deep inside me and, instead of turning from it, I let the wave crash over me.

"I know a lot happened to get you here, and I know you're not always willing to talk about it, but I'd love to know more about Marcus. He must be pretty great to do what he did, and…it was nice to talk to you about my mother. I want to know about the things that meant the most to you. If you don't mind sharing."

I study his face for a minute, then look down at my plate, allow a slow smile. "I don't mind, I just…Marcus was… nothing I'd ever experienced or could have dreamed would come into my life. I'm still not sure how he landed there, but from the day we met, there wasn't one I spent with him when I didn't smile. Even on our worst days, he always found a way…" I prop my elbow on the table and rest my cheek on my hand. "He was funny, and hyper, and thoughtful and made me feel like I was the center of the world." I play with my fork, warmth trailing the memories through me. "I know he loved me in his big, Marcus way, and I've realized through all of this that I relied on him for my happiness, and he let me. It wasn't the right thing to do. He didn't deserve what I did to him. He gave up everything for me, and I left him with nothing. I shouldn't be surprised he moved on with his life so quickly." I swallow, glance at Leo, and swipe a stray tear.

He doesn't say anything, just watches my face, so I unload the biggest thought I'm carrying tonight. "Anyway, I know there's only one way to make my very ordinary dream of peace and happiness happen now, so I'm ready to do it."

"And what is that, exactly?" He taps his glass with his forefinger.

"I've decided it's time to lure Nick out of hiding and take

back my life, permanently. Or maybe it's more like creating a new life for myself. I've accepted I won't be going back to the one from before. I'm even starting to be okay with it. But I want a future, and I can't have it until Nick is locked up."

Leo rubs the stubble on his face, frowning at the table "I'm not sure how I feel about this idea."

I lean forward and reach for his hand, my eyes holding his. "Well, since I'm all grown up now, I'm not asking your permission." I grin and raise my eyebrows. "I'm done hiding and I'm going to call the number I got at the prison."

"And make yourself a target," Leo says, flatly.

"Yes. A bright, blinking target with THE END written in bold letters across it. And then you'll put him in prison like it's any old, regular day for you."

I grip my new cellphone Leo bought for me and helped me set up a few hours ago, staring at the social media page I just created using my birth name, Zhao Xin Yao. My therapist said I could set up a profile to gain closure—create a digital footprint that will lead to the new version of myself. I'm no longer hiding, I'm becoming, and I'm starting here.

Positioning my new Buddha statue on the windowsill so he's looking out at the city, I take a few pictures, choosing the one where the afternoon light bathes him in gold, then add text:

Guess it's just the two of us now, big guy.

Adrenaline pulses through me, my fingers jittery. Before I can rethink this decision, I post it. But it's what I'm about to do next that makes my skin crawl. I told Leo I was ready for this, but it's never possible to be ready to face Nick. I've built a shield around myself, and to break it down and expose myself to the person who stole my life seems truly stupid. He's always taken more than I wanted to give him, more than he had the right to take, so what would stop him this time, now that his vengeance and hatred toward me have had nothing but time to solidify? The only difference between then and now is there's nothing left to take.

I grab the slip of paper from my meeting at the prison and text the number with stiff, cold fingers.

> I have a message for Nick Chao: Mei Li
> Zhang is looking for him.

CHAPTER 29

MID-AUGUST

Marcus: One full moon night, Marcus and Tavah snuck into the forest to eat the legendary love berries. Tavah took her magical singing spoon and Marcus took snacks. A 30-pound satchel full of them so he wouldn't die of starvation before he and Tavah could convince the love berries to be devoured in the name of true, smokin' hot love. Rumor had it, if you asked them nicely, they usually agreed. Marcus said if the love berries happened to be male, Tavah had to do the talking since her voice could make any male do anything she—

A girl squeal bursts from Johnny's room, and my head snaps up from where it's bent over my phone as I type a bedtime story for Tavah since she has a group project and can't be here with me.

I frown at Johnny's closed door. That squeal sounded a lot like Lin. I just got home from work and had no idea anyone was in his room with him, but I swear if he's hooking up with her, he's moving out, not me.

Murmurs float from under the door, but I go back to

typing my story. I'm almost to the best part when the door flies open and Lin bursts from Johnny's room.

"Marcus!" She darts toward me in a tank top and incredibly short pajama shorts, holding up her phone. "You have to see this." She's breathless, flushed, and I hope it's from whatever's on her phone and not whatever she was just doing with Johnny who ambles through the door shirtless, sweats riding low. I narrow my eyes at him, and he holds up his hands like he's innocent, then leans back against the door jamb, crosses his arms over his chest, and smirks.

"Look," she says, and my attention gives in to the phone Lin's shoving in my face.

A social media profile stares back at me. "What is it?"

"This?" She jabs at a Chinese name I can't pronounce, no matter how many years I've lived in Chinatown. "This is a friend request I just got from this very random girl, but for some reason, I was intrigued enough to find out who she is, and why she wants to be my friend. Because, I mean, I'm fine being friends with people I don't know, but just need to know if they're an eighty-five-year-old perv posing as a girl or something similarly nefarious first."

"So…why did you want me to see this, exactly?" I sit up and set my phone on the cushion beside me, rubbing my hair.

"Because I accepted her request and clicked around, and you won't even believe what I found. Like, there's no way you'll even believe who it is."

"I only know about ten Chinese people, so I'll probably believe you know one I don't."

"No. Really. You know her. Like really, *really* know her." She blinks at me, her face bright red with excitement I don't understand, her whole body vibrating like she's about to explode, and I need to run for cover. "I know your dad said she's dead or whatever, but I'm, like, 99.9999999% sure it's Mei Li."

The moment drops like a giant boulder between us, smashing into pieces. "Lin..."

"Just look." She jabs the screen, swipes. "Taiwan's her location, these pictures of a Buddha statue. Yeah, they're just pictures, but it's what they're saying without saying that's telling me this could definitely be our girl."

Our girl.

My eyes snap to the phone, then dart away, and I shake my head. "It's not her." I swallow. "It can't be, even if we both wish it was."

She narrows her eyes at me. "You didn't even look at it. Here—read the caption."

"I don't have to." I can't keep torturing myself over someone who doesn't exist anymore. "Mei's gone, Lin."

Johnny shifts uncomfortably, runs his hands over his hair.

"But what if she's not?" Lin's eyes devour her screen again. "Have you given up every hope that it's all some massive mistake or cover-up of some sort, and she's alive out there somewhere? That she ran from Gross Nick or something and had to hide or disappear or...I don't know. Anything but what we assume happened?" She blinks at me, clenching her phone. "Or would you even care now that you have someone new and can forget that whole 'love you 365-forever' stuff you said at your—"

"Stop." My voice is louder than I expected, so I get control. "Stop, Lin. There's a death certificate. Don't do this."

"Yeah? Where's her body, then?" She straightens, puffs out her chest like she's gonna fight me. "You can believe she's dead, but I don't have to. There's no way this is some random Taiwanese girl. This is her." She jabs her phone. "This is Mei Li and there's another explanation for all of this. I believe she's still alive, and she's trying to send me a message. Probably because she knows you won't listen even if she tried sending one to you."

I push to my feet, stride past her and her phone, past Johnny still standing silent and motionless at his door. Grabbing my jacket, I walk out the door without looking back and slam it behind me.

CHAPTER 30
MID-AUGUST

My feet hesitate after each step I take toward Great Harbor Bridge. I scan the area around me, my eyes jumping between bridge cables to hundreds of shipping containers lined up along the docks. As much as I'd love to hide inside one and let a ship take me away from what I'm walking toward, I won't get that far. Even though I don't see him, I can feel Nick's eyes watching me, heavy and sharp.

Less than two minutes after I texted the cryptic number on the slip of paper, a reply slid onto my phone screen:

> Great Harbor Bridge
>
> 9:30 PM
>
> Come alone
>
> Bring me what I want

I'd avoided my phone for the rest of the night and washed my hands dozens of times, but they still felt slimy, knowing Nick had been on the other end of that text.

I came alone tonight like he demanded, but I didn't bring

what he wants; I refuse to, even if I could've gotten into the locked evidence room and taken back the diamonds. So I walk toward my fate with only the echo of my timid footsteps and uncertainty about how this night will end to keep me company. It will end one way or another.

My legs fight me, tensing so I'll turn and run in any other direction as I step onto the empty bridge. The city and its distant hum of cars and life is far from done with the day, but this bridge stretches silently across the harbor.

My heart thuds in protest, punishing me for coming here alone and not telling Leo, and I flinch when my phone buzzes in my clenched hand. I pause, breathe through suffocating fear that hangs on me like cold fog as I read the screen:

Keep walking.

My heart stutters, trying to find a hiding place, and my breathing picks up speed even though I'm standing still. In my head, I'm running, and my whole body is ready to make it reality. But running is what got me here in the first place.

I take a deep breath, then two hesitant steps, falter, straighten, and push forward. I'm gripping my phone like I used to grip Marcus's hand during scary movies or storms or when he tried to get me to do something crazy. I hear him telling me everything is going to be okay. He's saying I've got this, just like he did when he convinced me to jump off a cliff into that lake. I feel him holding me from behind, his arms wrapped around me, protecting me like he did when we stood in front of the window and watched a wild lightning storm slash at the Las Vegas skyline. Has it been a whole year since Vegas? How did I get from there to here in one year? The thought digs in, and I drag it behind me as I approach the bridge's half-way point, but a whole new nightmare begins as the bridge rumbles beneath my feet and slowly rotates.

I swivel around, my eyes darting to the only point of

escape, which is now pivoting away from land as the bridge disconnects. The gap between land and the bridge widens, nothing but empty space and deep, dark water below. If I jump, I won't survive. But I might not survive on this bridge, either.

I swallow the lump of fear stretching my throat, and it goes down like a jagged rock, then drops into my empty stomach, sending ripples of nausea through it. My phone buzzes again, and I steady my breathing before glancing at the screen:

> Keep walking. Take the stairs to the top of
> the lookout.

My neck prickles, and my body goes numb like it's trying to fade into the night, so Nick's eyes will burn holes through empty air—black pits identical to his eyes and the darkness they're so used to. I press the record button on my phone before shoving it in my back pocket. Balling my fists, I prepare for Nick to jump at me any moment. Why didn't I tell Leo?

Chang Mama stopped me on my way out of the apartment and asked me a series of questions which I slipped around with vague responses, like that I was going somewhere for ice cream, maybe the McDonalds around the corner, maybe not. Her eyes had narrowed, and I had wondered if she would step in front of the door until I gave her specific details. But she'd asked if I would bring her a hot fudge sundae, and that was my ticket out without further scrutiny.

If only I were casually strolling toward a hot fudge sundae.

My legs tremble as I edge up the spiral wooden stairs, gripping the cold railing, hauling up one foot at a time. My mind flips through scenarios, each ending the same way: with this moment as my last. I can't see beyond it to one where I'm alive and free from Nick's chokehold. But as long as I record the conversation on my phone, and it automatically uploads to my storage like it's set to, let this night end however it's going to end.

At the top, the view expands and widens, nothing but black sky touching black water. But there's no Nick. I spin around, my eyes dissecting every shadowy corner, every angle big enough to hide a human.

The bridge stops turning, and I grab for the railing. The entire structure is parallel with the shoreline, no access on or off. If Nick's on the bridge, it's just me and him, and I was so, so stupid to come here. He set me up and my only options are to jump into the water or find a hiding spot among metal bars. But as I turn back toward the stairs, my eyes snag on a shadow moving toward me in the middle of the platform.

Nick pounces, grabbing my arm and dragging me to the edge before shoving me back against a bar. I cry out, the cold steel grating against my spine. But his eyes skewer me to the railing.

"And all this time you thought you could outrun me. Even tried faking your own death." He laughs. "I knew it was only a matter of time before we'd be together again." His words slice across me, and my breath cowers in my throat, stomach knotted. I close my eyes as a silent scream gnashes through me, desperate for a way out, but even if I release it, the only place for it to go is right back at me.

A tear burns my cheek, and anger at myself for letting Nick see my emotion in liquid form flares in my chest. He grips my cheeks with his coarse hand, leaning in so close, his lips brush my ear and my stomach writhes.

"I've waited too long for this." He moves only his free arm to pull something from his waistband, then presses it into my side. Cold steel bites at me before he runs the barrel of the gun up my side to my neck, along my collarbone. I hold my breath until his arm jerks back and pain shoots through my cheek, stars exploding around me.

I double over, but Nick grabs my face again, his rough hands hauling me upright as I try to catch my breath. He sneers something through gritted teeth, but it doesn't register as he shoves my face, throwing me to the wood planks. Tears sting as they rush my eyes, my palms on fire and oozing blood, smearing the wood with what will likely be the last of me while I attempt to steady the swaying world on my hands and knees. I tremble but push upward, stumble to my feet, the pain burning in my face and hands ushering in determination until I laugh a rough, sharp sound I've felt but never made, and my eyes land on him. "I must really be something if you'll go to such lengths to kill me. Moving a bridge? I'm flattered."

"Or merely an insignificant whore who took what didn't belong to her, including my freedom. Wasn't it only fair that I took away something you wanted?" He crouches, pets the gun in front of my face. "I enjoyed watching the detective's son bleed, knowing how much it would hurt you. I only regret that my aim was just a little off that day."

His words are knives slashing my heart.

"It was a great warm-up for my interaction with Chaz. My aim was spot on that time." He smiles at the gun. "He didn't seem the type, but he begged for his life. You will, too, no matter how strong you think you are. Impressively, the only one who didn't was the old woman. She put up a bigger fight than anyone ever has."

"What did you do to Guo Mama?" I hiss, rage pushing out of me until it slices the air between us.

"Let's just say she gets around much slower these days." Nick grabs my arm and yanks me to my feet, his gun pressed to my temple, but my phone clatters to the ground and my head snaps toward it. The red record button blares into the night, but I jerk my attention back to Nick so he won't look at it. "Wow. Hurting an old woman. Now you've really proven your strength and power."

He grabs my throat, still holding the gun to my temple. "Sadly, my men followed my instructions, and I didn't get the personal pleasure of hurting her, but I get the immense privilege of dealing with you."

"You assume you can hurt me." My words squeeze out as I meet his eyes, not even allowing a blink.

He shifts so his hips pin me against the railing and lowers his mouth to my ear. "And you assume I've done my worst."

His hand grips my lower back, pulling me tighter against him. "Before I kill you, I just want you to know that you may have outrun me after L.A., but not after Stanford. I followed you to Vegas and was there for everything. I watched you with the detective's son." He grabs my backside. "I watched you give yourself to him and when you weren't home, I slipped into your apartment and touched everything of yours. I was always there, even though you thought you'd outsmarted me."

I squeeze my eyes shut but can't hold back the tears that are frantic to escape and slide away from Nick defiling my most sacred memories. My throat thickens, and I choke on anguish while Nick laughs, slow and steady. It drags evil up from his depths, coils around me. He shot Marcus. Killed Chaz. He hurt Guo Mama and has done worse to countless others.

"Do it," I say, my voice tight but steady. "Don't monologue—this is your big moment and who am I to make you wait any longer?"

Nick smiles, then lifts his gun to my forehead, his eyes empty, black holes. "Give me what I asked for and I'll return the favor."

"You think I could just get evidence from a locked police facility? Again—I'm flattered but you really give me too much credit."

He's so close, the smell of his sweat clings to me, and I want to swipe at my face, but his gun is pressed into my temple, so I don't move. I meet his eyes and brace for the bullet that will end it all when a distant gunshot cracks the air followed by a blast so loud, I drop to the ground, a scream ripping from me as I cover my ringing ears and curl into a ball. The air vibrates right before pain seeps through me. Terror and confusion sit on my chest, my breathing fast and shallow as Nick writhes on the planks beside me, his hand pressed to his stomach, blood oozing between his fingers. Something warm trickles down my arm and I blink at the stream of blood, creating a puddle beside Nick who's gone still.

The world shakes, but my head's too heavy to lift, and I'm wrapped in dizziness until, seconds or minutes or hours later, arms wrap around me.

I struggle against them until a voice cuts through the blur, saying my name. My mind reaches it, holds on tightly, clinging.

"I'm here, Mei Li. I've got you," Leo says against my cheek, his voice trembling. "You're safe now."

CHAPTER 31

MID-AUGUST

The couch has grown around me over the past six hours since I got home from work. My eyes stare at the TV but don't really see anything, because my head's not here. First it was with Tavah at her family party I couldn't go to because of work, then wishing she was here with me on this couch instead of staying at her parents' house for the night. The Bay seems like a massive black hole when she's all the way on the other side of it. Then my head slid to social media profiles for a girl in Taiwan, and it's been stuck there as I've flipped through channels. Not even sure what time it is, just really late. Or maybe early. I tilt my phone up from where it lays on my chest. 2:47 AM. Johnny and Lin went to some party with the guys, and no one's back yet so it's just me and a weird lady with a 70s haircut talking about a cleaning product.

I text Tavah even though she won't read the message for a few hours.

> Marcus: Pretending you're lying beside me on my couch and we just had a conversation about moon dust. Is it real? Is it possible? How would any of us earth dwellers know? You brought up some great arguments, I had some but got distracted by your lips and we took a looooooong break from conversation and did some other stuff instead. How were your grandparents? Send pics of the destination T-shirts. I can only hope they're from places like Missouri or North Dakota. Thinking about taking the train specifically to sneak in your window. But what if I got the wrong window since I've never been inside your old house? What if I go in the guest room window and slide into your grandparents' bed? I'm too afraid. I'll stay here and not move until you get back tomorrow. Imagination's running absolutely wild. Love you, gorgeous.

I stare at the text, read it again, then add "So,so bad" before sending and staring at the screen, my fingers itching to stay busy so my mind doesn't wander toward social media profiles. But Lin's what ifs have been flashing in my head all day. What if that girl was Mei? What if Dad was wrong about her dying or was given false information?

If I found out Mei was alive, but not with me, would it change anything? Would it hurt less or more? Also…it would mean I'm still married. What was she planning on doing about that?

My mind and fingers team up and slide across my phone's screen to the app I've been tempted to open since I saw the profile on Lin's phone. But when it loads, I can't make my fingers type to search. Mei's dead. That girl can't be her. I'll just slide into darkness again and have to claw my way back out of it again.

Tossing my phone on the couch, I shuffle to the kitchen in

the dark for a drink. I fill a cup, gulp water, stare at my phone on the couch, like a blinking, red button I should never touch. I down another glass of water, stare harder at my phone until it beeps and I pause, because it's probably Tavah. Please let it be her.

I weave back toward the couch, snatch my phone, and drop to the cushions, elbows on my knees. Not Tavah—Johnny.

> Johnny: Won't be home tonight. This place is insane. U shoulda come. See you sometime tomorrow.

I flop back on the couch, stretch out, lay the phone on my chest, and close my eyes. A name I don't recognize blinks in my head like an obnoxious neon light and there's nowhere to switch it off. I clench my phone, hesitate, then swipe back to the app. I find Lin's profile and search names until I land on the one she showed me: Zhao, Xin Yao. Not even close to her name. My finger hovers over it before I tap, then close my eyes for 2.4 seconds, open them.

They burn, but I don't blink, just subject them to whatever pops up. The girl's profile picture is clouds, one word bio—Taiwan—then the latest post: a picture of a Buddha on a windowsill, staring out at some unknown city. My eyes gather all the words, ashamed but greedy. *Guess it's just the two of us now, big guy.*

My heart's pounding so loudly I can hear it in my ears as I scroll to the next post. A picture of numbers scrawled on skin in dark, bold handwriting. My stomach knots. April 12. June 21. January 24. June 21. My legs go numb, like those numbers are slowly cutting off circulation. April 12: the day I met Mei. June 21: wedding day. January 24 day she left. Beginning, middle, end. I bolt upright, hauling in air, sweat creeping across my forehead. But why June 21 twice?

I fumble through memories for the significance of the

second June 21. Maybe this isn't Mei. It's all coincidence. Meaningful for someone else, too.

My thoughts sprint, dart, gather, all of them knowing what this is—who this is—a crowd of them staring at me while I huddle in the dark corner, refusing to acknowledge them. June 21, wedding day, more recently our one-year anniversary, which I spent with another girl. My mind rewinds to that day and my stomach drops. Tavah and I at her apartment, getting ready to go on a hike.

Spam call from Taiwan.

Tavah answered. No one responded.

I close my eyes, suck in air like I'm having an asthma attack. Hold my breath, almost choke. I swear at my phone, stare at the dates. Scroll back to the most recent post of Buddha from two days ago.

But she's dead. And this is not her name.

I jump to my feet, pace the living room as I scroll, my fingers shaking, eyes glued to the screen and the photo of a table covered in food, which I examine for signs of Mei—the way she always garnished using Chinese characters. I zoom in closer, my chest alternating between ice and fire. There it is: a character made of baby carrots. My lungs ache as the screen slides to a post of lanterns strung across a busy street, a monkey on a bench, a blanket draped over knees, two sets— hers and someone else's? Is this some kind of joke? Did someone else create this profile in her memory? Are they messing with me? Did Lin do this?

The next post is just a quote overlaying a fortune cookie.

Saying goodbye to a life you were never meant to have is the hardest thing.

My chest tightens, then twists, and I clutch my phone, desperate to reach the pain inside me and rip it out. If this is Mei, how? And why now?

The silence in the dark apartment pounds against my ears,

and my finger reflexively taps the screen until I'm calling Dad. He's used to 3 AM calls.

"Marcus?" His voice is crackly when he answers.

"Is it possible Mei's still alive?"

The other end rustles and his voice is gravelly through the speaker. "What do you mean?"

"There's a social media profile. It seems like it might be her, but I need to know for sure. Can you help?"

CHAPTER 32
MID-AUGUST

A hospital room is the very last place I would have chosen to spend last night. After everything happened on the bridge, Nick and I were both loaded onto stretchers, hauled into separate ambulances, then driven to the hospital. When we arrived, they rolled me in one direction and him in another, which I hoped was toward the morgue.

A doctor examined me, then nurses stitched and wrapped my arm where a stray bullet from Nick's gun had grazed me when he was shot. Had I been standing a little closer, it could have been much worse. The psychiatrist didn't treat me like I was so lucky. He scrutinized the contents of my brain and wrote me a prescription I'll never fill. Then I was told they wanted to keep me overnight for observation.

Leo never left my side and while neither of us slept, we sat in silence, listening to the heart monitor's beep in the darkness. Leo was still here this morning when I gave my statement to an officer and when she left, he told me how he'd found me.

He'd been finishing up a few things on a case when Chang Mama had called him to say she was worried, because I hadn't returned from running for ice cream and she was certain something was wrong.

What I didn't know when he set me up with my new phone was that he'd shared its location with his phone so when I hadn't answered his calls, he'd tracked me to the bridge only to find it inaccessible. He'd called in a team and ordered them to shoot anyone on the bridge who wasn't me.

A few had gone to the bridge control center where they'd found the operator dead in an otherwise empty room. They'd overridden the controls and turned the bridge so Leo could get to me. The first bullet had taken Nick down, the second was from Nick's gun and had grazed my arm.

A nurse streams through the door with a tablet in her hands. "Good news! You're being released," she says in Mandarin.

Leo sits forward in his chair beside my bed. "That's great news," he says, nodding at me as I take the tablet from the nurse. His phone rings and he pulls it from his pocket and glances at the caller, then back at me. "I have to take this. I'll be right back," he says, answering as he walks out of the room.

I turn back to the tablet, signing myself out of this hospital, hopefully forever, then slip off the bed, careful not to jostle my bandaged arm and step into my shoes before going in search of Leo. I push through double doors to the waiting room, relieved to find him standing near a window, still talking on the phone.

I linger at the edge of the waiting area, giving him space and keeping the exit within a few steps, but his tone snags my attention.

"I was, yes." He nods, listens, talks to the floor. "I'm not going to pretend it wasn't a career high to see him cuffed to a stretcher and wheeled away."

Nick. Still somewhere in this building. Or better yet, dead.

Leo pauses again, glances out the window. "I can't give

you details about her or the—" Leo stops short, his jaw tight as he stares into the waiting room, listening to whoever's on the other end of the line. "I'm not sure why you need that information about her considering your person of interest is headed to prison." He stares at the tile again, rubs his forehead before he rushes, "Look, that information is confidential, no matter who you say you are."

My toes stiffen, holding me in place, because Leo's talking about me and my stomach twists when his voice hardens.

"You're a detective, figure it out."

He ends the call and shoves his phone in his pocket. I consider hiding behind a plant or darting out of the room so he doesn't know I overheard his conversation, but he turns and his eyes land on me.

"Hey," I say, "I was just coming to find you."

"Hey, sorry." He walks toward me. "I didn't know you'd be so fast."

"Is everything okay?"

He grabs my hand, and we walk toward the sliding doors. "Yep. Just the first of many calls from people trying to get information."

———

I wake up drenched. My heart pounds in my ears, so I breathe through my nose to stay centered like my therapist taught me to do when I get stuck in panic or fear. It's been four nights since the bridge; each night, I've woken from a nightmare. Usually, Leo is here to talk me through them, but last night he stayed in his own room since he would be leaving early for the hospital to interrogate Nick.

In tonight's episode, Nick held a gun to my head. He was yelling, his spit landing on my face, curse words flying like knives around me. The air was fuzzy with fear before a gunshot cracked the air and everything went dark and silent. Instead of me being shot, though, this time it was Marcus.

Swallowing the pain from the image of blood pooling around Marcus's lifeless body, I swipe tears from my cheeks and breathe to calm my heart. I lightly run my fingers over the stitches and angry red gash on my arm, grateful I was the one who was shot, not Marcus. He wasn't near the bridge or Nick. He's safe in his beautiful, perfect life as he was always meant to be. And I'm safe in mine, thanks to Leo who assures me that even though Nick is still alive, he'll spend the rest of his days behind bars.

And while Leo's been here to help me work through what happened, he isn't who I really want to talk to right now. Before I left, Marcus was who I talked to about everything. But he's no longer an option. Before Marcus, it was Lin, always eager to know everything even if what I told her was vague. She loathed Nick, and I can imagine her squeals of excitement over hearing he's headed to prison. I miss those squeals.

I glance at the time, do some mental subtraction. I have no clue where she is now, but I'm lucky to be alive and she's the only person I want to talk to.

My heart beats in my neck, echoes in my stomach as I push away thoughts of rejection and grab my phone from the nightstand. I've had her number memorized since seventh grade and when she answers on the second ring, her voice takes me back to nights on my fire escape, laughing and gossiping.

"Hey Lin, it's me. Mei Li."

Noise in the background drowns out her words until her voice bursts through the line. "Mei Li? Are you serious? Is it really you?"

"It's really me."

The pause swells, then bursts through the speaker with her voice. "Oh my gosh! Oh my gosh!" she rushes in a whisper. "Hold on—give me a second. I have to go somewhere quiet. Don't hang up, okay?" A door slams, and the background noise fades before she goes full Lin on me.

"Where have you been? Was that your friend request? I knew you were alive. I knew it. Tell me everything. Where are you?"

Her excitement lifts the heaviest layer of self-doubt and rejection, and I laugh for the first time in days. "It's so good to hear your voice." I smile into the purple morning. "I've missed it so much. And you."

"Mei Li, do you think I haven't missed you? I heard you were dead and now, I want to kill you for making me think that for so long."

"I had no idea that news reached you. How did you hear?"

"Marcus. Who heard from his dad who heard from who knows where, and he still thinks you're dead, by the way, even when I told him I didn't believe it. And then, the friend request was all the proof I needed, even if it wasn't your name. I can't wait to tell him—"

"No. Lin, please don't tell him. Don't say anything. Promise me."

"Why not?" she asks, and when I don't respond, she goes on. "Actually, never mind. Let's not waste time talking about him. Your bio says Taiwan. Is that right?"

"Yes."

"Why are you there? Is everything okay? Are you safe?"

"Yes, I'm totally safe. Not dead."

"Then why were you pretending to be dead? That's not something you can just not explain."

I search for the right words to sum up the last year and a half. "It's a long story. I'm not even sure where to start."

"How about with the basics? You can't come back from the dead and say it's a long story. Obviously, it's a long story."

I quickly give her the reasons for coming to Taiwan, Leo, and what's happened since I arrived, leaving out things I'm not sure I can say, and when I finish, Lin is quiet for too long. "You still there?"

"I still have so many questions."

"And I promise I'll answer all of them someday. I just wanted to call and tell you I'm alive and hear your voice."

"And I'm so happy you did, but when are you coming back? When can I see your face?"

"I…don't think I'm coming back." I brace for her reaction.

"What?!" she shrieks. "Why would you stay there?"

"I think it's for the best. It will be easier to start over here." Going back might actually kill me.

"So that's why you don't want me to tell Marcus? You want him to still think you're dead?"

I squeeze my eyes shut. Her casual mention of his name rips open the carefully patched hole inside me. "Have you seen him?"

"Uh, yeah. A lot actually. I'm at Berkeley, too, and sort of have a thing with Johnny, so I'm at his apartment almost every day."

"You and Johnny?"

"Are just having fun."

I put my hand around my throat. Knowing she sees Marcus in his new life every day deflates any excitement or curiosity about her and Johnny.

"You okay?" she asks, and I nod like it will help convince myself.

"Yes. Fine. Just…I miss him so much."

"Why didn't you tell him why you left?"

I gather my voice, pull it out of the puddle of waiting tears. "I don't know. I've wondered that every day."

"So does he."

My hand tightens around my neck until my nails dig into my skin. "I don't think he wonders about me anymore."

"I think you'd disagree with yourself if you were here and saw him."

"I called him a couple months ago. On our anniversary." The words scrape up my throat. "It was impulsive and desperate, and I instantly regretted it."

"You called him?" she shrieks. "What did he say? He never told us."

"He wasn't the one who answered his phone."

A few seconds pass before she responds. "Oh." Her single word is heavy with understanding and unspoken realities, and when she finally speaks again, her voice is weary. "I'm sorry, Mei Li. I can't imagine how that made you feel."

I mentally swat away the question buzzing around my mind, but it finds an escape route. "Is that his girlfriend?"

"Yes."

I move my hand from my throat to my chest, breathe through my nose. "Do you know her?"

"Yes."

I press my lips together. "Is she good to him?"

"Yeah, she is." Lin sighs. "Mei Li, my heart is basically bleeding to death for you, but no matter how much I love you, I don't blame him. He thought you were dead. I was mad at him for a really long time, but honestly, when he came back to San Francisco, he wasn't the same guy. He was in a million pieces and had to put himself back together without knowing why." She's quiet again before saying, "You know I'm Team Mei Li always and forever, but all that happened wrecked him. And Tavah's helped him put his life back together."

Tavah.

Tears flood the cracks between my shattered places. "I'm happy for him. Really," I say, failing to keep my voice steady. I take another deep breath, gain control so she can't hear the pain ransacking my soul. "I just really needed to hear your voice and know that you're doing well."

"Mei Li, I'm so sorry you—"

"I have to go, but will you please not say a word to Johnny or Marcus about me calling?"

"Umm…sure? But—"

"I'll call again as soon as I can, promise. Love you." I end the call and release the sob expanding in my chest, hand over my mouth. Even if Lin wanted to call back, she can't; Leo made my number untraceable, just like I have been as my life moved on without me. I'm invisible now—a ghost in Marcus's past.

CHAPTER 33

LATE AUGUST

"Dude, that game was insane," Johnny says as we walk home from the intermural flag football game we just dominated. "You still got it, Miller."

"That felt good." I grin into the night as we turn up the street to our apartment. "I needed that. Thanks for signing me up without asking me first. And thanks for forcing me to go when I told you no."

Johnny smiles. "It's been too long since we've been on a field together so I'll take what I can get. Plus, getting you off Tavah long enough to have some guy time wasn't easy but worth it."

I laugh. "Like you have any room to talk." I shove him and he laughs, holds up his hands. I look ahead as we walk. "But you're not wrong that she totally consumes me. And I'm totally fine with it. But I gotta say...tonight's game kinda cleared my head and got my feet itching to kick a soccer ball around."

"Say no more, my friend. You name the time, I'm your guy." Johnny smiles into the air ahead of us.

"Deal."

Silence settles between us until Johnny says, "Everything okay?"

"Why?" I grip my backpack straps as I walk.

"I don't know, just…you seem kind of distracted, and maybe it's that you can't wait to see Tavah since it's been a whole day and your hormones are calling but…just wondering if there's more. After that conversation with Lin and everything."

I haul in a deep breath, then blow it out, long and steady, words catching it and riding out of me. "I wouldn't say everything's okay necessarily. I sorta went down a rabbit hole the other night." I glance at him, then add, "A social media rabbit hole."

"And?"

Our shoes scuffing the cement is the only sound until he asks, "You think it's her?"

I kick a pebble, watch it bounce and veer off the sidewalk into grass. "It's all I can think about but still don't have an answer."

"What does your gut tell you, though?"

I close my eyes for a second, open them, let honesty roll. "I think Lin's right. I think it's her."

"Does Tavah know about it? The whole thing?"

I hesitate, then shake my head. "Not yet. Not gonna tell her unless I need to."

"Mmmhmm."

"Dude…this is crazy, right? Like, what's wrong with me that my life is always so messed up? Why did I ever think it was a good idea to fall for Mei? She just wrecked everything, and it feels like she's still trying to."

"You were blinded, man. She's so fine, you couldn't see beyond her. Every guy gets that, but…yeah…she just…" He trails off, looks at the ground, then back at me. "Look, Miller, there's…" He takes a deep breath, swears at the ground, shakes his head, looks away.

"You good?" I ask, watching his face, wondering what's coming next since Johnny's rarely serious.

"Yeah, just…I am, but…" He growls to the sky, scratches his head, talks to the sidewalk. "There's something I gotta tell you, bro. It's been eating me alive since this morning, because I promised Lin I wouldn't say anything, but I can't keep it from you. It's too big, so she'll just have to forgive me."

I frown, my pulse jumping. "Okay…"

He looks up, meets my eyes, draws in a deep breath. "You don't have to question if it's Mei Li's profile. Because it is."

I stop walking. "What? How do you know that for sure?"

Johnny stops, looks at the sky before facing me. "She called Lin."

His words are suspended in the air between us, so big and real, when they finally drop, they're gonna bust a hole in the ground. His eyes zigzag across my face as the world slams to a stop, pressing me from all sides, like its folding in on itself.

I wait for him to elaborate and when he doesn't, I blurt, "Are you for real?"

He nods spastically. "Yeah. I…" He blows out a frustrated breath. "I'm so sorry. This is definitely not how you should find out about something this big."

I bend over, grip my knees, breathe through my nose.

"I'm so sorry, man," Johnny says again. "Maybe I shouldn't have told you but feel like I owe it to you."

"What did she say?" I croak at the ground, wondering if I want to know.

Johnny hesitates, shifts, drums his thumb against his thigh. "Lin called and told me right before the game. I guess she wasn't supposed to tell anyone, but she was freaking out so hard, like excitement and anger and panic. Took a minute to calm her down, but she gave me the whole story, and I've been wondering if I should tell you and how and what's the best thing to do with this information." He swallows. "I knew it would wreck you, and I'm so tired of her wrecking you, especially since you're really moving on, so what good would telling you do? But I can't keep it from you, man. You gotta know, and I'm sorry. I don't know what this means for you, but...Mei Li's definitely alive. She's in Taiwan. And that social media profile is really hers."

My throat burns, my toes curl. I swallow to pave the way for whatever comes out of my mouth, then straighten, hands clasped on top of my head. "This can't be happening."

"I know. It's freaking messed up."

I close my eyes, talk to the sky. "Why did she call now?"

"No clue." Johnny leans against a tree, crosses his arms. "All I know is that Lin was expecting a call from the financial aid department so when she saw an unknown number, she answered, but it was Mei Li." He watches me carefully, his throat bobbing.

Nausea rolls, and I bend over to puke in the gutter. Squatting, I hang my head, breathe through my nose while my world unwinds, stripping everything bare again. "I just...I need to be alone right now. Sorry, man. Thanks for being a bro and telling me."

He shakes his head. "I don't think that's—"

"I just need to think."

He hesitates, shifts. "Share your location and I'll give you space, but promise me if things get too heavy, you'll call."

I drag out my phone and share my location, hands shaking. "Done."

"Okay. I'll be waiting at the apartment to talk about it. No matter how late you get back."

———

I trudge up the apartment building steps, jaw tight, head and heart locked, because they were too loud and couldn't agree. It's been a few hours since I left Johnny. He's texted a few times but has given me space to think like I asked him to.

I'd walked aimlessly, numb and stiff. I'd ignored all beeps from my phone. Puked in a campus garbage can. Twice. Wished I had a car or a motorcycle to take me so far away even though it wouldn't change anything. All I had were my feet, which stumbled along sidewalks and shuffled across parking lots and parks before barely hauling me back to the apartment.

As soon as I'm through the door, I collapse on the couch, stare at the wall as Johnny eases down next to me, texting while he waits for me to talk, and a couple minutes later, I speak for the first time since he left me alone to come undone. "What did she say? When she called?" My face and neck are clammy like a fever just broke.

Johnny sets down his phone, leans on his knees, talks into the living room. "It was a short call. She told Lin that she's in Taiwan."

My mind throws itself in reverse, back to the spam call Tavah answered and messed with the caller. The unknown caller. From Taiwan.

My eyes go blurry, but then I blink, laugh at the ceiling. "Not only did she leave and fake her death, but she did it as far away as possible." I stare into the stale living room and swear, lean forward on my knees, parallel with Johnny.

"This is so messed up."

"Beyond," I say, mostly to myself. "And the crazy thing is, after checking out her posts, deep down I knew it was Mei. She called me, too. I just didn't know it was her."

He turns his head toward me. "What?'

"Got a call on June 21—our one-year anniversary. From Taiwan. Thought it was spam. Tavah answered, but the caller didn't say anything, then hung up, and my head had already been circling Mei that day so from that moment on, my mind wouldn't let it go. The whole 'what if' thing." I talk to my feet. "But no one wants to admit out loud that their wife left and faked her death to get away. I'd so much rather hear she'd decided she's a lesbian. Anything but leaving and pretending to be dead."

Johnny whistles, long and low. "Wow. I'm so sorry, man." He cracks his knuckles. "She's messed with you too much and for way too long, and I'll always hate her for it."

"Wish I did."

He glances at me, doesn't say anything. My phone vibrates and I ignore it.

"Did she bother explaining why there's a death certificate with her name on it?"

"Not really. Lin said she was kinda vague."

I push up from the couch, rub my head as I head to the kitchen and yank open the fridge. "Doesn't get better than this," I say to the tortillas. "People come back from the dead all the time, make casual phone calls like their phone died for the last seven months." I swear and chug the orange juice meant for Tavah. I'll buy her twenty more, a whole refrigerator full, because it means she's alive and with me and not playing stupid games from some stupid country for a stupid reason that makes no sense. "Like she can just leave, then show up again and ruin what I've got with Tavah. Like she can rule my life alive or dead. But it's not happening anymore," I rant, gripping the orange juice bottle. "She left me in the hospital, wrote a one-sentence note to say goodbye, and that was it. She left willingly. Not because of Nick. Next thing I heard was that she was dead." My brain goes through the list again, checking to see if I've missed anything the other 2,000 times I've examined Mei's absence in my life. "That was the end, no matter if it's true or not. She's dead to me regardless, and I'm gonna leave it that way."

My thoughts land solidly on Nick, roll to Chaz. But then every word from her note flashes across my mind in slow motion, and my suspicions break apart and scatter into pieces of all the things I'll always fear but never know. We had a fight. We had a lot of fights. We were always good at making up, though, so I'm not sure why our last one made her leave and stretch it across miles and continents. She didn't fix anything like her note said she would. She blew everything up, and it can't be put back together.

My phone pings and jolts me out of my monologue. Setting down the bottle with shaky hands, I slide my phone from my pocket, shut off the alert, and call Dad, hoping everything's okay, because I'm not.

"Hey," I say when he answers, acting like this is any regular old Thursday night.

"M.C. Where've you been? Tried calling you about 30 times."

"Just…walking home."

"Got some news for you."

I tense. "Does it have to do with Mei, because if so, I don't want it."

"Uhh, what's wrong?"

I shut the fridge door, slide down it, land hard on my butt, swear. Bending my knees, I lean an elbow on one, hand in my hair. "Mei's alive."

"How'd you hear?"

"Johnny. She called Lin."

Dad swears through a sigh. "Yeah. That's why I was calling. I'm at the station, and things are blowing up. Just heard that Nick's in critical condition in Taiwan, and the news that's rolling in places a female with him at the time of the incident that put him in the hospital. I'm trying to keep up with the reports, but I'm pretty sure it was Mei Li."

I lean my head back against the cool metal.

"I made a call to the lead detective asking about her, but he was tight lipped. I'll keep trying to find out more."

CHAPTER 34

LATE AUGUST

Steam from the rice cooker hovers in the kitchen and mixes with the heat from the sizzling wok. I've already made a full batch of pork buns, dumplings, fried tofu and bean curd, and now I'm chopping the vegetables to add to the wok but my mind is far from this kitchen, replaying my phone call with Lin.

I should be so happy that Marcus is so happy. And I am. Except even coming out of Lin's verbal fountain of excitement, the news was lethal. I keep wondering if there was anything I could have done to save us. Part of me believes if I'd chosen differently, we'd still be together. If I'd stayed in Indiana, I could've been there while Marcus recovered. Yes, Nick still would've been out there somewhere, but Marcus and I could've made a plan together.

But it was never that easy. It would have just grown more dangerous for us, and one or both of us would have ended up dead. Even if we managed to survive Nick, Marcus's resentment would have continued to build and would have eventually torn us apart. But what if I had told Marcus's dad about Nick from the beginning? But I already know. In that scenario, I would have been deported, and I'm not sure our relationship would have survived. I could have told Marcus I was going to Taiwan, and he could have come with me. But he would have been so unhappy here and eventually would have left me. Of all the options we'd discussed before leaving San Francisco, none of them included him coming with me to Taiwan. I don't blame him in any scenario; each one involves a choice I made that would be too much for any relationship. Each one leads to the end, some faster than others. I've come to see it for what it is: fate or the universe or the Gods or whatever. Obviously, not one of those things thought we should be together in the first place, and it was only a matter of time before—

"Mei Li." Leo's voice cuts through my thoughts which were so deep, I didn't hear him come in but spin toward him, knife in hand.

He takes a step back, his hands up. "Whoa. Easy." He glances at the knife, a slow smile spreading as he looks at me again. "I've got some news but won't deliver it until you put down that weapon."

I glance at the knife out of the corner of my eye, then smile at him "Depends on the news."

"Well…" He lowers his hands and crosses his arms over his chest. "I think we should start with the bad news: there are only three people living in this apartment, but it looks like you have twenty-four pounds of bok choy on that cutting board."

"Why is that bad news?" I smile at the dark green piles. "Did I overdo it?" Laying the knife on the counter, I wipe my hands.

"Maybe? Unless you invited all the nuns at the monastery to dinner? And that will cause other problems like…eating space. Or dinner conversation. Or the fact you have meat on the menu." His eyes move over the kitchen and the food spread across its counters.

I laugh and toss the cut vegetables and chicken into the

wok, sending more steam into the air. "This is all for you, so your big news better be good or I won't let you leave the table until all the pork buns are gone."

Leo steps beside me, leaning back against the cabinet so he's facing me. "I went to the hospital today."

"That usually would be bad news, but I see where you're going with this, and I'm very interested." I smile as I stir the sizzling vegetables. "Did you get anything out of Nick?"

"I literally got nothing out of him."

I pause, gripping the wooden spatula. "I thought he agreed to give information in exchange for a lesser sentence or something. Not that I'm surprised he didn't talk."

"Yeah," Leo says, nodding to his feet. "I'm sure he would have if he could have."

I set down the spatula and turn to him. "What do you mean?"

"Apparently, it's really hard to talk when you're dead."

Oil pops and vegetables hiss, but my eyes never leave Leo's as I wait for him to continue.

He reaches over and turns off the stove, then grabs my hand and leads me to the table, pulling a chair out and motioning for me to sit down. "I was as shocked as you look right now," he says as he sits across from me. "I got a call on my way to the hospital that there had been an incident involving Nick. When I got there, his room was a crime scene and his body was in the morgue. A person posing as hospital staff put something in his IV, and Nick went into cardiac arrest before he was able to say anything to anyone."

"Are you serious?" I whisper, grasping at the thought of a world free from Nick.

Leo nods. "Yeah. And his killer would have gotten away with it, but he made a critical mistake and my team caught him. I interrogated him and it took some prodding, but eventually, he talked. It's amazing what these guys will do to save themselves."

The breath I was holding rushes out, and I meet Leo's eyes. "Why did he kill Nick? Who was he, and how was he connected?"

Leo rubs his eyes, leans forward, his elbows on the table, and clasps his hands. "Turns out, he was working for the same guy Nick was, but when Nick got caught, their boss wanted to make sure Nick didn't talk. I guess he was successful at taking care of Nick, not so much at staying under the radar."

I blink, waiting. "Who was his boss?"

"I can't say yet but it's a highly influential person in San Francisco who also appears to be directly tied to the diamonds, which—as suspected—are tied to the drug and human trafficking."

The hissing and popping in the kitchen fades and the world goes quiet, as do I. My thoughts whir to a stop, and I stare at the wood grain of the table until Leo's hand finds mine.

"The best news is, Nick's out of your life for good. You never have to worry about him again. It's finally over."

veer Tavah's car into a dirt parking area overlooking the bay. My legs are shaking too much to drive anymore. Throwing the car into park, I lean my head back against the headrest as I search for words that shouldn't exist.

"What's wrong?" she asks through a frown from the passenger seat.

I grip the steering wheel with both hands, eyes closed, my pulse bouncing in my neck as I swallow hard, then let out a long, trapped breath.

"Marcus? You're freaking me out right now."

I turn my head to look at Tavah, and her eyes are all over my face, searching. "T, I…I don't know how…" I rub my forehead, knowing I can't prolong this any longer. "I found out something that's so messed up, and I just need to talk to you about it."

She plays with her hair. "Okay, but now I'm less freaked out and incredibly worried because this is reminiscent of a balcony in Vegas."

"It's…a little like that." Or a lot.

She stares at her lap for a few seconds before pressing her

lips together and turning in her seat to face me, her glossy eyes on me. "Tell me."

I stare out the windshield, count to ten, then look back at her. "Mei's alive."

She blinks long and slow like the news is slicing through her in slow motion. Her hands go to her mouth, then a few seconds later, she opens the door and slips out of the car.

I throw my door open and round the car to meet her where she's standing, overlooking the bay. "I'm so sorry. I found out a few days ago that she might be, and I didn't believe it, but then Johnny told me she called Lin yesterday."

Tavah doesn't move, just stares, her hands still over her mouth, so I turn her toward me, wrap my arms around her. "This doesn't change anything."

"It changes everything," she whispers into her hands, her body stiff in my arms. "It means you're still married."

I bury my face in her neck, hold her tighter. "I don't know what to do, T. There was a time I hoped she was still alive, but then I accepted she wasn't and now…"

She pulls back and out of my arms. "And now what? What are you going to do now that you know?"

I shove my hand through my hair, shake my head. "I don't know what to do."

"Where is she?"

"Somewhere in Taiwan." I look up, meet her eyes, and when she hesitates, I wonder if she remembers the phone call. If she does, she doesn't say anything so I ask, "What would you do if you were in my place? Tell me what to do and I'll do it."

"Let her go." Her throat bobs as she swallows and nods. "That's what I want you to do, because I'm selfish. I'm not excited she's alive, no matter how relieved you probably are. I want you. I want us and what we've started, and I want you all to myself. I told you I won't share." She stares at the ocean, tears slipping from the corners of her eyes, down her cheeks, silver streaks in the weak moonlight.

"T…" I pull her close, wipe her tears, but she shakes her head, steps back, blinks to the sky as she swipes her face.

"This is my worst nightmare," she says, closing her eyes. "This is it." She pauses, her voice thick with tears when she speaks again. "I want so badly for you to forget her. But I know that won't happen."

I watch her, keep my distance like I'll add sharper edges to the pain I threw at her.

"The problem is," she continues to the sky, pausing when emotion swells in her throat, "if you ignored that she's alive and continued things with me, you'd always wonder. I've already told you that I won't share you, but I'm afraid you'll always be half with her, half with me and I can't do that, either. I won't. So I'm not going to tell you what to do. You have to decide how you feel and what you want. And who."

CHAPTER 36

EARLY SEPTEMBER

My phone navigation tells me I'm four minutes away from the station. I adjust the bag full of food on my shoulder; it's grown heavier the last twelve blocks. I've only gone to the station twice and, both times, I've carried something heavy. Last time, it was a tampon box filled with diamonds and this time, a bag of food and the weight of the last seven months. The girl I was when I got to Taiwan couldn't have predicted the curve her life would take. That girl spent months wanting to take back the decision she'd made. She was blocked by puddles of pain and under a sky made of sadness, fear, and regret. She couldn't see that around all the curves in the road, a stronger version of herself waited, so grateful to be alive, even without Marcus.

Gratitude was my bridge to this other side of my life I didn't know existed. And to Leo. Had I never come to Taiwan, I never would have met him, and now I can't imagine my life without him.

I round the final corner and skim the steps to the front doors. In the elevator, I picture how surprised Leo's going to be and smile into my reflection on the metal door.

The doors slide open, and I make my way down the hall,

beyond the reception desk, stopping at Leo's closed door. Through his window, I smile and wave at him where he's leaned back in his chair, phone pinned to his ear until he spots me.

I hold up our lunch, and he smiles, falling forward in his chair. He signals for me to give him a minute, and I nod, turning and scanning the office. Phones ring, keyboards click, and people bustle around me, asking questions, getting updates. When a woman waves at me from her desk, I recognize Ana from the gala, hoping she doesn't know what happened later that night between Leo and me.

She stands and walks toward me, smiling. "Mei Li, it's good to see you again." She gives me a brief hug.

"Nice to see you, too," I say before asking, "How are you?"

"Busy, thanks to you."

I give her a knowing look. "Normally, I would be sorry but not this time."

We both turn when Leo's door opens.

"What are you doing here?" he asks through a wide smile. "And how did you get here?"

"I'm not a shut-in, Leo. I can find my way around."

Ana laughs before telling me she needs to get back to work, but she's glad I'm keeping Leo happy these days. I nod and follow him into his office where I drop our lunch on his desk, then plop down on a chair and kick my feet up on his desk.

He eases into his chair on the other side, scanning my face, my feet, the bag. "But really, what are you doing here?"

"I brought lunch and a problem for you to help me solve."

He reclines in his chair, his hands clasped on top of his head. "Uhhh…the last time you came in with a problem, you had half a million dollars' worth of stolen international diamonds linked to a psychopath who'd tried to kill you.

Please tell me this new problem is a tiny bit smaller than that."

"Just a bit." I smile and drop my legs, leaning forward in my chair to open the bag on his desk. "Also, this time, I brought food to help us while we brainstorm solutions."

"You are very familiar with how I work," Leo says, taking each bento box I hand him. He opens one and groans, rolling his eyes to the ceiling. "I'll need a nap after this one. Hope you don't want any." He takes the chopsticks I hand him and goes to work on the vegetables.

I open the other one and sit back, using my chopsticks to trap a cube of tofu. "I started looking at jobs and apartments today and apparently, they all want some form of proof that I exist. So…that's where you come in." I pop the tofu in my mouth and wiggle my eyebrows.

He nods, finishes chewing. "You know you don't need to move, right? My apartment is yours, no expectations or obligations."

"I know," I say, covering my mouth as I chew and swallow. "But I'm ready to start my new life here. You've been a miracle, and of course I'll stay until I can afford my own place, which might take me years. But I need a job and an identity first."

Leo watches his chopsticks, nods before looking up at me. "I was actually going to talk to you about that as soon as the Nick dust settled, but…I guess now works just as well. Especially since the only Nick dust left is his own."

I watch Leo, grateful to be in a safe place where we can speak about Nick in past tense. He managed to take what meant most to me, but he doesn't get to decide how the rest of my life will go.

Leo turns in his chair and rifles through a drawer behind him, then swivels back and spreads papers across the glass desktop. He picks up one. "You were born Zhao, Xin Yao. And then," he says, laying my birth certificate in front of me before picking up the next, "you became Mei Li Zhang when you moved to the states." He lays my fake birth certificate next to the first and shuffles through the pile, examining another paper before holding it up. "When you ran with Marcus, you were Peggy Bromley, which suits you perfectly, by the way." He smiles and sets down the paper.

I roll my eyes but can only manage a weak smile because, of all the names I've ever been given, there's only one I ever wanted to keep. A rush of heat creeps up my neck when anger lights a fire inside me.

I shift in my seat to get away from flames and avoid looking at Peggy Bromley; she represents so much happiness but too much heartache. Leo hasn't mentioned the name I most want and the life that went with it. But of course he wouldn't—only five people knew it existed.

"I took Mei Li Zhang from you," Leo continues from across the desk, "but I can give her back if you want."

I clench my jaw to trap anger inside.

"You get to decide who you want to be. I'll give you whatever name you want."

My heart stutters, my throat tightens, my chest so hot, I shake my head and stand. "No, you can't. No one can. When I married Marcus, I may have been Peggy Bromley, but I was really Mei Li Miller. I wanted to be her more than anything, but of course, there's no proof that I was ever her or that I ever had him because Nick took all of that, too." I close my eyes, breathe to lower my voice, but I'm shaking. I clench my fists, look at Leo whose lips are in a tight line, his eyes gentle.

"And now it's too late to be her again. Someone else will have his last name. Someone else will be with him, someone will take my place, live my dream. She probably already has. I hope Nick rots in Hell. I'm glad his last moments on earth were filled with pain and even more thrilled someone took everything from him."

Anger boils into tears, and I cover my face as a cry

escapes. I turn away from Leo's desk, but he's beside me, wrapping his arms around me, holding me as I surrender to feelings I've shoved down. Anger and sadness twist through me, hollowing out a hissing, steaming pool of heartbreak.

Leo holds me until my chest is stretched from emotion, my cheeks swollen from tears that have been used up, evaporating my anger with them.

I take a deep breath, then let it out, and Leo leans back, his hands resting on my arms, his calm presence steadying me.

"Sorry. I didn't mean for that to happen." I wipe my cheeks.

"I'm glad it did because now there's more room inside you. And I'm honored I got to finally share in some of your emotions. There was a time I didn't think you'd ever trust me enough to let me in." He steps away to grab a tissue, then hands it to me. "I don't need an answer right now. Think about the name you want for as long as you need to. Take your time."

But one pushes its way through the layers of leftover emotions, and I hesitate, then say, "I think I already know."

"Yeah?" Leo stands in front of me, hands in his pockets. "Tell me, I'll make it happen."

"Mitchell. Mei Li Mitchell."

Leo's eyebrows meet. "Where did that come from?"

"There's one thing you didn't find about me in your research. My biological father is named Peter Mitchell. I've never met him, but I think I'm going to."

Leo nods and straightens. "Okay, then. Consider it done and nice to meet you, Mei Li Mitchell."

CHAPTER 37

MID-SEPTEMBER

wish you didn't have to go." Tavah talks to her hands, which are in her lap where she sits in the driver's seat, the late afternoon sun non-existent in the shadowy short term parking garage. She stares out the windshield, her cheeks are still blotchy and swollen from a sleepless night and the emotional ride to the airport. I told her last night Dad could take me, but the look on her face changed my mind, and while it hurts a million times more to leave her this way, at least we got to spend the last thirty minutes together. Even if all we we're doing is falling apart.

"I get why you need to, I really do, but…"

I swear under my breath and slouch in the passenger sea. "I don't. And I don't wanna go to freaking Taiwan. I don't wanna see her. And I don't wanna leave you for five days. Don't wanna leave you for a few hours or ever. I hate this."

Tavah swipes at a tear, still staring out the windshield. "I should be feeling jealous, but I'm too terrified."

I slide my hand across the console, fingers tangling with hers. "What are you scared of?"

"That you'll see her and remember I'm not her." She closes her eyes.

"T..." I twist in my seat, lean toward her, rest my forehead against hers.

"No, Marcus, I know the power she has over you. You gave up everything for her and she was completely, 100% yours. I'm attempting to take her spot and want it so, so badly. But since you told me she's alive, I feel her squeezing between us. I don't like it. There isn't room for three of us. So this is like..." She keeps her eyes closed, wraps a hand around my wrist, holding on. "This is when I feel like I have to prove myself and not stand in your way or be selfish, and if I handle it perfectly, I'll be the winner." She opens her eyes, and her steady emotional ground crumbles beneath her.

"Tavs...hey..." I run my hand down her face, eyes searching hers to understand how weird this all must be for her. I lived an entirely different life with someone else—all she can do is imagine it and wonder if I'm headed right back into it. And if I'm being fully honest, I don't know. I have no idea how to do any of this. I never have.

"I don't want to lose you, Marcus. I can't even picture what my—"

I stop her words with my mouth, hoping to take some of her pain or soothe mine, I don't know, but the last thing I want to think about is whether or not Mei is what the next five days will bring, so I'll stay in this moment with this girl and make it last until I have to get out of this car and onto a plane.

———

This can't be right.

I followed the directions to the address Dad gave me, but it's a freaking monastery so either Dad's source has a sick sense of humor or these directions are way off, because all I see are monks with shaved heads in brown robes. The biggest golden Buddha I've ever seen in my life. But no Mei.

I stand on the sidewalk in front of the massive red and gold gates, traffic winding in and out of lanes behind me. My backpack is filled with boulders of doubt and fear, and I wanna shut down. Instead, I push forward. But to where? And what?

Tourists and monks intermingle, patches of brown mixed with red, gold, orange. This is not a place a guy finds his missing, resurrected wife.

I scan the immaculate grounds again. I should've known. Buddhist temple, lots of Buddha, but just like me and God, Buddha and I haven't been on the best of terms recently, and I have no patience for his million identical friends smiling at me right now.

Definitely the wrong place. There's no way Mei left me for this, no way she's really alive, no way any of this is legit and I'm stupid enough to have spent half my savings to come here on a ghost hunt.

I turn around, scan the street, the hotel on the other side of it. Seems like a normal place to go until I can get back on a plane and out of here. Forget "closure." I lived without it from my mom for eighteen years and can do the same with Mei.

I cross the street, the tallest guy in the crosswalk full of people who look like they know where they're going. I hold my backpack straps like I can hold myself to this ground instead of running toward home and Tavah. I gotta get back to her. But I keep walking, because there's that other part of me—about 48%—that's so completely messed up enough to think that finding Mei alive at a monastery would be a relief.

At least I'd know for sure Nick didn't hurt her. That she's alive and safe. And if she's really living at a monastery, at least I'd know she didn't leave me for another guy. But…if she really ran here, I turned her into a monk. Like, not even lesbian—a freaking monk who faked her own death.

No way. I clench my jaw. She's not here. I pull my phone from my pocket and text Dad.

> Marcus: In Taiwan at the address you sent. It's a Buddhist monastery.

I shove my phone back in my pocket and check in at the hotel. Twenty minutes later, I'm standing alone in the middle of my room on the seventh floor. I stare at the window while I wait for the time difference to make it not the middle of the night for Dad. My mind wrestles from my grasp and runs back toward the monastery, the Buddha statues in every corner of the grounds. Then it flashes to the night I met Mei—when I took her Buddha statue hostage and started the whole thing between us. He'd started it, so why shouldn't he be here for the end?

Problem is, all the Buddha smiles make me wanna fight, because there's nothing cheerful or funny or happy about this. And wouldn't it just be ironic if I found my wife in a garden full of them?

A monk...

Wow, Mei—that's...wow.

We'd had some pretty religious experiences together, but apparently, she'd taken them to a new level. There's no way she's there. And if she is, am I even allowed on the grounds since I have a wife and a girlfriend? Will the spotless cement crack under my feet? Will the Buddhas come to life and rush me?

I bolt for the shower, then take my time, letting the water pelt my back before getting out and drying off. I throw on some clothes, brush my teeth, and grab my phone to text Tavah, but there's a missed text from Dad on the screen.

> Dad: Glad you got there safe. Location's right. She's there.

My heart picks up speed, adrenaline pumping through me, and I'm out the door, out of the hotel, on the sidewalk that leads to the monastery gates. I'm not sure what I'll find here, but if I wanna get home, I gotta do this.

I stride through the wide-open gates onto the grounds and look around for the building's main entrance. Is there, like, an office at a monastery? A monk secretary? Do I check in? Give a secret knock before someone will tell me if my wife is a permanent resident here?

An Asian guy's hauling a box down the stairs toward me. He doesn't look very monk-ish, unless they wear designer jeans and tight T-shirts. And work out a lot.

I catch his eye, and he stops, sizing me up. "Can I help you?"

English.

"Uh, yeah…" I rub the back of my neck. "I was just looking for somebody and…I'm pretty sure she's not here. I mean, maybe you don't even know, but is there a Mei Li here? Mei Li Zhang? Or she might be going by Zhao, Xin Yao. Or maybe Peggy Bromley? Mei Li Miller? I'm honestly not sure what name she's using these days."

He swallows and his eyes scan the air above my head, jaw tense as he considers my words. "What's your name?"

My stomach crashes through the cement stairs and confusion and stupidity screech to a halt in my veins. No freaking way…

"Marcus." I pause, catch my breath. "Miller. Marcus Miller."

The guy hesitates, then nods. He gives me one last look before turning and slowly walking up the steps. "Wait here," he says over his shoulder, and I freeze.

He's messing with me. Right? Or maybe there's another Mei Li Zhang/Zhao, Xin Yao/Peggy Bromley/Mei Li Miller here. Some old woman will come out and I'll be out the gates, back on the plane, back with Tavah, back to my life that doesn't include monasteries or monks or Mei. The wrong person is gonna walk out that door at the top of the steps. Just another person with the same name. She won't be my Mei and–

There's a girl. She's walking down the steps. She has short hair. A nose ring glints in the sunlight. Her body's lost in her oversized hoodie. I know that hoodie. I wore it the night we met. I'm back on a fire escape. Nervous. Wondering when my brain shut off and my courage took over. I thought I'd lost that hoodie, but there it is, on a girl I thought was also lost forever. But this girl is alive. She has circles under her eyes. Brown eyes. Deep and full of pain. I'd know them anywhere, no matter how tortured or disbelieving they are. They lock onto mine and I'm rooted, my feet refusing to move.

Mei.

My Mei.

CHAPTER 38

MID-SEPTEMBER

mpossible.

I blink once, twice, slower the third time. He can't be standing at the bottom of the steps. I've taken these steps hundreds of times and he's never been there before, staring at me like a crack in the past has opened and he's reaching through it with his eyes. It can't be him—he's on the other side of the world, living another life. My dreams have caught up with me, blurred reality, and I've leaped across the threshold of insanity, no looking back.

But if I'm insane…I'll stay this way as long as I can because it's Marcus. My Marcus. And yet…

This Marcus is bigger than mine. He has the same broad, muscular shoulders, but they aren't thrown back, ready to take on the world like my Marcus's were. My Marcus had a wide, brilliant smile that drew lines at the corners of his mouth as it stretched its limits. The guy at the bottom of the steps isn't smiling. My Marcus would have closed the gap between us, but this one is rooted to the ground like one of the Buddha statues, separated from me by an invisible wall built of a lifetime lived apart.

He squints in the sunlight, his eyes so blue, the afternoon

sky must have crept inside them. They're the same eyes that belong to the same Marcus I fell in love with so long ago. The boy who saved my life, then became my life when I promised to love him for the rest of mine. It's the one promise I've kept.

My hand presses to my chest, over the outline of my infinity ring hanging securely on a chain around my neck. And just beyond that, my heart beats frantically. It's been so silent until now, but it recognizes him, and it's waking up the rest of me that has also been reluctantly existing without him.

Marcus's mouth parts, and I lean forward, like the breeze will carry him and his words to me.

Instead, he puts his hands on his hips and stares at the concrete, swallows, shakes his head. And when he lifts his eyes to mine again, pain and confusion flash across them.

He has every right to be mad.

He doesn't understand. Neither do I.

I touch my shaved head. Is he repulsed by what he sees? I wouldn't blame him.

My soul cowers inside me, leaving me exposed and unsupported as my trembling legs give in to anguish, and I sink to the unforgiving steps, hands over my heart to keep it inside me.

Marcus turns away, and I open my mouth to call to him, but the silence filling the stagnant air between us chokes me.

When he glances over his shoulder, his eyes grab mine, hold them, and I feel what they say: *"You were dead."*

I stop breathing as my soul struggles to leap across the gap between us, my body paralyzed by disbelief. *"I was."*

He takes a step away from me, then another.

No.

Another.

Please!

He staggers away. Two more steps, his back to me as he takes another two steps.

Two minutes.

Two minutes ago, I was packing clothes in a box for a local orphanage when Leo walked in. He set down the box he was holding, and I smiled and hugged him, but he held me tighter than usual.

"What's wrong?" I'd asked, pulling back enough to read him.

He'd glanced away, avoided my eyes.

"Leo, what happened?"

He'd run his hand through his hair and stepped away from me. "There's someone here for you."

And then…I was standing in front of the someone and two minutes tilted my world, sliding me off the stable place I've been standing on, into a free fall.

Marcus is across the courtyard now, all my feelings and hopes clinging to him, dragging behind him because they won't let go. When he slips out of sight, my legs carry me down the steps after him.

I reach the gates, rush onto the sidewalk when a hand grabs mine, and I whirl around.

Leo's mouth is moving, but my insides are roaring too loudly as they rearrange and make room for feelings to emerge from their burial ground deep inside me.

My tears blur Leo's face, then I frantically search the other side of the street. Marcus in his blue shirt is a block away, disappearing through a hotel entrance.

I turn to Leo who's still holding my hand and, for a split second, I think he's going to pull me toward the monastery. Instead, he walks me toward the street.

"I don't understand," I say, breathless, my feet skimming the cement, my body and mind far ahead of me and through the revolving door with Marcus. "How did he find me?"

Leo talks to the hot, humid air as we cross the street, passing a group of old people. "I hope you don't hate me for this, but I told him. Not him, exactly." Leo interlocks our fingers, turns right toward the hotel. "I talked to a detective with the San Francisco Police Department."

My heart drops, my thoughts scattering from the impact.

He stops in front of the hotel's revolving door, his eyes looking beyond it. "Detective Miller called me asking questions about you. At first, I told him nothing. But then I found out he was Marcus's father and after Nick died, I called him back and gave him the monastery's address."

I blink, the haze in my head clearing in the wind of Leo's confession.

"I had to, Mei Li. When I found out who you really were and how many people were looking for you and suspected you dead, I…I had to." Leo shakes his head. "I didn't tell you because I wasn't sure he would actually come here, but it didn't take him long." Leo lets go of my hand, pulls me against him. "I love you and know leaving him is your biggest regret. So…this is your chance. Whatever comes of this, I'm here. Always."

A tear slips out and drops to the sidewalk, and I wordlessly follow him into the hotel lobby, across the marble to the desk where he pulls his badge from his pocket and asks the woman behind the desk for Marcus's room number.

She types, then looks up from the screen. "Room 742."

Leo turns to me. "I'll stay down here and wait if you want me to."

I glance at the elevator, then back at him.

"Or," he says, nodding, "you can call me. If you need me."

I study his face, then watch the elevator door open, a woman in a black dress stepping out of it, leaving it empty, ready. I meet Leo's eyes again. "I'll call you."

He rubs the back of his head, nods, and I step past him toward the open elevator door that will carry me up and backwards into my past.

make it to the toilet in my hotel bathroom in time to puke, then spend some quality time on the tile, my back against the wall as I replayed the moment on the steps. My head still doesn't believe it even though the rest of my body got it loud and clear.

Mei's alive—confirmed. It changes nothing.

I grab my backpack, pulling out my mouthwash and rinsing before shoving it, my toothbrush, and stale travel clothes into the backpack.

"Did you get that, Mei?" I say, my voice trapped in the quiet room, loud in my ears. My hands tremble as shock from seeing Mei recedes, leaving me empty. "I don't care anymore. I don't care that you left me behind and let me think you were dead. I don't even care anymore that I had to start all over without you, because I have. Thought it was impossible, turns out it wasn't. And if this is what closure feels like, who needs it?"

But Mei on the steps a few minutes ago…

There was pain in her eyes. More than I could translate in one glance.

Everything—being in Taiwan alone, seeing Mei, missing

Tavah—balls in my chest, grows, stretches, pushes against me. My hands shake so badly as I yank on the zipper, my fingers lose their grip and drop the bag on the bed.

I swear and shove it off, my clothes spilling out of it before I drop to the edge of the mattress, close my eyes. "I don't care, don't care, don't care," I whisper into the silence I stunned with my outburst. "I can't care that I used to love you." My heart slows, adrenaline draining from me. "But more than everything, I hate that I still do."

I hate that my need to protect her is still so deep inside me after all this time that I want to run back to the monastery, pull her against me, and shield her, even if she doesn't need me to.

I clutch my chest. I'm gonna die if I don't get outta here. I've seen her—alive, in the life she chose over ours for whatever reason. That's closure enough, especially after seeing that guy with her. The way he looked at her.

Grabbing my bag off the floor, I shove everything back inside it, then head for the door, flinging it open.

And wish I hadn't.

The girl I saw minutes ago—and every single day of my life for almost a year before that—is standing on the other side of the door. Seeing her face shoves me backwards into another time. It's one big memory made from millions of them.

I can't speak even if I could find something to say; I'm trapped between lives, hotel room and escape route, Mei in the middle of it all.

I meet her eyes, then drop mine. She's skin and bones, but her presence is heavy enough to crush the atmosphere around me.

Gripping the doorknob, I keep the door a barrier between us, my body half concealed behind it. I consider shutting it. Wonder if I could crawl out a seventh-story window, scale down the building somehow. Wonder about the accessibility of the ventilation system, but when Mei steps toward me and whispers my name, all thoughts of escape plummet and shatter in a pile of dust.

"What are you doing here?" I ask, shaking my head.

"I…" she swallows. "I came to ask you the same question."

Her voice shakes loose more feelings that I try but fail to hide, my heartbeat and breathing too fast, palms sweaty, chest tight. I shake my head again, still staring at the floor because if I look up, I'm flooded. I'll drown again and I just resurfaced.

Her gaze moves to my backpack over my shoulder, then back to my face. "Before you go, I need to explain." Her voice barely makes it through the gap in the door, but it's strong enough to leave a mark. I close my eyes, grip the doorknob until I swear I'll snap it off.

"It would've been nice to know you're still alive a good, solid seven months ago." I stare at my feet, my jaw pulsing, and her eyes flick to the ceiling, glossy and ready to overflow. Like any of this will change anything now.

"You need to know why I left," she says, a little louder, as if I didn't hear her the first time.

"Finding you here alive is all the explanation I need. Got it. Loud and clear." I clench and unclench my jaw, concentrating on my shoes instead of the nausea creeping through me, but when I look up, our eyes collide, and I look away, refusing to let her trap me. Straightening, I talk to the air above her head, like I'm waiting for someone to walk down the hall and save me. "I don't need an explanation now. It won't change anything."

"Marcus, I—"

"No—really. I don't need to know why you couldn't tell me what was wrong. I don't even want to know now."

She presses her lips together and I shift, my eyes going to the ceiling, my breathing speeding up.

"You deserve to know."

Hurt surges, hot and thick, and I shake my head and direct a single syllable laugh to the overhead lights. "I deserve it? Like I deserved the months of silence and grief over your death that, turns out, was fake?" I swear and fling the door away from me, turning and walking back inside the hotel room.

"Marcus, please." She catches the door before it slams shut and walks into the room after me.

My whole body stiffens. We haven't been in the same room—on the same continent—since Indiana. I keep my back to her, because I can see more clearly when she's out of sight. I've gotten used to it. If only I could just slip out of here without looking at her.

"I'm so sorry for what I've done to you." Her voice is steadier, more determined as it drifts toward me, curls around my arms and legs, pulling me backward through time, back to how it felt to be near her. I squeeze my eyes shut, breathe.

"I should have told you," she continues. "I should have included you instead of trying to protect you, like I even could have. Everything fell apart when I left. I immediately knew it was a mistake, but by then, it was too late."

Her voice smooths the rough edges that cut through me the moment I saw her standing on the steps, but they still poke out of me, too many holes releasing too many feelings. I drop to the edge of the bed, my eyes on the tile.

"I know you have a new life, and I will never ask you to change that. I'm just asking for a few minutes to explain. Please, Marcus."

Looking over my shoulder, I slowly raise my eyes to hers, the jolt from their connection like lightning ripping through my body, a white blast in my head. Nothing but sparks and stillness and Mei's eyes.

CHAPTER 40
MID-SEPTEMBER

Marcus turns to face the window, his shoulders tense under his T-shirt. He must have felt it, too—the pulse that visibly rippled the air between us the moment our eyes met.

An orange haze from the setting sun rests on the skyline, reaching for him and outlining his profile in gold. The sound of traffic clutters the quiet, people going home from work completely unaware that seven stories above them, everything is changing.

Marcus is silent. I don't blame him. I never gave him a chance to understand in Indiana; why should I expect him to listen to my reasons after all this time and distance? We've been apart almost as long as we were together.

My heart beats up my throat while I try to stay grounded. If I don't tell him now, I might never have the chance to explain, so I swallow my fear and ease into the conversation. "How's Charlie?"

Marcus rubs his neck, still staring out the window. "He's living with Guo right now."

"Good." I nod. The fact he didn't give Charlie away sends a trickle of hope through me. I wait for him to say more until the truth that's been waiting to be set free gets restless. "I left to keep you safe, Marcus. Chaz found me at the hospital, and he wanted to get rid of Nick as badly as I did. To do that, I had to take the diamonds to Taiwan—to the detective who knew how they connected Nick and every bad thing he's done. It was supposed to be quick. Easy. I couldn't tell you because I knew you'd follow me and put yourself in more danger. You'd already gotten hurt once, and I wasn't going to let it happen again. I planned to be back in a week." I bite the inside of my lip, steady my voice. "But I had to go into hiding instead."

The story falls out of me, heavy and off balance. I empty every detail, leaving nothing behind. I tell him about living in a monastery, why Leo created a fake death certificate, changing my appearance, moving in with Leo, and confronting Nick on the bridge. I describe how he died.

When I finish, Marcus is facing me, his hands gripping the windowsill behind him.

The details settle between us, and I grip the edge of the mattress when emptying myself leaves me shaky. A door across the hall slams, the elevator whirs behind walls.

"What did Nick do to you?" Marcus's voice eases toward me, offering a bridge across the silence.

"Does it matter?" I ask the tile, my toes curled into its cool, steady surface.

"It matters to me."

I breathe through my nose, slowly releasing anxiety and the bitterness of the memory. "He hit me. Threatened me. The same thing he's always done."

"And?" The flame in Marcus's eyes competes with the struggling orange glow of the sunset. "Did he get what he always wanted?" His words fracture the frail air.

"He didn't get the diamonds."

He rubs his hands down his face, crosses his arms as he

leans back against the wall. "You know what I'm talking about Mei."

"No." I shake my head. "He was shot before he got the chance."

Marcus nods quickly, swallows as he blinks at the floor. "I'm glad. I wish you'd never been close enough that he could hurt you at all, but I'm glad he didn't do worse." His voice is weary, cracked, and he squeezes his eyes shut before opening them and looking at me. "I just wish…I wish you would've let me in. Maybe this never would've happened to you. We wouldn't be here right now. We'd be doing what we always did, and I'd be happy doing that. We'd be together instead of a lifetime apart."

My fingernails dig into the comforter. "You would've left eventually. Nick would've forced us apart."

He scans the room, his eyes jumping from the tile floor to the door to me on the bed. "You're wrong, Mei. I made my choice, and I was happy with it. I made mistakes, but you were never one of them. I would've done anything, given up anything to stay with you. I thought I proved that to you."

"Whether you believe me or not, I thought I was doing the only thing that would keep us together. I never could have predicted this. Never imagined that, in a matter of months, I would lose you forever."

Marcus turns back to the window, leans over as he grips the sill, and my hand presses to my chest, digging in as I watch him—everything I've lost but still want more than my own life.

"Was it you?" he asks, the question tight and hesitant as his back rises and falls.

I know exactly what he's asking. It's a moment I want to bury so deep in my memory, it dissolves. But he's digging it up from where it lies, still as painful and sharp as it was the day it happened.

"On the phone? On our anniversary? Was it you?"

The 6-21 on his wrist flashes through my mind. But it faded long ago so I direct my answer to the new numbers and letters on his wrist in foreign handwriting. "Yes." I finally answer, and before he can respond, I continue. "I gave in and called you like I'd wanted to thousands of times but couldn't because I was supposed to be dead. When I heard her voice, I knew it was too late." I nod to confirm what I'm saying. "That was the moment I actually died."

Marcus swears, runs his hand through his hair. "I didn't want to move on, Mei," he explodes, facing me but keeping his distance. "I didn't even breathe for months after you left. And then I found out you were dead, and I prayed all night every night for answers. They never came so I stopped asking." He stares into the room like those nights are trudging across the tile. "I had to accept that I'd never see you again. I gave all of myself to you and had nothing left to live for. So I found something." He drops his eyes, lowers himself into a chair across from the bed and leans forward, elbows on his knees as he rubs his neck. He swears again and squeezes his eyes shut. "Why didn't you just let me in? Did you not believe me when I said I wanted you forever, no matter what?"

Tears spill onto my cheeks. "Being with you..." I take a deep, painful breath. "Being with you was the best choice I've ever made and will ever make. I would make it a million times."

He looks at me from under his lashes, his voice low and steady. "You can't say that, Mei, because it makes no sense to me."

"It's as honest as I can be. What do you want me to say?"

"I don't know!" He throws his hands in the air, slouching in the chair. "Tell me I wasn't enough or that I didn't treat you right or that you regretted running away with me and our months together were too much. Or you couldn't trust me, or I didn't love you the way you wanted me to. Tell me you think marrying me was a huge mistake—anything would make more sense than telling me you'd choose me a million times but couldn't even tell me what was happening with Nick or Chaz or in your own head."

"I didn't leave because you weren't enough, Marcus. I left because you were everything to me, and I refused to be the reason you got hurt again. You'd already given up everything to protect me, and you would've kept doing it despite what you wanted or needed. But I couldn't have lived with myself. And you couldn't protect me from the things I had to do." My voice rises, tears swelling in my throat.

He shakes his head, swipes his face, hangs his head and stares at the floor. Moments slide past us, taking some of the tension with them until a hundred heartbeats later, he asks, "Who's the guy, Mei? At the monastery?" His jaw pulses as he grips his hands between his knees. "What is he to you, besides being in love with you?"

Confusion and hurt swirl in my head and heart, breaking apart my explanation, and when I don't answer, Marcus pushes himself up from the chair, grabs his backpack, and strides toward the door.

"His name is Leo," I blurt before he gets across the room. Standing, I stare at his back, his hand on the doorknob. "He's the detective who helped me. He's the one who told your dad where to find me. He's been here through everything. He took care of me at my lowest. Without him, I wouldn't be here. I almost wasn't."

Marcus's back rises and falls, muscles strained, and seconds later, he drops his bag and turns to face me. "Taking care of you was my job. You let him do it when it could've been me."

I bury my face in my hands, his words filling, then emptying me.

"What the hell?" He strides toward me, and as I lower my hands, he grabs them, turns them over, his eyes all over the scars on my arms. I try to pull away, but his grip tightens, and I wish so badly I'd put the hoodie back on after showing him the bullet wound.

His eyes meet mine, his fingertips running over the scars. "What happened?"

In a flash, I show him everything I so badly want to hide, especially from him. Proof of my weakness and inability to live without him. Proof of my final loss and my descent. He holds my wrists while his eyes search mine, and I tell him about the pregnancy and how it ended. I tell him about the darkness and hopeless moments that descended and settled into places where happiness had once been.

"I'm so sorry, Marcus. I couldn't even keep that part of you."

His eyes wander my face before he lets go of my wrists and wipes my tears. His hand moves down my cheek, thumb caressing my neck before his pointer finger hooks the chain from under my shirt, pulls it out.

He lets out a shaky breath. His pulse bumps in his neck, jaw tensing before he talks to the ring between his fingers. "How did we get here, Mei?" His voice is soft, deflated, and I watch him stare at the ring, my eyes tracing his face, stopping on all my favorite places: the permanent smile lines around his mouth, high cheekbones, dark, expressive eyebrows arched over eyes filled with the sky. When he speaks, my heart leaps toward him.

"Do you remember," he says, easing into the feelings rising between us, hot and unsettled, "the time I told you I'd love you even if you were bald?" He meets my eyes.

I smile through tears and nod, undone by his closeness. "It's growing," I whisper, my heart thumping loudly enough for him to hear.

"I like it." His eyes rise to mine, his finger reaching to touch my nose ring. "And this."

I reach up, slip my fingers through his hair. It's different. Just like him in so many ways.

His hand drifts back to my wrist, which he lifts to his mouth, his eyes never leaving mine as he kisses the fading scars. "I'm so sorry I wasn't here," he whispers into the sliver of space between us. "I'm so sorry, Mei." He pulls me into his arms, wraps them around me, and I cling to him, afraid he'll disappear if I let go. "If I could go back," I breathe against his throat, "I would do everything so differently."

He pulls back, his trembling fingertips smoothing across my forehead and down my face before sliding down my sides and over my hips, possessing me as they have so many times before. He leans in, our breath suspended, curling together, and when his lips slowly meet mine, the growing ache inside me turns to liquid heat, and I melt into him, my body pressing against him as he deepens the kiss.

CHAPTER 41
MID-SEPTEMBER

My eyes follow the familiar curve of Mei's hip where she lays on her side, facing me, her eyes closed now that she's drifted to sleep. She needs to sleep, or so the dark circles under her eyes tell me. But I'm wide awake since my body thinks it's the middle of the day and my mind refuses to waste a second sleeping now that Mei's right here in front of me, alive, breathing.

My phone has vibrated a few times in my pocket, but I haven't moved, just laid here and watched Mei as my mind unwinds.

When she'd told me why she'd left and everything that had happened since, I'd lost it. So many months of wondering and hating myself and her. Watching her face, her lips, as she told me she felt like leaving was the only way we could be together, I'd believed her. Now, with her so close, I feel nothing but gratitude that it brought us here. It's infinitely better than where we've been.

Her shirt has ridden up, exposing a smooth ribbon of skin, and I hold myself back from touching her. I know what her skin feels like; my entire body has it memorized.

She stirs, like she felt my thoughts, and curls into me in

her sleep, her shirt slipping further up her waist, exposing part of a tattoo inked on her side. My fingers twitch, eager to explore this new part of her.

Instead, I slip the Sharpie out of my pocket and ease down the bed until I'm eye level with her stomach, just above the waistband of her pants. Glancing at her to make sure I haven't disturbed her, I uncap the Sharpie with my teeth and softly write *365 4 Ever* right above the spot where, if the tiny life we'd created together had been real, would have grown. My cheek presses against the sheet as I stare at my message and let moments stream through my head, most of them happy, some a kick between the legs.

My phone buzzes again, and I slip it out of my pocket without looking, silence it, then slide it off the bed, because I just want this moment with Mei, even with the guilt gnawing at my stomach. I've gotten surprisingly used to it recently.

Mei stirs, her fingers finding me, spreading through my hair like they used to every morning she woke up beside me.

I scoot back up the mattress until we're face to face again. I watch her, catching her eyes when they finally flutter open and let me back in. *"I told you not to let me fall asleep."*

"But you're too cute when you're asleep."

She smiles a lazy smile, and I smile back, then whisper, "I missed you," partly meaning during the last few minutes when sleep stole her from me, but mostly meaning over the past seven months when time and distance erased her.

She closes her eyes again, like she's holding tightly to my words, and if we were back in our old life, we'd spend hours showing each other the feelings we don't have big enough words to express. I'd whisper how much I loved her over and over, then lead her to the place where she'd come completely undone and take me with her.

"Every second with you was my very favorite, Marcus," she says like my thoughts are whispering between us, too. "Take me back."

I search her face. "To where?" A hundred places and times flash through my head. "To the night we met at Guo's? Or to Seattle, in separate bunkbeds?" I smile and her eyes light up. "When you loved making me suffer on the top bunk, alone with my very dirty thoughts?"

She laughs and shifts closer until I'm on my back, her head on my chest. "I think you're remembering that wrong. I tried seducing you almost every night."

"Oh, I remember," I say through a smile, lacing my fingers through hers and holding our hands on my chest. "I wasn't sure what we were or…what we weren't and where things were headed. Kind of like right now."

She lifts her head, her eyes searching mine, and I ask without speaking, *"If we could, would you go back?"*

"Yes." She nods.

"If you could choose any part of it to relive, what would it be?" My mind offers options: our first time, finally learning all the secrets about each other we'd only imagined? The same night. Lying awake, facing each other, talking without words like we have tonight? Or would it be the night in Vegas when we'd laughed so hard, the neighbors had knocked on the wall and then we'd given them something to knock about?

"I would go back to the beginning so I could relive it all." She drops her eyes, then lies back on my chest, drawing a pattern on my shirt with her fingertip, just like she used to. "As painful as some of it was, we were together, and it's better than dying inside. Nothing hurts like that. What about you?"

My mind moves in reverse, looking for a place to land. But I wouldn't go back to Indiana where everything dropped off a cliff and exploded. I wouldn't go back to Vegas where everything unraveled, then twisted with new fears and stress. I wouldn't go back to losing Stanford. And any time before that was nothing but a gaping, wide unknown.

I turn on my side, and she shifts until we're both on the pillow, our faces inches away. "No." I shake my head, my three-day facial hair growth rasping against the pillowcase. "I'd stay here because going back only leads to the end again and I can't repeat that. It killed me."

Mei's eyes scan my face, gathering information I don't have to say. "You're different."

"I am."

"We both are."

"Yeah. I think the people we were died in different ways. This is kind of a new place for us."

This isn't San Juan Island or Vegas or Stanford or Indiana. It's not San Francisco. This is Taiwan, and I have a plane to catch back to my side of the world in a few hours. My backpack is waiting by the door.

My fingers trail down her arm. "But some things didn't change."

"Like what?"

"Like…" Honesty sits on the surface, waiting to usher my thoughts up and out. I used to hide them from her like they might scare her, but she's stronger than I ever gave her credit for being, and I've learned from Tavah that honesty is the only way. "Like my feelings. They're the same. They're still in there, and I'd love to pretend they're enough to put everything back together, but then what? We'll leave this room eventually, and we have nothing but memories to hold onto." The questions that spilled through my head all night leak out. "What are we supposed to do with all the stuff from our past? How does it fit into whatever comes next? If there is a next for us? We'd have to do something with all of that, and I don't even know what that would look like. I'm not sure I want to. We've started over so many times. Maybe we've just run out of start overs." My thumb strokes her hand. "I think I used my last one when I thought you were dead and was forced to move on without you."

"But now you're not alone."

My chest tightens, but I look her in the eye. "I'm not."

She pauses. "I'm glad."

"And you have Leo."

She nods, her eyes still on mine. "I do. But that will never change how I feel about you. I'll always want you, even if I shouldn't, and even if we can't just step back into each other."

Her words land heavily, sink fast and deep, and I pull her to me when they settle. Her leg slips over my hip like it used to every night and when she apologizes and pulls away, I slide my hand down her thigh, holding her in place. She sinks into me, our hearts slipping back into their old rhythm.

My love for her wrecked my life. It was a force strong enough to cripple me for the rest of it. There's no way to go back to when I was whole and hopeful. I don't know how to be either of those things anymore, and I don't know what comes next for me. I remember in gory detail how I got here, though, and facing it feels like being dragged backwards. So I'm not gonna think about past or future. I'll just be right here, right now, only with Mei.

CHAPTER 42

MID-SEPTEMBER

"So…" Marcus says, his eyes holding mine from across the table as he takes a bite of his breakfast sandwich.

My fingers settle in my lap, and I blink slowly, transported to every morning of our life together: Marcus's gaze on me as he scooped cereal into his mouth, never looking down even as he grabbed his protein shake and took it down in one long gulp, like he didn't want to miss a minute of our silent conversations.

The memory fades, and I realize I'm still staring at him, my hand on my neck to steady my pulse.

His chewing slows and he glances away, swallows, looks at his plate before lifting his eyes to mine again, voice low. "Tell me about the new tattoo," he says before taking another bite, his eyes skidding over my face. "I like it." He plays with his fork on the table. "What does it mean?"

My face flushes, and I bite my lower lip as goosebumps run up my side like his fingertips are tracing my tattoo right now.

"I got it when…" I drop my focus to my untouched food.

"It was the day I decided I was done letting my situation control me."

"What is it?" His eyes reach for me as he picks up his cup and drinks his orange juice. He never liked orange juice when we were together. Another part of him that's changed.

Turning my teacup in my hands, I answer, "It's an Asian cherry tree in bloom. Some of the blossoms float away with the breeze, then turn into birds when they realize there's nothing holding them back."

I swirl my tea, take a sip, and when our eyes meet, his say, "*I underestimated you.*"

My eyes are fixed on his. "*What do you mean?*"

"Of the two of us, you were obviously the stronger one. I should've given you more credit and…I'm sorry."

For a fleeting moment, I think he's going to reach toward me, and I hold my breath but his fingers curl around his glass instead. I press my lips together. "I feel like we made a pretty great team."

He nods, glancing up at me from under his dark lashes before talking to the table again. "Yeah," he breathes. "We did." The words are solid with finality, and I hear the lilting voice of his girlfriend in my head again. What is she thinking while he's here with me? Will he tell her why the words and feelings in his eyes haven't faded or that time and distance shrunk to centimeters last night?

I lift my eyes but meet his halfway. No. He won't tell her. I know he won't, even if he should. Because he might love her, but it's not strong enough yet to overshadow how he feels about me; I'm swimming in it as we wordlessly stare at each other across the table.

When the server approaches and asks if we want refills, we blink away from each other, and I answer in Mandarin that we're finished. Marcus scoots back his chair, avoiding my eyes as he bends to grab his backpack, hauls it onto both shoulders like he's buckling into reality again, then grabs the tray from me and heads for the garbage can by the door.

I hesitate because once we walk out the door, our time is up. My lungs and heart struggle against this moment, my breathing sputtering. Frantically blinking away tears, I fumble in my bag for my lip gloss to distract myself as I follow Marcus through the door he's holding open for me. When my feet hit the sidewalk, I pause, then hurry back inside and grab two plastic spoons.

"What are those for?" he asks when I stride past him through the door again and onto the sidewalk.

I turn to him as the door closes behind us. "How long do you have before your flight?"

He checks his phone. "About twenty-five minutes before I have to leave for the airport."

"Then we have to hurry."

———

The garden of Buddhas glistens in the early morning light as I lead Marcus to the one I love most and kneel in front of it, my knees in the dirt beneath it. I hand Marcus a spoon. "Help me dig," I say before shoveling small scoops of dirt into a pile.

He drops beside me, digging and glancing at me. "This feels illegal. And maybe sacrilegious."

I smile. "Maybe, but I used to talk to you here." My hands shake as I dig deeper, closer to the box. "I used to walk through these statues and talk to you like you were walking next to me. I think this statue looks the most like our Buddha, so most of my talking included him."

Marcus stops scooping dirt, silent and still on his hands and knees before he turns his head toward me, his eyes soaking in the blue sky. "I used to talk to you, too. At night. On Johnny's couch when everyone else was asleep."

I glance at him, then back to the dirt, stopping when I hit

something solid. Scraping the remaining dirt off the box, I pull it out of its burial site and sit back on my legs, staring at it as I brush the dirt off with my hand.

Marcus sits back, his eyes going from the box to my face. "What is it?"

"It's for you." I set it on his lap, then get to my feet, dusting off my pants.

"What's inside?" he asks, staring at it as he stands.

"Wait until you're on the plane to open it. Please."

Marcus towers over me, so close I can smell the fabric softener on his shirt and the earthy smell seeping from the box clutched in his shaking hands between us. I want to step closer, but his phone buzzes and yanks me from the current of feelings swirling around me.

He pulls it out and his jaw tightens as he drops it back into his pocket. "My ride's a few minutes away," he says over my head before unzipping his backpack and setting the box inside. He silently follows me back through the garden, down the steps, and through the gate until we reach the street where his ride will pick him up and take him away from me forever. Just a car door, backseat, four tires to end it all.

The new ache that throbbed to life this morning when the sun lit the sky pulses stronger as we stop at the curb. I look at the sun-bleached cement, blinking back emotions that are pleading for him to gather them, mold them into something new. Marcus's fingers wind around mine, and he pulls me gently toward him until I'm staring into his chest, the diamond patterns on his shirt. But my beating heart shoves my eyes upward to meet his.

He holds my hand so tightly, our pulses bump together in my palm. They're still a perfect fit. But it doesn't matter. That won't stop them from pulling apart, and being separated by ocean and memories—me on my side of the world, Marcus on his.

"So this is what closure feels like," he says into the air

above my head, and I blink away the sting in my eyes, then close the distance and bury my face in his chest, his arms wrapping me tightly against him.

People walk around us, gasoline fumes breeze over us, and the world moves on despite how desperately we cling to each other. I give in to the sob building inside me as I press closer, wetting his shirt with my tears.

"I'm still in love with you, Mei."

My breathing catches on the sharp pain inside me, and hope surges but recedes just as quickly because, no matter the words, he's not staying and no matter how much I want to, I can't go with him. "I know."

We stay wrapped around each other, motionless on the outside but a torrent on the inside, until Marcus's ride stops at the curb. His hand slides down my arm to thread his fingers through mine again, and he lifts my palm to his mouth.

I close my eyes, feeling everything in one touch of his lips on my skin.

"I will never not be in love with you," I choke, our hands clasped between us now like they were the day we got married.

"I know." He lifts my chin so I'm staring at him, then smiles as he blinks at the sky, his eyes glossy. "I saw." He pauses, then leans down and presses his lips to mine, hesitating before urging mine open, and I dive into him one last time.

Our mouths linger before Marcus pulls back and steps away, his eyes still on mine as he lets go of my hand one finger at a time before turning from me.

He takes a few steps toward the car, and I blurt, "I wouldn't go back, either." When he turns back, I add, "I thought about it, and I wouldn't relive any of it." A tear escapes, and I swipe it away. "But in another life, I would start again with you anytime."

He closes his eyes, opens them, then nods before sliding into the waiting car that takes him away.

———

Hours later, after Leo has picked me up from the hotel and driven me home, I lock myself in my room and come apart until the sun barely dangles over the skyline. I pick myself up, leaving all the broken pieces on the floor, and walk to the shower, raw. When I pull off my shirt, the mirror reflects something black on my stomach. I stare at the numbers scrawled just below my belly button in black Sharpie:

365- 4ever and right under that, 6-21.

CHAPTER 43

MID-SEPTEMBER

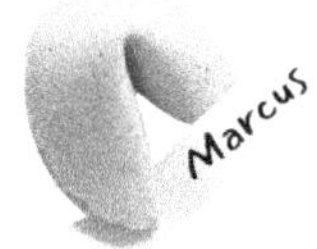

sit back in my airplane seat and yank down the window shade, the afternoon light's too bright. It's not even close to last night's moonlight slipping through the hotel window and over Mei and me, outlining the curve of her body against mine. If it can't be that light, I don't want any other.

Her body has changed since the last time I touched her, but it still fits perfectly. Maybe even better since we were forced to let go of who we tried to be for the other and just were.

Now, I'm crammed in a row with a Chinese girl and an old white guy, and neither of them care that I'm leaving a trail of my past in the atmosphere.

They don't care that I just ripped out my soul and left it with someone else and have to grow a new one.

Taiwan and the last words Mei said to me are 38,000 feet below and hundreds of miles behind me now. Except for the part sitting on my lap, dirt still clinging to the box. Whatever's inside is going to hurt just as much as leaving Mei after she said she'd try again.

I glance out the plane window. No land in sight, only flat,

deflated clouds. Shifting the box on my lap, I pick at the tape and unwrap, ignoring the looks from the guy next to me. It takes ten minutes, but now all I have to do is lift the lid and let whatever's inside finish me off completely.

I ease it off, breathe. Look inside. Sharpies, at least a hundred of them, notes attached to each one. I flex my fingers before grabbing the one on top, reading the note.

Day 1 of mourning you.

I slap the lid back on and stare at the seat in front of me, panic reflected in the screen.

Sharpies and notes and Mei's perfect handwriting, her smell and fingerprints and trapped memories all tempting me to get lost in them.

There's too much *us* in this box. Going through it is gonna take me too far back and I'll get stuck there again.

I close my eyes, sweat misting my palms. Mei kept part of me hidden in a box. But it's the old me. That guy doesn't really exist anymore. But what does she remember about him…?

My heart thuds in my throat and I swallow, pulling off the lid again, my shaking hand pulling out one of the Sharpies. I've never seen one like this, and I've seen a lot. Mei used to look for new ones to add to my pretty extensive collection. Guess she still does.

But they're not what makes me feel like I'm having a heart attack at 20. It's the words written on the notes attached to them:

Day 3 of mourning you: This color reminds me of the night we walked to 7-11 for Slurpees and you tried to teach me how to get a brain freeze.

Suddenly, that night is all around me—cold throat, warm night, my astonishment at learning she's physically incapable of brain freezes. Her cold lips. Blue raspberry tongue.

I grab another Sharpie:

Day 11 of mourning you: The Gummy Bear Incident

I drop the box under the seat in front of me and unbuckle my seat belt, then squeeze past my seatmate and up the aisle to the bathroom. I barely get the door latched before I puke my guts out, my body squirming from the blazing trail of Mei left all over it. Every place she's ever touched is lit up like Vegas.

A few minutes later, someone jiggles the door, and I flush the toilet and wash my hands and face. Kinda wish I could open a window and hurl the box into the atmosphere. But… even if I could, I wouldn't. I've already done the impossible and walked away from her. This can't hurt worse than that.

My head throbs as I slide back into my seat. With the box on my lap again and self-destruction in mind, I pull out another Sharpie, ignoring the stares from the guy next to me.

Day 14 of mourning you: The day we kissed for ten minutes at the door before you left for work. Five minutes later, you were back. You didn't even make it around the corner.

I was very late for work that day with a stupid smile on my face.

Day 12 of mourning you: Remember that time we swore we saw Hitler walking down the street?

Day 15 of mourning you: The nights you'd lay on my stomach and make up lyrics to the sounds it made. Your laughter is my favorite sound.

I close my eyes, my face burning. What am I doing on this stupid plane? I lean my head back against the seat, concentrating on breathing so I don't puke again. I can't go back to Mei, but I also can't go back to Tavah now that I've confirmed and admitted I'm still in love with Mei. That's never gonna change, either; I knew that for sure the second the car took me away from her and toward the airport. When the parts I thought were healed inside me ripped open because she was still holding onto them even as I moved away from her. I opened my mouth to ask the driver to turn around, but my body was in shock. I just sat motionless in the backseat, watched life move forward, emptier than it was when I came to Taiwan because most of me stayed with her.

I walked away from Mei, and I'm gonna have to do the same to Tavah because there's not much left of me to give to anyone else.

Gripping the armrests, I talk myself through a freak out. But what's Mei gonna do now? Will she end up with Leo? I don't care if he's the reason I found her again; I still wanna punch him.

I lean forward, head in my hands. I'm gonna puke all over myself and my seatmates if I keep thinking about her with him.

I reach for another memory to distract myself.

Day 10 of mourning you: The way you used to talk about our future kids. You were so excited to meet them and always said they'd be cool like you and beautiful like me.

I rest my forehead on the seat in front of me, fighting cold sweats until the guy next to me asks in a thick Australian accent if I'm okay.

"You look like you've had better days."

I jerk up, sitting back in my seat, arms crossed. "Yeah." I clear my throat. "Had better years, actually."

"Girls?"

I hesitate before nodding.

"Recognized the agony. They'll mess you up every time."

A picture of a smirking Ray Miller rises in my head. "So I was warned."

"Learned it for yourself, eh?"

I glance at the window shade, then shift in my seat. "Yeah."

The guy smiles and nods knowingly. "You're young enough you haven't caused too much damage yet."

"Just walked away from my wife who I thought was dead but who was really alive in Taiwan under a new name. Headed back to my girlfriend in San Francisco I never would've been with if I had any clue my wife was alive. But now I love my girlfriend, too, so…how's that for damage?"

He lets out a low whistle and shakes his head. "Kind of young to have stories like that, aren't you?"

Everyone I met after I married Mei had the same reaction. One of my co-workers in Vegas asked why I brushed off all the "attention" I got during our shifts, then choked on his soda when I'd told him I was married. 'You're married?' he'd asked, like I'd admitted I was an escaped serial killer. 'Dude…you could have any female in this city.'

I'd thanked him for the vote of confidence but told him when he met my wife, he'd get exactly why I'd married her.

The Australian guy continues, holding up his hands. "Don't know the story but seems like you're still in love with your wife."

I glance at him, then back at the seat in front of me. "I'll always be in love with her."

"Then her being alive should be a good thing, right?"

"The very best thing."

He raises his eyebrows. "And your girlfriend?"

"Yeah. Her too."

"Is it possible to love two women at the same time?"

"I've managed to," I answer, turning my head to look at him. "But what do you think?"

"Sure." He watches my reaction, then adds, "Don't think there are any rules about it, but it seems like there's always one that settles more deeply into your soul."

When I don't respond, he goes on.

"I don't know what you've gotten yourself into, but it seems to me you're afraid."

I let out a long breath, relieved that he said the word and not me. "Yep." I nod. "I'm afraid of everything,"

"So I guess your job is to decide how afraid. And of what."

"Already know." I curl the end of the nylon seat belt around my pointer finger. "Gotta change my life again. Start over. Without either of them."

The plane jumps and we both brace ourselves as the pilot interrupts with an announcement about turbulence and the seatbelt sign flicks on with a ding.

"My next question would normally be 'why', but it seems you aren't sure at the moment, so…" The guy buckles his seatbelt, then slides a laptop out of his backpack. "Sounds like you've got some sorting to do. Wish I could help, but women are a mystery to me. Good news is you have ten more hours before we land."

"Yeah. Great news." But there's no sorting to do. Decision was made the second I decided to spend all night with Mei while Tavah waited back in San Francisco.

The plane's on the ground. Has been for at least ten minutes, and I've watched passengers shuffle down the aisle, a blur of jet lag. But I don't blink or move, just wait for my legs to want to move. But they don't, because they know I have to walk off this plane and into the airport…toward Tavah.

My grip tightens on the box. I've read every memory inside it. Twice. Some even more. If I keep them, they'll weigh me down, drag behind me forever. So when I stand, I set it on the seat and rush down the aisle, bracing myself on every seat along the way.

I grip the escalator railing so tightly, my knuckles turn white as I scan the crowds for Tavah. When I see her, my heart stirs from where it's been lying face-down, quiet and resigned.

I step off the escalator and Tavah launches herself at me. I wrap my arms around her, but they're stiff, even as she slides through them and takes my face between her hands, kissing me in a way that, before I left for Taiwan, would've led straight to a horizontal surface.

I should stop her. I just kissed Mei. Can she tell?

I pull away and grab my backpack straps to keep myself grounded. Her eyes go to the 6-21 I drew on my wrist in metallic blue Sharpie somewhere over the Pacific.

I drop my hand, press my wrist against my leg, and her eyes follow the movement, then search mine.

She tucks her hair behind her ear as she talks to the floor, her face flushed. "You saw her?"

I clear my throat, glance at her before looking away. "Yeah." This airport is too bright—I need darkness and privacy and quiet. I need somewhere to hide from that look in Tavah's eyes.

"And?" Her voice is strained by the tension between us.

Isn't it obvious? It's written all over my face—all over my

body in blazing Mei trails. It's on my wrist in Sharpie. But I bite back words Tavah doesn't deserve. None of this is her fault and this isn't the place to explain anything. "Can we go somewhere and talk?"

Her eyes shine with the promise of tears, and I look down, flex my toes in my Adidas.

"What happened, Marcus?"

My chest burns as I shake my head. "Nothing. I mean… it's not what you're probably thinking happened."

She closes her eyes as a single tear slips through her eyelashes. "Or maybe it's exactly what I knew would happen."

"Tavah, I—"

She turns her head. "Why didn't you tell me before now? Before I came here, believing and hoping the best after battling thoughts of the worst since the second you left?" She takes a desperate breath. "Why do you struggle so hard to let me in?" Her composure crumbles, and she puts her hands over her face, standing alone even though I'm right in front of her.

"Tavah, I'm so sorry. I just need to—"

"Yeah, you need to do a lot of things, Marcus." Her eyes are locked on mine, tears sliding down her cheeks. "And you can start by finding your own way home."

CHAPTER 44
LATE SEPTEMBER

"Are you sure you're okay with this?" Leo asks, holding my hand as I lie on the bed, head supported by a pillow. After saying goodbye to Marcus, I told Leo I wanted to move forward with my life, not let my past hold me back from happiness. He'd told me Chang Mama had an unconventional but proven way to help, and I'd agreed to try it. I was willing to try anything that would help me forget what I'd seen in Marcus's eyes.

I nod before he reluctantly lets go of my hand and slips silently out of the room as Chang Mama lights incense and waves it above me. She tells me to close my eyes and breathe deeply so I do, letting the sweet, woodsy fragrance fill my nose.

Even with my eyes closed, I feel the steadiness of her hands hovering over me as I slip into my subconscious.

Pressure gathers in my head, an intense grip that clutches my deepest memories, then pulls them from their hiding places. Fear clings to each of them but Chang Mama softly chants for me to let go, and after the words lull me into a rhythm, I release them in a gasp.

I'm eleven…walking home from school. A cat is in front of

the restaurant, playing with a shoestring. I bend and pick him up, cradling him as I rub his tummy until he scrambles from my arms and continues playing. I open the restaurant door and step inside. The room is dim but there's noise coming from the kitchen, so I move toward it, stopping when shouts and metal grinding against metal as a gun is cocked leap at me.

I crawl under a table just before a stranger flies through the swinging kitchen door, followed closely by my father, gun in hand. He shoots twice and a silent scream surges inside me, hands over my ears, but the man is already outside, and the bullet hurls itself into the wall, leaving a starburst in the red wallpaper. I tighten myself into a ball under the table, vowing to never speak of what I witnessed in case Baba's wrath turns on me.

But as this memory trickles through me, it dries up until it's only a few drops hanging in my mind, and Chang Mama's hands smooth over my neck, wiping away the last drops. All my warmth follows the movement, leaving behind the memory of a gun held by another man. The details escape as Chang Mama's hands massage my neck. My muscles tighten and suffocation squeezes me as Nick Chao's fingers grip my throat, squeezing life from me. I spiral into darkness, a memory blurring past me on my descent.

I'm almost naked on a cold floor, my shoulder blades grating against marble as I fight for my life. Energy leaks from me, and I cry out, my body trembling just as Chang Mama hovers her hands over my chest. Warmth floods me and Marcus is right behind it, smiling over Oreos floating in a bowl of milk. We're laughing as we run in the rain, and he's saying things with his eyes at our wedding, then jumping off a dock into the frigid ocean. Sweltering nights in Vegas, cold nights in Indiana, holding Charlie, Marcus smiling the smile he saved just for me.

I grasp at all of them, pulling their light toward me. But

they dissolve, replaced by Marcus's laughter echoing through our threadbare apartment as he chases me, a water gun in each hand after he'd confiscated mine. He emptied both until we were rolling on the kitchen floor, laughing and drenched. But the joy fades, and I watch myself close the door of our Indiana apartment. In sharp detail, a montage of the disastrous results rush my mind, and when Chang Mama's hands tremble above my stomach, I sink into pain so intense, it splits me in two. I lose the one thing that tied me to Marcus all over again and even though the baby was never going to grow, the memory still leaves me gaping and raw, turned inside out.

With a wave of Chang Mama's hands, the wounds close, the pain dissolves behind wide open skies in my mind and heart, leaving clarity: the course of my life was changed when Marcus entered it. He took me from my pain, replaced it with beautiful moments and the happiest memories. But he won't take me from it now, and I'm stronger than I was then. I faced my greatest fear and took its power. I looked Nick in the eye. I've lived without Marcus. I've started something new. It's different than I'd hoped or wanted, but it's mine, and I will live in my present, grateful I get to choose my future.

"You may open your eyes when you are ready," Chang Mama murmurs in Taiwanese.

My mind is airy, blank, my body loose, and for the first time in a very long time, I'm relaxed, safe and whole. Except for the swirling in my heart under my palm.

Slowly, I open my eyes, blinking back into the dim room.

"You did well, Mei Li." Chang Mama lays her hand over mine on my chest. "I sensed much movement and clearing." She nods, patting my hand. "Except there was something inside here…too deep to reach, unwilling to detach." Chang Mama gives me a gentle smile. "When I tried to coax it out, it held on tighter, which means it is not time for you to let it go. That doesn't mean you cannot continue moving forward, it only means whatever occupies that part of your heart is too precious and sacred to part with." She takes a step back, nods, then leaves me alone with the part of my heart that still belongs to Marcus, which my body and mind apparently refuse to give up.

I lie back on the bed, my palm still resting over my heart as I smile to the ceiling and thank my body and mind for holding onto Marcus so tightly. I was never meant to live without him, and now I never will, no matter what side of the world we're on.

CHAPTER 45
LATE SEPTEMBER

use my key to Tavah's apartment and slip inside, hoping no one else is home. I know she's here, because she's still sharing her location with me, and I've stared at that stupid dot for three days. I deleted it on my walk here.

Setting the key on the table, I keep my eyes focused on her bedroom door, knowing after this, I'll never be here again. This thing between us has grown into more than I ever imagined it would, but it's only going this far. If I'm being real with myself, it ended the second I decided to go to Taiwan. She knew, even if I didn't.

I hesitate before knocking on her door, but when there's no answer, I turn the knob and slip inside like I've done so many times before.

She's at her desk, her feet pulled up, knees to her chest. She's staring into the dark and when I close the door, she turns her swollen eyes on me. I don't say a word, but her face crumples.

I cross the room, kneel in front of her, and pull her into my arms, leaning my head on hers. I swallow hard, trying not to cry. I've made this decision, and it's the right one for both of us, even though it's ripping me apart.

"I knew you were coming," she chokes into my shirt, clenching it so tightly that her hands shake. "I woke up this morning, and I knew it would be today."

I hold her tighter, wishing I could absorb all the hurt I've caused her. I know what it's like—being the one left to suffer. I'm the one walking away and it's all suffering, knowing how close we came to being Us. But I can only handle me for now. Maybe for the next forty years, and I'm not dragging her through my mess any more than I already have. Finally, I'm doing the right thing for her.

But am I? Holding her in the space she's created in my arms, I second-guess my decision. Mei will never know. I could stay in this life, see Tavah smile again, hear her laugh instead of cry. I could let my life with Mei and the fragile hours we spent together in Taiwan slip behind me for good, replace it with Tavah. I've done it once, I can do it again, and this time, I have closure with Mei. Besides, I've dated Tavah longer than I dated Mei before running away and marrying her.

Our wedding day flashes in my head, and I'm reminded once again how much I was willing to give up for Mei. It was never about time with her—it was about that first look we shared in Guo's shop. It's about the way my life looked with Mei in it—like happiness in crappy apartments and figuring out our arguments and laughing until we cried—crying until we laughed. It's about the way she looked at me and our wordless conversation on the monastery steps that shattered me all over again. I'm not gonna bother picking myself up or pretending that what happened in the hotel room didn't mean anything.

I still want 365 forever. I want to keep 6-21 sacred and even though it didn't last, I don't want anything else.

"Come here," I whisper to Tavah and stand, pulling her to her feet and into my arms.

She clings to me, and I close my eyes, my cheek against

hers, our tears blending. "I love you." My voice breaks and I swallow.

"Just not enough," she whispers into my neck.

I shake my head, my stubble rustling against her hair. "Too much to keep dragging you through my mess. And I need to figure out who I am."

"I'll never get over you." Her voice breaks again.

I swear and squeeze my eyes tighter, clenching my jaw. There's no way I can do this. No way I can let her go. No way I can turn and walk away from her toward nothing. She's been my bright spot for too long. I love her. And it isn't just gonna go away because I saw Mei one last time. Tavah's like Sharpie all over my head.

But Mei's always been a tattoo.

I let her sob in my arms as I smooth her hair, run my hands down her back. I need to throw up so bad, but I close my eyes, force it down. I wish I could take the hurt away. I wish I'd never created it. Wish I had a fast-forward button for both of us. I wish I'd never let either of us get to this point, but then the memories come flooding back, and I know I'll never regret them, no matter how much they hurt.

So I hold her. It's the only thing I can do. The only thing I want to do. It's the only way I know how to say goodbye.

———

I leave Tavah's apartment at 2 AM, after she stopped crying and fell asleep, curled against me on her floor where I sat, back against the wall.

I wander the empty campus until a security guard pulls up beside me on his bike while I'm puking in a garbage can and asks if I've been drinking. I've never had alcohol, so I've never been drunk but imagine the way I'm staggering to keep my legs moving forward instead of backward looks a lot like it. I'm pretty sure being smashed would feel infinitely better than how I feel right now.

All my blood has pooled into my feet, leaving the rest of me numb and cold, but I manage to unlock the apartment door. I throw my keys across the room, drop to the couch, and run my hands through my hair, swearing into the dark at the hot, black pain.

I'm lost between lives. My past life, what I thought was my future life, and this murky space that's acting like my present. I threw myself into Mei, then Tavah. But I never took the time to figure out who I am without either of them shaping my world. I've remodeled myself so many times, I'm pieced together and need to demolish everything that used to be me and start fresh.

I clutch my chest and roll to my side, staring at the window, knowing Mei's beyond it, thousands of miles across an ocean. Which is more than what's between me and whatever comes next—a whole lot of nothing.

I shift on the couch, and my phone jabs my thigh. Sliding it out, I flick it on and stare at the first picture—Tavah blowing a gigantic bubble, her eyes wide. I smile. She always prided herself on her gum-chewing abilities. I swipe to a picture of her lying on the beach, sunglasses on, her smile making the whole picture glow.

Not sure how I'm gonna get through my days without that smile. Without that girl.

I flip through more pictures. I'm gonna miss this…and that. That…and the way she did that. Ah, man…that—I'll definitely miss that. Maybe most.

I'll miss the way she always has random facts for me and how she loves windy days. I'll miss the way people respond to her and her infectious laugh. I'm pretty sure I'll hear it echoing inside my head, battling with Mei's, blending. Both of them laughing at me.

I take a deep breath and select all of Tavah's pictures, then hit Delete. Nobody will ever be Tavah.

But no one, not even Tavah, could replace Mei for me.

I open the app that holds proof of my life with Mei. I haven't opened it since I sent every picture but one to it, but that's exactly the picture I'm after. It's like looking at love itself: me and Mei, her head on my chest as we'd lounged in our Vegas apartment one Sunday afternoon. I'd taken it from above and had never gotten over how beautiful she is. How she'd created complete happiness inside me without trying. How she'd made my life too big for anyone else to ever fill the space she left. She'd taken me so high and then so, so low. I'll never forget how low and will never be that low again. Tavah was the only one brave enough to try and pick me up, and I'll always love her for it.

But the girl looking at the camera with those deep, gentle eyes…she's The Girl. Always will be, and if I can't have her, I don't want anyone.

CHAPTER 46

MID-OCTOBER

The bus looks so harmless but standing in front of its open door feels like my soul is tearing apart, one slice of it staying here while the rest is eager to take the steps inside and move on. The impending goodbye wraps around my ankles and holds me to a place I never dreamed would feel like home. It's not the place that made it that way but the person standing in front of me as I search for the right way to say goodbye. I've learned too many times that there is no right way. It always hurts.

Marcus came and left almost a month ago, but our night together is still fresh. When his message on my stomach faded, I made it permanent in black script on my shoulder blade. I won't see it every day, but I'll know it's there, behind me but important enough to hold onto forever, just like our time together.

Then, a few weeks ago, I'd logged into an email account I hadn't used since before Marcus and I left San Franscisco. After filtering out all the spam, there were two messages left: one from Mama sent almost a year ago that said she was staying with my aunt and uncle in Kending, and one from Chef Marco. He said he'd become the director of a culinary institute in San Francisco and would love for me to apply to his program. The email was sent when Marcus and I were still in Indiana. I wrote him back, not expecting a response after so long, but one arrived a few minutes later, telling me he'd still love for me to apply. So I did. Two weeks later, I got an acceptance email with scholarship information. The next day, with Leo's help, I'd applied for a student visa using my new name and passport and a few days later, I was approved. Leo took me to dinner to celebrate.

I don't feel like celebrating now, though, as we stand in silence in front of the idling bus. My eyes are on the pavement, my hands shoved in my jacket pockets. I don't want to look into Leo's face because it's one more thing I'm going to miss. I love him, and that's a new realization, too. I didn't know I could ever love anyone besides Marcus.

"I hate this, Mei Li." He takes my hand, holds it to his chest.

"Me too."

"I just wish…" He releases a long, slow breath. "I wish things were different. And that you would stay. Yeah, that makes me selfish, and I hate being selfish, but if I had my way…"

I look up into his eyes which are cloudy, flashes of pain and hope peeking out. "You could never be truly selfish. It's not your style."

"Maybe I should give it a shot." He smiles and blinks up at the sky then back at me. "I love you, you know."

"And you know I love you, too." I reach up, trace the outline of his face to commit it to memory. He gathers me in his arms and buries his face in my neck as I listen to his heart. The ache inside throbs and pushes out tears. Today, I don't stop them as final boarding is called.

This is it—another end.

Leo pulls back just enough to wipe the tears from my

cheeks, then gently presses his lips to mine before stepping back. "I've wanted to do that since the last time."

Slowly, reluctantly, my fingers release his and I adjust my satchel strap and pick up the duffle bag waiting at my feet.

"If you ever need me, you know where to find me," he says. "Or if you don't need me but just miss me." He shoves his hands in his pockets.

"And if you're ever in San Francisco and miss me..." I smile and walk to the bus steps, then turn and rush back to him, throwing my arms around him. "Thank you. For saving me," I whisper against his cheek.

He leans back, shakes his head. "If that was saving, I hope I get the chance to do it again someday."

I step back in line, keeping my eyes on him. He holds up a hand in a wave. I commit his face to memory as I find my seat and watch my present turn into yet another past.

CHAPTER 47

There are still sounds that take me back. Like the alarm that used to wake me at 4 AM for soccer practice. Chain link fence handles and a coach's whistle, grass shrieking beneath my cleats. I close my eyes like I can hide those memories from myself. But I can't hide from the sound of the blender growling from the kitchen. It's a harsh reminder that I'm back at The Clubhouse—full circle.

A week after I got home from Taiwan, I withdrew from Berkeley and started looking for apartments near USF. Neutral ground. But for now, I'm back at the beginning, like I've been nowhere and done nothing in the last year and a half. Guess I rewound time too far, because I'm alone, just like I was before Mei. This time, though, I know for a fact that girls can not only mess me up, but they can completely break me.

I stand from where I've been sitting on the edge of my bed, wondering like I have every morning for the past month how I got back in my old room that pretty much looks the same but smells like lavender candles instead of fabric softener and grass stains. But my room looks exactly the same—

with me and only me in it. No matter how hard I pretend every night that Mei's in here with me.

I take a deep breath, sigh, then stretch and avoid the window. She's nowhere even close to her old apartment, but every time I see it, I hear her laugh, and I just can't do that right now.

Glancing at my watch, I swear and snatch some shorts from my desk chair. Gotta get a run in before work. My leg hasn't hurt this week, and I've been running farther, pounding out the thoughts stuck like chipped cement in my head. Gotta get rid of the clutter so I can focus and earn my spot back on the USF team I turned down for Stanford. I got accepted and registered for next semester but until then, I've got a lot of training to do for my one-on-one tryout next week. Going back to my first love never felt so good.

Snatching my phone off my nightstand, I put in my earbuds but scan a text from a girl who comes into the bike shop and asked for my number a couple days ago. Not sure how she misread my concrete wall of indifference as interest. Just to mess with me, my coworker gave her my number, and I've got the perfect way to get back at him.

If the world thought Ray Miller was woman-averse, I'll crush his eighteen-year record.

I delete the text and click off my phone, then walk into the living room where Kenna's doing yoga.

"Making me look bad again, eh?" she asks through her arms from her downward dog. "Running your daily half marathon while I do 30 minutes of mild stretching."

I gulp down a glass of water, then wipe my mouth and smile as I stride toward the door. "You can join me anytime."

She laughs and it squishes out of her as she moves to cobra. "I'm almost 40, Marcus. I'm at the point in my life where I get to choose what I want to do, and the only time I'll run on purpose is if I'm being chased by a man with a chainsaw. And even then, I might consider other options." She smiles at the ceiling as she continues. "But burn some calories for me, please."

I laugh. "On it," I call as I pull the door shut behind me and skim down the stairs, push open the building door, and step outside. Guo's shop won't open for another two hours, so I don't have time to visit her or Charlie today even if I haven't seen either of them in over a week. He gives me the saddest looks every time I leave, and I can't take it. I'm purposely looking for apartments that allow pets so he and I can be bachelors together. The last time I visited Guo, she was oddly quiet, and Charlie was nowhere to be seen. She assured me he was fine, but it felt like she was hiding something from me. Or didn't want to say what she was really thinking, which would only happen if she'd had a stroke and lost her ability to speak. I asked, she said she hadn't. I told her all about how I was starting over—how I'd broken up with Tavah after coming home from Taiwan and was accepted to USF for winter semester and had a strong chance of getting on the soccer team. I'd avoided all things Mei adjacent even though I have burning questions about still being married to her. Are we? Aren't we? Was it ever legit? I can't drag up the question to ask, because I don't wanna know. Either way; that whole scene in Taiwan is locked inside me and will eventually wither if I don't give it air or sunlight. Then I might find the guts to ask.

I jog down the street, round the corner, head uphill, eager to feel my legs burn. I grit my teeth and run faster and harder until sweat rolls into my eye and I swipe it away, hauling in cool, fresh air tinged with salt and the moisture it collected as morning fog moved over the bay. My mind goes static as music thumps through it until my phone rings. Tilting the screen toward me, I swipe it when Johnny's face smirks up at me.

"What's up?" I pant, not slowing down as I run another hill.

"Not running my guts out like you, that's for sure."

"Left my spleen a couple blocks back and feeling lighter already."

"Pretty sure your spleen has enough muscle to walk out of you by itself. You're a machine these days, man. Leave some masculinity for the rest of us."

I stop at a light, hands on my hips as I wait for it to change. "Always looking for a running partner."

"Tempting, but you know…Berkeley's treating me way too good to come back over the Bridge."

"Her name's Berkeley?"

Johnny laughs. "You wish."

"Still Lin?"

"Ehh…yeah? No? I don't know, man. She's intense, but it's like I can't stay away so I don't know what'll happen. Good times, though."

"Happy for you." The light turns, and I look both ways before darting across a street, keeping my head down and hauling myself up another hill.

"Yeah, thanks, even though I know you're lying. How you doing, anyway? Haven't caught up since you moved out. Has it been bad being back?"

"Nah." I drag in air. "It's been fine. Better than I thought." I swipe sweat off my forehead. "Kinda nice to live the reclusive bachelor life. Fits me pretty well, actually. But I'm trying to get on USFs team, so…going back to my first love, hopefully."

"Oh yeah? Not bad, Miller. Getting your groove back and making the magic happen as always." Johnny's quiet for a minute, and if I wasn't surrounded by traffic and buses, I'd actually be able to hear his thoughts clicking into place. But I wait for him to say whatever he's hesitant to say while I jog in place and wait for another red light to change on my way to the wharf.

"So I don't even know if you care or anything, but I just

heard some crazy news and you're the guy I always share crazy news with so…"

"Think I retired from crazy news." I jab the crosswalk button again. "But one more time, I guess."

"Tavah withdrew from Berkeley and went to Costa Rica with Alli and her friend, Siri who lives in some crazy jungle house there."

The traffic blurs, the roar of loud mufflers and whir of electric cars fades before rushing at me again. "For real?"

"Yeah, Lin just told me last night. Tavah packed some stuff and announced she was going to Costa Rica. No one saw it coming. She didn't even tell her parents."

I stare at my running shoes while the information sinks in. "Wow. No, that's totally not like her."

"Nah, man. She's been so quiet and closed off. Barely left her room since you broke up. You messed her up bad. Marcus Miller damage is life changing, turns out. You've got two girls on different continents because they got too close."

"Dude, seriously?"

"Kidding, kidding, but look at the facts, you know? Your lovin' puts them over the edge and they bolt. You've got serious powers, and I've always known it. But now I'm looking at the proof and need some of your magic dust."

"You want Lin on another continent?"

Johnny bursts out laughing, "No. Nope—never mind. Keep your dust."

I drop to a bench, deflated, my body achy. "Costa Rica, really? Tavah never mentioned a thing about Costa Rica." I sit forward, elbows on knees, hands clasped in front of me. Maybe I didn't know her as well as I thought. "I hate how it ended. But it had to, no matter how much I wanted to be with her."

"Because you still want Mei Li bad. You never told me all the details of what happened when you saw her, by the way. Stuff went down, right?"

I stand. "Can we not talk about her?"

"Yeah, yeah, you got it. Sorry, dude. Your life's just way more exciting than mine."

"Remember how I said reclusive bachelor?" Except not really a bachelor since I'm technically still married. I think. I really need to ask Guo. Eventually.

"Want me to come by for tea some day? Play checkers with you? Read the newspaper while we discuss the economy and politics?"

I jog across the crosswalk, shivering now that my sweat has dried and I'm headed into the breeze coming off the ocean. "If you can wade through the piles of cans and pizza boxes to my gaming chair, maybe we could stay up all night virtually shooting each other."

"Girls? Who needs girls? Be there tonight, Miller. With my headset and a stash of Oreos."

CHAPTER 48
MID-OCTOBER

Nerves ignite when my staccato knocks against my aunt's door echo through the hallway. I haven't seen Mama since before I left San Francisco with Marcus, but I'm about to. I shouldn't feel nervous to see her, but I'm the reason she had to leave the U.S. Her email didn't sound mad, but will we have anything to say to each other after everything that's happened?

The door opens and my aunt's eyes shine when she finally recognizes me and waves me into her apartment. She chatters on, telling me how good it is to see me, that I'm too skinny and need to eat, that I shouldn't have cut my hair so short, but that I'm so beautiful despite it. I was eight when I last saw her, but she swoops me in like family anyway, and then Mama's there, smiling and radiant. She's always been beautiful but now her shoulders are open, her hair pulled up on the sides, showing off her golden eyes that have new light in them.

She beams as she rushes forward, and I take a step toward her before she reaches me and wraps me in her arms. She holds me like I always imagined a mother would hold her daughter, and my tears flow freely, my body trembling with relief and years of locked away resentment that was misplaced and misdirected.

"You have no idea how happy I am to see you," she whispers through her tears. "When I got your email saying you were coming, I was too excited to sleep or eat."

I smile. "Sorry it took me so long to write back."

"I am just glad you are safe and here now." She releases me and her eyes grow serious. "I heard about Nick."

I nod. "Yeah, but I don't want to talk about him if that's okay."

"Yes. Let's not." She bustles over to a closet and snatches a purse. "Are you hungry? There is a small noodle shop just around the corner."

"I'm starving, actually. That sounds perfect."

On our walk to the restaurant, we talk about my aunt and uncle and what life is like in Kending and how good it's been for her to be out of San Francisco and so close to a warm beach. We order and sit at a table for two where she chatters about how happy she is to see me and that she talks to Guo Mama almost every day and is so excited to tell her about our meetup.

"How is she?" I ask, leaning my elbow on the table. "I called her about a month ago. Before I decided to go back."

"She is exactly the same. Still making mischief. Even if it is a little harder for her these days, she still manages very nicely."

I look at the table. "I hate what happened to her. She did nothing wrong. She didn't deserve it."

"Did anyone deserve any of this?" Mama tilts her head, her eyes soft. "Did you?"

I glance at her, shake my head.

"None of this was your fault. We both know who is responsible and lucky for us, one is dead, one will die in prison. Yes, everyone got hurt in some way but now...it is over."

She assesses me, and I consider telling her I visited the man we used to live with, but she continues. "And you are safe and that is all that matters to me." Her stare is final, not allowing further discussion about regrets. "I know your heart is hurt and for that, I am very sorry. I am also sorry about Marcus."

I play with the infinity ring dangling from my necklace and frown. "About which part?" I haven't talked to her in over a year, so I'm not sure what she could possibly know about Marcus and me. The deep ache stirs.

"Guo Mama updates me every time she talks to him."

"Oh." I blink at the table, shift in my seat. "Does she talk to him often?"

Mama shrugs. "I am not sure how often, but Guo Mama told me you two are no longer together. But that, of course, she still has hope."

My eyes dart to the teapot in the center of the table, trace its pattern. "I used to have hope too, but he said goodbye. And I get why he had to. So…tell Guo Mama she can hope, but we've made choices that will take us in different directions."

When Mama asks where I'm headed now, I tell her all about Chef Marco's email and my acceptance, and she covers her mouth with both hands as tears slip down her face this time. She can barely choke out how proud she is of me and when I tell her I'm going to stay at Lin's for a few days, she practically leaps in her chair, her palms flat on the table as she leans toward me.

"Make sure you visit Guo Mama when you get to town. It would make her so happy. I guess she is being a grandmother to your cat. Do not be surprised if he is overweight when you see him again. She loves to give him treats."

I smile at the thought of an overweight Charlie happily eating his treats in the corner of Guo Mama's shop. "I plan on it. Just have to get there and settled at Lin's first. I'm going to stay there until I find a place closer to the institute. It's comforting, though, knowing she's there, so I'll definitely visit her."

"Also, if I may point out, even though you and Marcus chose to go in different directions, it appears, you are headed in his."

I smile, my hand finding the infinity ring again. "I'm aware. But I'm not going back for him."

"Not even a little?"

I sip my tea, not answering, as I force that thought out of my mind and turn my attention toward the folder Mama gave me before I left San Francisco. I still have a very big question I've been carrying since then and it finally gets its turn. "Can I ask you a question?"

She nods and looks at me over her teacup. "Of course."

"Will you tell me your story? About Peter Mitchell?"

Mama reaches out and touches my arm. "I have been waiting for twenty years to tell you about him." She plays with her necklace, her thoughts clearly going back in time as she talks. "I met him when I was sixteen. My family rented a beach house on Peng Hu Island for the summer." Her eyes shine as she continues. "Peter Mitchell. From America." She smiles at the table. "I was playing in the ocean and he body boarded into me. He told me that was his plan all along and from then, we spent every possible moment together until one day, he told me he loved me."

She grins into the air like he's sitting beside her, whispering in her ear. "The night before my family was going home, I invited him to the beach house while my parents and sister were at dinner. I was in so much pain over leaving him." She looks down, playing with her napkin. "I was young and stupid but so in love with him."

Before meeting Marcus, I wouldn't have wanted the details of what happened between my mother and some guy to bring me into existence, but I can't deny the similarities between our stories—American boy, sneaking around, completely and totally in love so young. She feels more like a friend than a mother now. Still, if her feelings for Peter were anything close to mine for Marcus, the details of what happened between them are sacred to her, so I stay quiet as she continues.

"When I found out I was pregnant, I wrote him but kept it a secret from everyone else. Months passed without a word from him, and my pregnancy became obvious, so I had to tell my parents." She meets my eyes. "Baba wanted me to get rid of the baby—of you—but I was too far along and never would have agreed to it anyway, so he arranged my marriage to his business partner's son who was planning to move to America. Somehow that made me feel better, to know I would be in America, closer to Peter, even if I had to be married to someone else. I had caused my family a lot of shame already, so I agreed.

"A few days before the wedding, I received an email from Peter. He had been away at school, and he did not see my email until he went home on holiday and was closing his old account. He told me to come to Rhode Island, and we would figure things out together. He even bought me a plane ticket." Mama's smile fades and a shadow passes over her face.

"But you didn't go," I murmur, and she shakes her head, eyes glossy.

"I was too afraid. I could not shame my family again, so I married someone I did not love and never would."

"Mama…" I shake my head, my heart bleeding for her.

"Regret is a funny thing, Mei Li. It finds you immediately after you make the wrong decision and never lets go. I have regretted not using that plane ticket my whole life. On my wedding day, I swore to myself I would never be weak again, and that is why, when your baba became involved with the wrong men, I kept records, knowing one day I would need them. That day came when you were forced to go to L.A. with Nick."

She looks at her lap, studying her hands. "I gave it all to the police right after you left, but it was too late to save you from what Nick did to you. Guo Mama told me what happened in L.A. and I hated myself for not being brave sooner. But you and Marcus were so brave, and I was relieved and grateful when I learned you had left San Francisco together."

My eyes skip from her face, around the shop, gathering pieces of what she's not saying.

She nods. "You were not the one who sent us from America. It was me. I was too weak to be the mama you needed. I wished every day I could be, but when Marcus came into your life, I knew he was what you needed most, and I made sure your baba never knew where or when or how you left."

I swallow the throb radiating from my heart into my throat.

"That boy was so in love with you," she says through a smile, squeezing my hand. "I was taking out the garbage the night you two met at Guo Mama's and knew it was big, just by the look in his eyes." She tilts her head, smiling. "I watched every day as you two walked by our building on opposite sides of the street. You kept your head down, pretending not to know him, but I saw the smile you tried to hide and the way Marcus could not keep his attention on anything but you. And then there were the notes you wrote each other."

My face flushes, my blood surges, then recedes. "You knew about those?"

She presses her lips together, then nods before grabbing her purse and pulling out a very familiar yellow folder with "Calculus" scrawled across it as she blurts, "I read them and think you should read them again too."

My heart stumbles over itself, face burning. "You kept them? Read them?"

She nods, smiling. "There was no way I was going to leave something this important behind. I went through your room before I left, just to make sure there was nothing important. And I'm sorry I read them. I could not help it. It was the only way I could participate in what was happening between you two. It was the only way I could confirm that he was as perfect for you as I suspected. Each note made me love him more."

I cover my face. I, too, had loved him more with each note, but some of the things we'd written were not meant for anyone else's eyes, especially not Mama's.

"But…there was one," she says, as my hands slide down my face and I look at her over my fingertips. "After you broke up with him and left for L.A. with Nick, he gave a letter to Guo Mama for you. I never read it, but I put it on the very top."

I open the folder to an envelope. I stare at it, not moving, not breathing while my heart thuds in my ears. But I can't read it here with Mama smiling at me or in the middle of a noodle shop. Closing the folder, I shove it in my satchel as Mama sits silently, her eyes flicking between my satchel and my face.

Mama once seemed so weak to me. She spent so many years wishing for what she really wanted, but in the end, her weakness had become a strength. For the first time in my life I wish I could be just like her.

"If you were given a second chance with Peter, would you take it?"

She looks down at her clasped hands on the table and then meets my eyes and sighs. "If I ever saw him again and fate had made it so he was not married, I would like a second chance."

We walk back to my aunt's apartment, my arm linked

through Mama's until I stop before following her through the door. "I'll be inside in a minute."

As soon as the door closes behind her, I back against the wall, my trembling fingers pulling out the letter Mama carefully saved inside this envelope.

Two days. Mei. I've left messages, sent texts. I came by your house, but I haven't heard from you or seen you and I'm going completely out of my mind. So I'm going old school and using paper. It's harder to ignore. I don't care when you read this, I just need you to.

Two days ago, my life made sense. But now I don't even recognize myself. I don't wanna go back to what I was before you, but I don't like who I am without you. I'm so messed up and can't stop thinking about the last time I saw you and what you said over the phone, and I don't know what it means. Actually, no—I do. We're just scared because we've never been here before and everything's so real and my feelings have changed everything for me. But the longer we're apart, the more scared I get because you being gone is my new real, and fear's got me pacing at 3 AM. I'm sick to my stomach and can't breathe and I'm skipping school because...I don't know, Mei. I don't know what to do, but I'll do anything. Ask me and I'll do it, I swear, because I love you, and that will never change. We're not over, Mei. We never will be.

CHAPTER 49

LATE OCTOBER

zip my hoodie all the way up, then shove my hands in my pockets as I hurry toward the trolley stop, eager to put space between me and the divorce papers I downloaded. I didn't even type in my name before I closed my laptop and shoved it under my bed.

Heavy October fog hangs over the streets and in all the cracks and alleys between buildings. I walk faster, hoping to put out the Mei bonfire that ignited inside me last night when she blazed to life in my head, my heart, all my vital organs after I opened the papers. I'd ended up on the fire escape at 2:30 AM, convinced I was seconds from combusting.

I'd been so distracted all day by soccer tryouts and a double shift that I'd actually dared to consider during my pre-bedtime shower that I was making progress: only a mere 600 or so Mei thoughts, down from the usual 4,000 a day.

I've seen the sunrise every morning this week, like my body's still in Taiwan after almost a month.

I huddle against a lamppost while I wait for the next trolley. There was a time when I would linger at this exact stop, always the last to board, hoping to catch a glimpse of Mei, my eyes scanning all the sidewalks, every crosswalk, just in case.

Today, I hunch my shoulders, keep my eyes down, and let my heart hurt.

When the trolley squeals to a stop, I dart up the stairs, scan my card, head to a corner seat and quietly implode, especially when I realize I'm looking right at the bench where Mei sat the night we met. When I got on the trolley and she was already there, sitting sideways, feet pulled up, knees against her chest as she put on lip gloss. It was the lime kind that would become my favorite but all I could do then was wonder. Now I know what it tastes and feels like.

That night, I'd kept my eyes on my phone, pretending to care about the memes Johnny was incessantly sending while all my attention was stretching across the trolley car toward Mei. It wasn't the first time I'd noticed her, but I never would've talked to her if we hadn't both gone into Guo's shop at the same time. I would've just watched her from my peripheral vision, held my breath when I felt her eyes on me, then gotten mad at myself for making up hot crap in my head. I would've just walked up the opposite side of the street and kept my eyes focused straight ahead, smiling to myself when she tripped on a crack. I'm still not sure why I crossed the street that night, calculating my timing to run into her at Guo's shop door. I think I wanted to see what it felt like to be on her side of the street—if the air was different over there so close to her, or smells and tastes and colors were heightened near her.

I scoot over when more people pile onto the trolley and dare to glance out the window. Just because she's been creating neon trails through my head doesn't mean she's walking down the street at 8:20 AM. But from the corner of my eye, I watch every person who gets on the trolley, terrified and desperate to see her while knowing there's no possible way she's in any of these crowds. I'm trying so hard not to be desperate and being on the soccer field yesterday helped. But right now, I made a huge mistake getting on this trolley and the slow slide down all the memory lanes that are San Francisco streets. Like that girl over there, weaving through groups of people, all graceful and fluid like Mei. Or like the Asian girl waiting on the corner, smiling at her phone as she texts, her long black hair draped over her shoulder like Mei's used to.

My phone's just blank, waiting for a text or email from USF coaches.

I don't remember being single feeling so exposed. But I am and have been since I stupidly left Mei with her Taiwanese model boyfriend. And Tavah's on a Costa Rican beach in her green bikini, the sun glinting off her smile. There are probably guys there, watching her while I huddle in the corner of this cold trolley with Mei's ghost on my way to work.

My phone buzzes, and I tip the screen toward me to read a text from Meemaw: How's my big, beautiful baby boy this morning?

I dial her number, and she answers immediately.

"How's my grandbaby."

"Hey, Meemaw. I'm good. Fine."

"Let's try that again. How are you really doing this morning, sugar?"

"I'm…feeling sorry for myself, if you really wanna know." I slouch back in my seat, watch out the window. "I've become most excellent at it lately."

"Oh, I don't like this news at all. You should be sitting on my front porch swing with me right now. The big tree in the front yard is losing all its leaves, and I'm fixin' to make a big ol' pecan pie just because it's Fall. Why don't you come for Thanksgiving since Raymond and Kenna can't?"

"I wish. Gotta work the day after so…not enough time."

"Well, my cornbread dressing would make you stop feeling sorry for yourself now, wouldn't it?"

I groan through a smile. "The torture's not helping."

She laughs. "Why don't you tell me what's going on, baby."

"I've gotta get off the trolley in three stops so short story… I started divorce papers then went too deep in memories and I just…" I lean forward in my seat, elbows on my knees, phone at my ear. "I miss Mei. Tavah, too, but Mei's kinda killing me today. I don't know. I thought I wouldn't still be in this much pain since I made the choice to leave her but dude…it's brutal and the papers made it worse."

"It surely sounds like self-torture, hon, and I'm sorry you're experiencing all this heartache. The only cure is time, unfortunately."

"How much time?"

She hoots a laugh. "If only there was a rule for that."

"Guess I'll use Dad's eighteen-year rule."

She laughs again. "Good one. Your daddy's a great man but his heart isn't nearly as big and squishy as yours."

"Mine feels pretty shriveled and trashed right now, and the more time goes by, the more it hurts, so…challenge accepted." I smile, my eyes scanning the sidewalks outside the window, lingering on every Asian girl, just in case.

"You ever thought maybe you didn't make the right choice and your heart's letting you know you should turn around?"

"What do you mean?"

"I mean…maybe you made the wrong choice, leaving that beautiful Mei Li in Taiwan. Maybe you thought you were making the right choice in the moment because everything was too big and confusing but now, you've gone down the road a bit and realized it's not the right one."

I close my eyes. "Too late, Meemaw. It's done. All of it." Especially when I finish those papers.

"Is it too late?" The porch swing creaks in the background. "As I see it, that's exactly why U-turns were invented."

CHAPTER 50

LATE OCTOBER

"Oh my gosh! Oh my gosh, oh my gosh, oh my gosh!" Lin squeals so loudly, everyone gathered near the baggage claim turns their heads to watch her rush me when I step off the escalator. She practically jumps into my arms, and I drop my bags and her, both of us crumpling to the floor in a pile of laughter.

When I told her my arrival time, I didn't know she would come with flowers, giant balloons, and a glittery sign held by her embarrassed little brother who's grown a foot since I last saw him. But the added touches of love and excitement make the pure joy of hugging her for the first time since we said goodbye in Seattle even more perfect.

Her brother drops the sign in the nearest garbage can and plays a game on his phone as we walk through sliding doors to short term parking. He slumps in the backseat while Lin and I try to shove as many words into the 45-minute drive as humanly possible, pausing only long enough to drop her brother off at home before heading to Lin's apartment.

"I'm beyond excited you're staying with me," she says as she turns onto Berkeley's campus, and a weight drops on my chest. I've never been here, but it feels like part of me has, ever since I learned Marcus came here after Indiana. When I called to tell her I was coming back, she let me know Marcus dropped out and hasn't been back since, and assured me I wouldn't run into him.

"I mean," Lin chatters on, her head swiveling as she looks for cars before making a right turn, "how lucky that one of my roommates moved out so you could move in, right? I was sad she left and everything, but when you called, it was like, meant to be."

"As much as I love you, I need to find a place closer to school. So you've got me for one week."

"Okay, yes, but know what we get for this one whole week?" She reaches over and squeezes my arm, going too fast as we bounce into a parking lot. "Nonstop fun, that's what!"

"How's Johnny going to feel about me taking you away from him?"

"Oh, don't get me started on him," she says and then launches into the drama that is her and Johnny's 'relationship'. She isn't even close to done when she veers into a parking spot. Shutting off the car, she continues the story as she grabs one of my bags and I take the other, then follow her up the stairs into her apartment. I keep my head down until we're inside, because even though she told me Marcus left Berkeley, I worry everyone who knew him will know I'm The Girl Who Left Him and Faked Her Death.

I follow her into the apartment lit by multi-colored twinkle lights shimmering from the ceiling and a pink artificial Christmas tree in the corner, decorated with random objects. "All my roommates are either at work or gone for the weekend, so it's just the two of us!"

She opens a door, swinging it aside and dropping my bag in the room. "You can stay in here since my room roommate gets freaky weird about people lying on her bed. Kinda my fault since she once found me and Johnny on it so...this is empty and waiting for you. Plenty of space for your too-skinny self." She flips on the light. "I put on clean sheets so you can make yourself nice and comfy."

I set my bag on the bed and unzip my satchel to pull out the miniature stuffed red panda I brought her for her collection. Her face lights up and she hugs me again.

"I love it! And you! Life could not get any better right now."

"I love you too, and you win undisputed best friend of the year yet again."

"I'm not sure anyone else is actually up for the award since you were dead only a few months ago, but obviously I win." She laughs and squeezes me so tightly, I squeak and break free, laughing.

"This will be so fun. I've never done the college thing before."

Lin raises her eyebrows. "Yeah, you decided running away with a hot guy sounded better and you weren't wrong. Right? You don't regret it? Or do you? Maybe you do and if so, I'm sorry. We just haven't really talked about it in depth so…" She hunches her shoulders, then drops them and waves her hand. "But either way, don't worry about running into Marcus. He really isn't around. I promise I didn't make it up just to get you here. I haven't seen him in forever, actually. Johnny told me he moved out, that's all. I'm not even sure where he went, just not here."

I nod and swallow. "I believe you."

She tilts her head, studies my face. "Sorry." She pulls me in for another hug. "I shouldn't be so insensitive. Sorry, sorry, sorry." She rocks me back and forth until we're both laughing and I blink away a few rogue tears.

"I'll answer all your questions but just not tonight, okay?" I pull away, swiping my cheeks. "I'm kind of exhausted and confused about what time zone I'm in."

"You got it, babe," she says, stepping to the door and

blowing a kiss. "And…welcome back!" she squeals one more time before shutting the door.

My eyes jump from the pastel bedspread to the velvet purple chair, a hint of vanilla hanging in the air. I unpack a few things, then take a quick shower and brush my teeth before tugging on Marcus's old hoodie I can't bring myself to get rid of, then crawl into bed. But my head whirs with Marcus thoughts until, after an hour of fighting them, I move to the purple velvet chair by the window and stare into the dark night. Lin said Marcus isn't here anymore, so why do I feel like he's not far? Is he with his girlfriend? I knew letting him go in Taiwan was sending him back to another girl, but now that I'm this close, I feel the heaviness and finality of my decision. He could be with me tonight instead of her, if only I'd asked him to try life with me again, not just hinted at it.

I take my phone off the charger and text Leo that I arrived safely at my new and temporary apartment. He'd be just getting home if he's not working a case. If I were still there, we'd be sitting down for dinner, chatting about our day. Laughing. Content. Happy.

He responds immediately and even over text, he calms me.

I miss him so much.

I send a message to Mama who responds to tell me she's glad I'm safe, then reminds me to visit Guo Mama as soon as I can.

I hesitantly click off my phone and set it back on the charger, staring into the dark, ready for the rush of Marcus memories that grew stronger the closer I got to San Francisco. Grabbing my bags, I take them to the closet, hoping unpacking will take my mind in a different direction. But the floor of the closet is filled with boxes and when the door bumps one, it topples, spilling its contents onto the floor.

Turning the light on, I bend to put everything back in the box, then pause. The rock in my palm has a heart drawn on it with marker, a T+M written inside it. I smile at it, wondering if Lin's old roommate is the T or M. When I pick up the T-shirt, the scent of fabric softener washes over me, hurling me backwards through time to being wrapped in Marcus's arms, my face against his chest, tangled in sheets that smelled just like this. It sends a jolt through me, and I reflexively hold the shirt to my nose and inhale deeply, opening myself to the river of hurt that rushes in before squinting at the design. It's a Yosemite shirt identical to one Marcus used to have, and my hands freeze as a wild, urgent thought sweeps through my mind, unsettling me until my hands shake and I drop the shirt in the box.

My chest hurts, my breathing rapid as I pick up the notebook slathered in stickers that fell out but just as quickly drop it like it scorched me. My heart drops into my feet, and I put my hands over my mouth.

I only caught a glimpse—a glossy blur—but it was enough. I squeeze my eyes shut to force out the pictures of a beautiful girl with my Marcus. Multiple stickers with multiple pictures.

I glance at the notebook lying face down on the carpet, then take a breath to prove to myself I'm still alive before slowly picking it up and turning it over.

The girl…my Marcus. No, not mine. Not anymore. He's now with her, and they're standing next to each other—too close—at a concert, his smile bathing her face in warmth, hers aimed at the camera, shattering it with beams of light. They're on a swing in the forest, his lips on her ear. Marcus and this girl dressed in Hawaiian shirts and poker hats, holding up a sign that says "Winner" in gold lettering.

Despite the pain shooting through me, I inspect every photo sticker, spending extra time on the ones of them kissing. So many of them kissing. Others of their arms wrapped around each other at a beach, holding up a skim board, them dressed for a formal event, a crowd of people around them, all unfamiliar faces. Close-ups of them, their cheeks pressed together as they laugh at the camera.

I gather the moments of Marcus and this girl—Tavah, intruding on their happiness like I'm intruding in her room. This has to be her room; she's the "T" on the rock, Marcus the "M". Why didn't Lin tell me? Why would she do this to me? Why would Marcus do this to me—be with this girl like he was with me? And is he with her right now, doing all the things he's done with me?

I want to wake up Lin and throw my pain in her face, but first I'm going to torture myself a little longer so it will hurt so much I go numb. Because he's not mine. He's hers. I knew that when I said goodbye in Taiwan. This is the reality of it. This is the other side of us. It's what him not being mine anymore looks like.

I pick up a pink plastic spoon with a message written on it with Sharpie in Marcus's familiar handwriting. "Marcus Licked This." There's a tube of lip balm with a handmade label taped over the original one: "Marcus Flavor." A small stack of postcards spread in a line. I flip one over, scan the writing. A note from Marcus to "T." I close my eyes, remember his voice in Taiwan saying her name that was a knife to my heart.

I don't get past the adjectives he used for her on the first postcard. I won't read the rest. I can't be that cruel to myself, and I can't get back into her bed. Was Marcus ever in it with her?

I cover my mouth as I silently cry, then pull myself together and grab my bags, leaving Tavah's things where they spilled.

I rush into the living room and dial Guo Mama, desperately hoping she'll answer at 2 AM.

The other end clicks and rustles before her voice crackles toward me. "Wei?"

"Guo Mama," I breathe, still trying to keep myself breathing.

"Xiao Mei!" Her voice lifts me from the pit of my dark, sleepless night. "Are you alright?"

I shake my head, press my lips together. "No. Can I come stay with you?"

"I insist you stay with me. I have an extra room, just waiting for you. This is exactly as I hoped."

"I won't stay long, just—"

Guo Mama cuts me off with a snort of disgust. "Don't be silly. I could use some help around the shop. You are the perfect girl for the job."

A desperate 'yes' leaps out of me, but my mind flashes a memory of Guo Mama's guest room and the last time I was in it. After L.A.

But where else will I go? I can't stay here. I can handle the past better than the present because at least I know how my past ended. I won't stick around to watch Marcus live his present with someone else.

"Thank you," I rush. "I'll be there as soon as I can." Ending the call, I turn toward Lin's room. Asleep or not, she brought me into the emotional mess in that room, and she's going to get me out of it by taking me to Guo Mama's right now.

CHAPTER 51

LATE OCTOBER

really gotta get out of Chinatown and into some fresh scenery.

Dropping my keys and backpack on my desk, I peel off my work clothes and pull on sweats while I stare out my window at the street below. If I can just get a spot on the USF soccer team, get into a new apartment far away from here and all the memories 'here' induces, everything will get better. Until then, I gotta stop looking out this stupid window at Guo's shop and the building next to it. She's not here. She's not in the city, the state, the country.

I grab the cord and yank down my blinds, but they knock over Buddha where he was perched on the windowsill. Pulling them up so they hover just above him, I set him back on his stone feet. I pat him on the head before dropping onto my bed, pulling out my phone to check my email. Work was nonstop today so I couldn't check it the usual 500 times. Before I got on my bike to ride home, I checked but there was still nothing. Maybe now.

There's a stack of new messages, but my eyes screech to a halt on the one I've been waiting for. I sit up and my heart picks up, trying to push my finger to open the message. But what if he's telling me I didn't make it?

Swallowing, I force my stiff finger to move and click on the message, my eyes all over it. Then I'm on my feet, standing in the middle of my room, staring at my phone with a stupid grin on my face as I read the email again. One more time. Confirmed—I'm in. IN. There's a spot on the team and it's all mine. A jersey with my last name and number. Next season, a few months from now.

I scan his email again. No, not a few months. I start training with the team tomorrow, 7 AM at the official USF training facility.

Closing my eyes, I grip my phone, let the adrenaline rush through me. I'm back. Not at Stanford, yeah, but on a field, running toward a goal, part of a team again.

I burst out of my room, round the corner into the living room where Dad and Kenna are curled on the couch, reading something on Dad's phone. Their heads snap up when I push energy through the room toward them.

"I got the email." I grip the wall, my body rigid with a year's worth of hope and shock. "I made the team."

Kenna bolts up on the couch. "Are you serious?!"

"Dead," I grin, and Dad and Kenna both jump up and cross the room toward me until we're in a group hug.

"I feel like there should be fireworks or a street party," Kenna says, grinning up at me. "This is huge! Your life is falling into place again. Final piece."

I blink a few times as Kenna's words punch me in the gut, but I nod. At least life won't have a gaping hole in its middle anymore. "Yeah. Can't believe it. It felt like such a long shot."

Dad opens his mouth to say something, then shakes his head like he's decided against it and pulls me into a back-slapping hug.

"If I could lift you, I so would right now," Kenna says as she wipes at tears, then wipes Dad's.

"You getting soft on me, old man?" I ask as I pull away and swipe my face. "That's a lot of tears coming out of your eyes."

He grabs me around the neck, and we wrestle while Kenna scurries out of the way, laughing. He almost has me pinned, but I twist and take him down instead.

Kenna hands Dad a tissue where he lays on the floor, breathing hard, and I smile as I catch my breath. He reaches for my ankles as I head back to my room, but I laugh and maneuver out of the way.

"Nice try," I call before shutting my door behind me.

I flop back onto my bed and close my eyes. That email was the shot of confidence I needed. I can handle anything now. Bring it.

———

I have fifteen minutes before work, so I walk my bike into Guo's shop, lean it against the wall, and scan shelves and racks for her white hair. Winding through robes and bags, I stick my head around the corner of a shelf where she's humming as she dusts. "Guo!"

Her head snaps toward me, and she jabs me with her duster. "Boy, you will give me a heart attack someday, for one reason or another."

I bend and give her a tight hug, and she grins up at me. "Your face is brighter today. What happened? Did you hear good news?"

"I did!" I grin down at her. "I'm officially on the USF team. Just like that."

Her eyes pop from her wrinkles, wide and bright. "Marcus Miller, you are a superstar. I'm so proud of you, boy." She grips my arm and beams up at me. "Everything is working out perfectly, yes?"

"Definitely," I sigh, nodding. "Is Charlie around? Thought

I'd say hi before I head to work. I promised him if I got on the team, I'd take him with me, even if I'm not supposed to have cats in the dorms. He's been a fugitive before, so he knows how to keep quiet."

Guo studies me, then scans the aisle. "He is upstairs. Lazy morning for him." Her eyes

skitter toward the backroom door as she flicks her duster over a shelf of ceramic temples.

CHAPTER 52
EARLY NOVEMBER

Everything's the same; the shops are where they've always been, the musicians are still playing the same songs on the same instruments on the same street corners. The food vendors fill Chinatown with the same familiar smells. Tourists still walk the streets, cameras and shopping bags in hand.

It still feels like home, even without the restaurant's glowing lights. Maybe it feels more like home now without the fear and anxiety that plagued it in the past. Now, there's a bright yellow breakfast place where the restaurant used to be. My old bedroom window is filled with plants. The fire escape ladder is pulled up and secured.

When I told Lin I was leaving because I couldn't stay in Marcus's girlfriend's room, she felt so bad. She had no idea what was in the closet and apologized profusely. She didn't think I needed to know it was Tavah's old room since she wasn't his girlfriend anymore, which Lin hadn't been totally certain about since Tavah didn't tell anyone anything before she left for Costa Rica. According to Johnny, Marcus had broken up with her a few days after returning from Taiwan. That's also when he'd withdrawn from Berkeley and moved out of Johnny's apartment, though she wasn't sure where he ended up. She said she's pretty sure he didn't follow Tavah to Costa Rica but didn't want to bring it up, just in case.

Guo Mama shuffles into the kitchen, holding onto her walker as she hums a tune I can't place, then smiles. "Ah! Xiao Mei. Today is the day when everything falls into place for you!"

I laugh. "I guess if falling into place means my first day of culinary classes, then yes! Today is the day."

"Yes. A good day indeed."

"Is there anything you need me to do before I leave?"

"I do have something, but it needs to be done between now and 8:10."

It's a very specific request from a usually vague Guo Mama, but I nod. "Okay. I'll do it. I just have to leave in…" I check my phone. "About an hour."

"Oh, you do not need to finish today, just start working on it. After 8:10, you can go if you need to." She smirks as she shuffles her walker past me, and I raise my eyebrows, wondering what I've gotten myself into.

"Follow me," she says, motioning as she passes me, her walker creaking as she makes her way to the front of the shop. "It's the window display. I need a new one."

We stop at the front window, and she waves her hand across it. "I want it to be something…meaningful. Something with a message of hope."

"Wow. That's…unexpected and oddly specific?"

"You will think unexpected." She pats my arm, then turns her walker back toward the counter.

"What's that supposed to mean?" I ask, smiling at her hunched but determined form, her purple shirt hanging on her bony frame.

"You're running out of time," she says over her shoulder. "Just stand there and see if you find your inspiration." She jabs a bony finger toward the window. "Don't leave that spot until 8:10. Something will come."

Hopeful window display? In a souvenir shop?

I step closer, inspect the stacked, hanging lanterns and Chinese fans splayed as a backdrop for the current display. There's not a speck of dust or sun fading on any of them. Like Guo Mama just redid this display.

I sniff the air. It even smells like new plastic and paper. I glance back over my shoulder to where Guo Mama is humming behind the counter as she counts money for the register, then turn and reach for the lowest hanging lantern. I'm afraid to even leave to get a ladder. If I leave before 8:10, will the glass explode or something? The shop doesn't even open until 8:30.

I unhook lantern after lantern, keeping a close eye on the clock, but as I step onto the display platform to reach the fans, I glance out the window and freeze. Three people stand on the other side of the street, talking, laughing. My mouth goes dry, and I can't find my breath as I gulp in air to fill my writhing lungs.

Ray Miller is holding hands with a tall brunette woman who smiles up at him, but it's the third person that's making my heart slam against my chest.

I jump off the platform and bolt around the corner, peeking out just far enough to watch them, my eyes clinging to Marcus who's holding his backpack straps and talking to his dad and the woman. She laughs and Ray waves his hand like he's dismissing whatever Marcus said. Marcus pokes Ray in the shoulder before waving and walking down the sidewalk.

Marcus. Here. Walking down the other side of the street like he did when we were hiding our relationship from the world. I was always on this side and he was always over there until we were safely past Dragon's Gate. Why is he even here at 8:05 in the morning? Why is he here, in Chinatown?

My breathing is so loud but not dumping enough oxygen into my bloodstream because I'm dizzy.

Guo Mama chuckles, and I cover my face with my hands to step out of the moment and think, hoping when I pull them away, I'm somewhere far away from here. I can't stay here if Marcus is here, too. I can't be this close to him again and not be with him.

The door chimes, and I jump, whirling around. Ray does a double take when our eyes collide and he stops walking, the woman smiling at me as she holds Ray's hand.

Heat floods my face as Ray raises his eyebrows, opens his mouth. "Mei Li?"

"Hi. Hello." I toss a jittery smile his way. "How are you?"

The woman's eyes are wide and stuck on me.

"Wow. What a surprise!" He studies my face, shakes his head. "I did not expect to see you this morning. When did you get here?"

"Umm, about a week ago. Maybe? Yes. I think so. A week ago." My words fire out of me.

"Wow." He nods, looks around the shop before meeting my eyes again. "It is so good to see you. A surprise, but a nice one. How have you been?"

"I'm…good." Are we just going to pretend he doesn't know what happened? How much does he know?

"By the way, this is my wife, Kenna. Sorry—I was so shocked to see you I forgot my manners."

"Oh!" It's my turn to raise eyebrows. "Congratulations. Nice to meet you, Kenna." My smile wobbles, insecure as I reach for her hand. Marcus said nothing in Taiwan about his dad getting married. I thought he hated women.

Her eyes are a spotlight on me. "It is so, so nice to meet you, Mei Li," she says, like she's going to add, 'I've heard so much about you.' But she doesn't. She just beams at me and presses her shoulder into Ray's.

"What are you doing back in San Francisco?" he asks like

I'm still just the server at Zhang's and not his secret, dead daughter-in-law reincarnated.

"I…got accepted to culinary school. So I'm here for a bit."

"Your school here in the city?"

I nod. "Yes. Near the Mission. Yep." I nod again and paste the smile on my face harder so it won't fall off.

"So you're staying."

I laugh nervously. "I have my student visa, promise."

His loud laugh booms through the shop, and Kenna watches him before turning her eyes back on me.

"No, no, no." He waves his hands. "Not here to arrest you, Mei Li." He smiles and shakes his head. "And I'm sorry about how things went for your mother and you." His eyes are warm and so sincere. "She was a huge help in our investigation."

A lump wedges in my throat, but I straighten, wave my hand. "Thank you. It's fine. I'm okay. And so is she." I don't know what he knows.

"Good, good. Glad to hear it." He studies my face again. "Really. It's so good to see you. You look great."

"You too," I say. "And congratulations again." Unspoken words squirm between us, and I surrender first. "Actually… before I lose the chance, I have to say something I should have said a long time ago." I draw a quick breath to give my courage enough life to continue for one more minute. "I'm not sure what you know about…everything. About Marcus and me."

I'm desperate for any sign in his face that will tell me I should stop. Instead, he shifts his weight to one leg, runs his hand through his hair, and nods. "I know everything, And I'm just so—"

"I need to apologize for my part in how things happened. With Marcus. For the wedge I put between you two. You didn't deserve that, and I just want you to know how sorry I am."

Ray is silent for a few deafening heartbeats and Kenna slides her arm around his waist, sending me a sympathetic look. He glances at the tile, rubs the back of his neck, and now I'm looking away because it's such a Marcus gesture. Then his eyes catch mine, shiny. "Thank you for the apology, even though it wasn't necessary. It means a lot, though. And for what it's worth, all of this has made my son a better person. He hasn't figured that out for himself yet, but he will."

Guo Mama approaches and Kenna walks up the aisle to meet her, giving her a tight side hug. Ray follows and I watch how life moved on without me. Kenna seems to be part of the neighborhood now. If so many things had been different, maybe I could have really been part of their family, too.

When loneliness seeps in, I go back to the window display, glancing out the glass to where I'd seen Marcus five minutes before. At exactly 8:10.

I look at Guo Mama, then at my feet, shaking my head. Of course she knows everything about Marcus and his schedule, where he's living, exactly what time he leaves in the morning. I could ask her all of it. I could ask Ray, but it's really none of my business anymore.

I look back out the window, picture Marcus again: his hair ruffling in the breeze, his hoodie tight on his arms. He seems taller now, but his long, purposeful stride is exactly the same. If only it had brought him toward me instead of away.

Ray said I'd made Marcus better, but that's impossible because Marcus was unstoppable until I pushed pause on everything he had perfectly laid out in front of him. If anyone made anyone better, he did that for me. No one's ever been loved like he loved me.

When the shop door chimes again, my head snaps toward it, but it's only a group of women, chattering on their way inside.

I look at the display, then start taking down fans, one by one, stopping only to wave at Ray and Kenna as they leave. I watch them through the shop window as they walk down the sidewalk.

Guo Mama shuffles over, planting her walker beside me, staring out the window. "You should have asked him."

"Asked him what?" I reach for another fan, tug it down.

"The thing you most wanted to ask him."

"And what is that?" I turn toward her, lanterns and fans dangling from my hand.

She looks up at me, her face calm but smug. "The same thing you could ask me because I also have the answer."

Pressing my lips together, I set the lanterns and fans down, straighten and look at her. "Apparently you know everything about Marcus, including his schedule, but I have too many questions. I don't even know where to start."

"Yes, yes, but there is one." She holds up her crooked pointer finger. "Biggest of them all."

"How do you know that?"

"Because. It is what anyone who just saw the love of their life would want to know."

I shake my head, close my eyes. "It's none of my business."

"None of your business to simply hear that Marcus Miller is back where he belongs? That he lives right there once again?" She watches me but points toward Marcus's apartment building. "I think it could be anyone's business who happens to look outside every day at 8:10 and sees him leave for work. That is not so secret, is it?" She blinks up at me, a smile hovering.

I swallow. "He's back? Living with his dad?"

"Mmm, well." She shrugs and grips her walker. "I guess you will have to work on this window display every morning between 8:00 and 8:10 and decide for yourself."

———

I was almost trapped in a window display this morning, then found out Marcus is back in Chinatown and an hour later, I started my first official class at the institute. As weird as today has been, I'm exactly where I'm supposed to be, finally.

After class, I opt to walk through the city rather than take a bus back to Guo Mama's. I wander to all the places where Marcus and I have been together, which are also the places I fell a little more in love with him.

I walk to Dolores Park where we watched Sabrina and ate Red Vines, and he told me he wanted to kiss me but didn't. At least not that night, and if I'd known what kissing him did to me, I never would've waited for him to make the first move.

I stand in the exact spot on the grass of the Palace of Fine Arts where Marcus and I lost track of time on his dinosaur blanket during our first official date. I take the bus to Golden Gate Park and bridge where my feelings for him spread out like wings and took me wherever he was.

And now, as I approach Guo Mama's shop, I stop across the street from Marcus's apartment building. My eyes slip to his window, well trained and familiar with its patterns of light and dark.

Including that Buddha statue on his windowsill.

My chest swells, and I take a step closer to the curb as I visually devour the statue, silhouetted by lamplight sliding through the gap between partially lowered blinds and the windowsill. It's our Buddha, the same my Nai-Nai made for me before I left Taiwan and the same I gave to Marcus before he left there, too. But why is it here? Marcus always placed him in his window as our own, private signal.

As I stare at Buddha, a thought gathers in my mind, and when I turn to walk through the shop door, I know exactly how I need to do the window display. It's hopeful and meaningful, unexpected, if only to myself.

I rush upstairs to my bags and pull out my calculus folder and all of Marcus's notes. I sit on the floor, paper spread around me as I carefully re-fold each note into their original shapes: a paper fortune teller, a 3D heart, a dog, a bowtie, a crane, a pigeon, frog, flower, and starfish.

When Guo Mama taps on my door to tell me she's off to bed, I'm still folding, reading, feeling, falling. I deep dive into memories, letting emotions flow through me. Then, I go downstairs into the dark shop, turn on a lamp, and haul the notes and Guo Mama's giant jar of fortune cookies to the window. I will have this display done by 8:10 tomorrow morning, even if I have to stay up all night to do it.

need to talk to Guo. She'll know exactly how I should feel about Kenna's and Dad's big announcement at dinner tonight. She'll tell me how to pretend I feel differently than I do about being a "big brother" in five months.

As if my life didn't feel messed up enough. Now, a tiny human who doesn't even breathe oxygen yet is already taking over The Clubhouse. My room will undergo another identity crisis. Guess it's a good thing I'm moving so Dad can have room for his new family. For his new kid who'll have a life that's completely different than mine was with Dad. This is Ray Miller's official do-over. Version 3.0. Which makes me Marcus Miller 4.0, big brother and lifetime bachelor. Almost-dad.

My mind squeals in reverse to Mei, so small and nervous in the hotel room as she told me that she'd taken part of me with her to Taiwan—something that, if it had lived, would've been half her, half me.

The thought squeezes me through the hallway, down the stairs, and out onto the sidewalk where I inhale, desperate for fresh air. Scanning the street, I dart across it toward Guo's shop but slow as I step onto the sidewalk, my focus yanked to the window display that wasn't there yesterday. Hundreds of fortune cookies and folded paper shapes dangling from a suspended, cardboard fire escape mounted to a fake backdrop of a lit window. A small golden Buddha statue perches on the landing.

My hands go numb as blood drains and collects in my feet, making them throb and itch. I step closer to the window, balancing the food containers while I squint at the folded paper shapes. My fingers twitch, remembering every fold and crease and tuck to make sure Guo couldn't open them before Mei did. My heart thuds in my neck. Those are my notes to Mei. Every single one. But how? Better yet, why?

My feet burn, so I push through the door into the shop that smells like a big lemon got stuck in the vents today. My eyes sweep the aisles and racks, on high alert. But Mei's not here. Even if her notes somehow are. Maybe Guo stole them when we ran and she's messing with me?

No. This is so stupid. Fortune cookies, fires escapes, and Buddha statues are everywhere in this neighborhood. It's Chinatown. They're nothing special—just part of the theme.

But those notes…

Swallowing, I walk toward the backroom, but stop as I pass the register, my eyes all over the hoodie draped over the chair behind the counter. I step closer, scanning the store again before leaning over the counter.

Yeah. It's mine. The one Mei had in Taiwan. The same one I had in Indiana before she took it when she left.

I back away like it's a flame thrower. I'm losing my mind. It can't be mine. It's one just like it and for some super weird reason, Guo has it draped over her chair.

But there's one way I'll know for sure.

I reach for the hoodie, my fingers trembling as I pull out the silky tag, flip it up. M.C.M stares back at me in faded green Sharpie.

I back away, the bulldog logo blurring as I stare.

Mei's here. The window display strongly hinted at it, but this hoodie proves it.

Hurrying back through the store, I practically sprint to the sidewalk, stand in front of the window, visually ransack the folded notes. That one—the starfish. My Sharpie exploded. I was in class and had already spent twenty minutes folding the paper, so I wiped the blue splatter with a practice shirt in my backpack. The blue smudge bled through to the other side, giving the starfish a bruise.

I turn on the sidewalk, look at The Clubhouse, back at the window, stuck and confused, but whirl around when Guo's walker clicks behind me.

"Why are you running away so fast, boy?" She tilts her head.

"Guo, what's this about?" I point at the window.

Her eyebrows jump and she grins. "Ah! Do you like it? I can introduce you to the artist."

Her statement drops, rumbles beneath me. "Where is she? Why is she here?"

"Oh…" She talks to her gnarled fingers gripping her walker. "She says she's back for culinary school, but we all know she is here for the usual reasons a girl would travel from the other side of the world and land across the street from a certain boy."

———

Dad sits on the floor across from me in our building's hallway, silent while I stare at my Adidas, my eyes blurry.

"I know hearing about the baby was hard, M.C."

He'd opened the door to take the garbage to the chute and found me just like this—slumped on the floor against the wall outside The Clubhouse door. He'd dumped the garbage, then sat across from me, legs out, settled in.

"It's not that."

He squints at me, silent before his eyes widen. "Did you go to Guo's?"

I nod.

"You saw Mei Li?

My eyes snap up to his. "You knew she's here?"

He swears under his breath, rubs the back of his neck. "Yeah. Kenna and I ran into her the other day, but I had no idea how or when to tell you. And, honestly, wasn't sure it was any of my business. Figured I'd let things happen as they were meant to happen."

More silence floats from my side toward him, from his side toward me, bumping into each other and creating a plume of dust and smoke from the burning thoughts and chaos in my head.

"So you saw her?"

I pause, making room for anger at Dad for not telling me, but I don't have energy to be mad, so I shake my head. "Didn't see her. Saw the window display. And my hoodie." He has no clue what either of those things mean, but somehow, he translates.

"Look, M.C..." He rubs his head, shakes it, drops his hands to his lap. "I've made a few mistakes while raising you and a few more recently—like dropping baby news on you today—but making you think all girls are bad was maybe the most harmful."

His voice is too loud. His words are in another language. I let them dissolve around me.

"You managed to find not just one, but two great girls, and I'm beyond impressed with the lengths you went to keep Mei. You didn't get that bravery from me. I never would've done what you did. But now... after talking to Mei Li, all the pieces came together, and I realized I never really knew you. Not this side of you, at least. You showed it only to her and it was big and strong. And I'm so proud of you."

A lump lodges in my throat and I clear it.

"I can't stop thinking about how bad your mom messed up, never meeting you."

I glance up at him, then back at the carpet. "I met her."

He frowns but doesn't say anything so I unload the whole story of meeting Olivia in L.A. and all the apologies I owe him for feeling like he was keeping me from something great.

He stares at the wall above my head as the information settles over him. "Wow." He whispers, shaking his head. "Okay, then. I guess now you know."

"And now I know Mei's back." I close my eyes, concentrating on breathing, though I haven't really breathed since I talked to Guo.

"M.C. there's one more thing you need to know now that you've met your mom."

"I don't wanna—"

"Hear me out." His eyes reach across the hallway and hold me firmly in place. "I'm glad she left me, but I wasted a whole lotta time feeling otherwise. I could have and should have moved on years ago. So all I'm saying is, if you let Mei Li slip away, you'll be just like the old me, before Kenna— bitter, cynical, and guarded for no good reason but to torture yourself."

He waits for a response, but I don't have one, so we sit in silence as thoughts of Mei and seeing her again set me on fire.

CHAPTER 54

Charlie's on the window seat, his green eyes following me as I close my bedroom door. I hold up the Buddha Guo Mama let me swipe from the shelf in the shop when I got home tonight. It was the one that looked most like Marcus's and my Buddha.

I set him on the windowsill, then curl up on the window seat beside Charlie, draping a throw blanket around me. Charlie crawls onto my lap and his purr rumbles against my legs when I pet him.

Neon signs are still ablaze on the street below, but China-town is quiet and calm now, except for my head which is bursting with Marcus thoughts I can't shake. They crowd and jostle their way to the front, loud and eager as my eyes cut a trail across the street, then back before repeating the pattern and continuing toward The Clubhouse. I never would have slept if I'd lived in Guo Mama's apartment when Marcus and I were secretly dating; I have a clear view of his bedroom window from this one. But I guess it doesn't matter if it was then or now, together or apart—I'm not sleeping as long as there are Marcus memories on repeat in my mind. I wonder if he's behind his dark bedroom window, sprawled across his bed, sheets tangled around his legs, pretending it's me instead? Set loose, my mind runs wild and reckless toward memories of Marcus and I tangled in each other when want and need collided.

I take a deep breath to dilute the very vivid daydreams of us that stroll through my head, hazy and hot, but they move through me, tempt me.

No. Nope. Torture is not an option tonight.

Maneuvering toward my nightstand in the dark, I grab my phone before returning to the window seat. I punch in numbers I know by heart and wait for him to answer.

"Hey!" Leo's voice is wide awake on the other side of the world, and I'm no longer alone.

"Hey." I pet Charlie as he crawls onto my lap again, annoyed, but as soon as I scratch under his chin, he purrs. "How are you?"

"How am I? Bored, that's how. All of the excitement in my life left with you, and it's just a quiet apartment except for Nai-Nai's humming." Leo laughs and I join him, remembering her incessant humming all too well.

"There's no excitement here either. I must've lost it somewhere in Taiwan."

"How are your classes going?"

I straighten, my back against the wall, knees to my chest. "Amazing, actually. Like you with your detective stuff, I've found my calling. Chef Marco told me I've only gotten better since he worked with me last. Guess that's from all the cooking you forced me to do for you."

"Whoa, whoa, whoa. You chose to keep me ten pounds heavier. I just didn't complain." When our laughter merges, silence follows before Leo says, "I'm so happy for you, even if I wish you were still here."

"Thanks for believing in me." I look up at the moon casting its light over buildings and into dark corners of the street. "I miss you."

He sighs. "I miss you too. And I know exactly how we could fix that."

My eyes shift to the street outside and a figure walking up the sidewalk. I lean toward the window, squinting to get a better look.

"You still there?" Leo's voice yanks me back to the conversation, but my eyes stay on the silhouette, my heart picking up speed. The walk…

"Sorry, yes—think I'm hallucinating, I'm so tired and I have class in the morning. I better try to sleep. I just needed to hear your voice."

"Sounds good. Talk soon?"

"I'll call you this weekend," I promise before hanging up, my eyes glued to the window. I don't need to see his face. I don't need to hear his voice.

It's him.

My mind flashes to the night we moved into our Stanford apartment. We'd just finished unpacking our two bags and all 12 of Marcus' hoodies. One after another, I'd put them on him and when I was done, he could hardly move. He'd walked to the mirror but tripped over his shoes and rolled back and forth on the floor, trying to sit up. We'd laughed so hard, neither of us could stand, so I'd straddled him and peeled hoodies off one by one.

I blink away the memory and watch him walk up the sidewalk, my heart pounding so loud he might hear it and look up to find me watching him.

Every embarrassing scenario flashes through my mind until I can't breathe. Panicked and appalled at my self-torture, I swallow the anxiety clawing up my throat.

Marcus stops, his gaze on my window like my heated thoughts sent a flare directly at him, and I flatten against the wall, my nerves screaming. I ease behind the curtain which is sheer enough to see him but thick enough to blur me.

He stares at my window for way too long and my pulse

leaps through me, then plummets when I realize what he's looking at.

Buddha. Sitting on my windowsill, just like our Buddha is sitting on his. I could be downstairs and out of the shop in seconds. I could tell him everything I wish and hope and that I want him in this new life with me maybe even more than I wanted him in my old one because now, I know what it is to have him. And lose him.

Marcus crosses the street, hands shoved in his pockets, then stops in front of the window display, the exterior shop lights spotlighting him.

My heart is flopping around in my stomach, and I scoot closer to my window, my breath making foggy circles on the glass. He stares at the display, perfectly still except for the breeze curling through his hair.

The lights smooth over his forehead, his jaw, his nose. My fingers flex, ready to feel his lines as they have so many times, and I'm on my feet, the throw blanket landing in a heap on the carpet as I dart out of the room and downstairs, Charlie trotting after me.

I skid through the shop in my socks, headed for the door, and when I reach it, my eyes frantically scan the sidewalk outside the windows, but I'm too late.

The street is empty, Marcus is gone.

CHAPTER 55
EARLY NOVEMBER

should've taken backstreets to avoid the window display, the new Buddha statue, and always—always—the magnetic force that is Mei. But my legs were tired from running the practice field, kicking the ball hard enough to hopefully shake Mei thoughts, so I took the shortest route home. Now they're running again, this time toward the bus stop.

My breathing is loud, my heart pounding in my ears. I need somebody to navigate me through the Mei explosion and the smoldering, melted remains of my common sense toward the more rational side of myself. Because right now, all my head's doing for me is creating images of us together. It's not like they're super creative since they're memories, but the astounding amount of detail is wearing me down.

When I finally make it to Audrey's apartment, I punch the door code and crash inside like someone's chasing me. Audrey's sitting at the table with a guy, her forkful of pie frozen halfway to her mouth. I hold up my hands, apologizing as I sail toward her bathroom and shut myself inside.

I climb in the shower without turning it on and sit in the

dark corner. I forgot to lock the door, though, and Audrey slips into the bathroom a few minutes later.

"Tell me what happened," she says, sitting on the closed toilet lid.

"I didn't mean to interrupt. I just needed to go somewhere and think where Dad and Kenna aren't all over each other or talking about baby names but maybe you were hoping to be all over that guy before I barged in. Sorry, Drey. Go do what you were gonna do—I'll chaperone from here."

She stands and flips on the light, repeating herself. "He left. Your timing was actually great, because I had the slightest inkling he might be gay and was trying to figure out how to tell me he's not into me." She blows her bangs out of her face. "So…talk. You can't come undone in my shower unless you tell me what happened."

I let out a long breath and rub both hands down my face, then growl in frustration before shaking my head. I stare at the hexagonal tile pattern until Audrey reaches for the shower handle and I jerk up, grab her hand. "I'll talk—I will. Just need to figure out how to start. Where, when. I got the who, still waiting for why."

She settles back against the toilet, crosses her legs, folds her arms. "You gonna be okay, Sippy Cup?" Her childhood nickname for me tugs at the tears and they all fall together. The whole tear extended family, friends, neighbors.

"Marky, whatever happened can be fixed, I promise."

I get control of myself, run my palms down my face, embarrassed.

"Must be pretty big to get that many tears out of you."

I swallow, close my eyes, shake my head once, slump over my bent knees, then spill the story of Taiwan, my decisive intentions to move on that don't feel decisive anymore, and how the window display, then Buddha threw me so far backward.

When I finish, she shakes her head and inhales through her teeth. "Yikes—I don't know. What do you think?"

"Trying not to."

Audrey's silent for a minute, then she slides off the toilet and sits on the fluffy pink rug, her back against the wall, the glass shower door between us. "You know what? Why don't you take a real shower. A nice, long, hot one. I call my shower the Thought Portal because I always get answers to my questions there, so…give it a try. I'll call Ray and let him know you're spending the night so he doesn't sound the alarms, then order some baklava, yeah?" She jerks her head toward the bathroom door.

I nod and she leaves, shutting the door behind her. I drag myself up and out of the shower. I reach for my backpack on the counter, but it tips and Magic 8 rolls out.

I freeze, stare at it. I forgot it was in here.

Reaching for it, I hold it in front of me.

My brain's still not convinced Mei's real. I've thought about her so much, it's 100% possible I hallucinated her. But my hallucinations and fantasies don't usually include Guo, so…

I stare at Magic 8, squint, then close my eyes and shake it as I form the question in my mind: Was Mei really at Guo's shop?

Heart pounding, I turn it over, tilt the screen toward me: Yes definitely

But why? She's not here for me. But why is she here? Why did she come back, knowing I was coming back to someone else?

"Do I deserve to be alone?" I ask Magic 8, shaking it harder than necessary, then apologizing like it has feelings.

My sources say no.

Liar. You should check your sources.

My mind slides back to the first night I saw Mei—the night my life took a serious detour and slipped from my control. The night Mei took over my world, and I'd let her because Magic 8 said so.

And then something inside me unwinds, and I'm seeing more than just that night. I see the night in Vegas, when we wrapped a blanket around us and went for a walk at 1 AM, using Magic 8 as our directional decision maker. Another night in Indiana, stretched out on the couch together in the dark, laughing as we made up conversations for the raging party on the floor above us, using Magic 8 as our inspiration. The night we spied on our crack-head neighbors in Vegas, both Mei and I peeking over the windowsill where Magic 8 sat, watching the whole thing with us. We were in a supermarket in Stanford. I was trying to convince Mei to get in the grocery cart to save us time. I explained how easy it would be for me to push her around and get just close enough to the shelves that she could grab whatever was on our list without me having to stop. We'd used Magic 8 to tell us what we should and shouldn't buy.

We were eating dinner, speaking eye language, our feet making out under the table, Mei asking Magic 8 questions. We were curled up in front of the fire, reading a book together, using Magic 8 to make it a choose your own ending story. I was walking her to work, then bursting through the door after my shift, breathless to see her. Every memory, every day, every night, every smile, every tear, every touch spills over in my head, and I'm drowning in Mei. And Magic 8 was there for all of it so why shouldn't it decide where I go now?

I gasp, trying to control my shivering, but my body's uncoiling, my mind surrendering, too full and overflowing. I pull off my clothes and yank on the shower, swearing when the cold water rains on me, then sink against the wall when it runs warm.

I close my eyes and let the heat and steam move down me, over me, keeping my body anchored, my mind and heart running out of Audrey's apartment toward Chinatown.

Toward Mei.

I blink the water out of my eyes as I shake Magic 8 and ask my question over the spray: "Will I ever get over Mei?"

The blue triangle struggles to the surface, then fizzles away. I shake it again. "Tell me! Will I ever get over her?"

The triangle gathers and I can barely make out the words:

My reply is no.

My breathing sputters and I try another question, my decision suddenly dependent on Magic 8. "Should I go back to Mei? Will she take me back? Can we ever be us again?"

I shake it harder until I dare to look at the answer:

It is certain.

CHAPTER 56

EARLY NOVEMBER

A car horn blares from the street below and my eyes snap open. I didn't sleep much and the memory of Marcus on the street still hangs on the edges of my mind. Was he really out there or did I dream him there?

All I want to do is stay in bed and hide from the day that will bring more of the same when what I most want is just across the street but unreachable.

Hauling myself out of bed, I shuffle to the shower, then blow dry my hair. I pull it up in a messy bun before adding just enough makeup to hide the dark circles under my eyes, then head downstairs for another day.

Guo Mama sits at her kitchen table, sipping tea. There's a second mug in the empty chair across from her.

"Sit." She nods to the chair and when I do, she tilts her head. "You look tired. Did you sleep last night?"

"Not well. I overslept and missed my first class." I take a deep breath and grab the mug, cupping it so it warms my hands. "I'm going to have to make that up, but since I'm here, what can I help you with today?"

"Well, let's see." She taps her chin and settles back in her chair. "I think it's important that the front window stays very,

very clean so everyone can see your gorgeous display." She grins at me, her eyes sparking.

"Guo Mama, no…"

"What?" She holds up her hands. "I have standards for my shop. And while I think everyone important has seen it, we can never be too sure."

"What do you mean?" I watch her face, hope fluttering in my chest.

"You are not always here, you know. You do not always see who might stop by for a visit. Or stop by and admire your very meaningful, hopeful work. I believe it has been…very touching for some."

"You're being cryptic again. What are you saying?"

"I'm saying…" She pushes herself up from the table and pulls her walker closer. "Get to work on cleaning the front window, please, Xiao Mei." She glances at the clock as she pushes the walker toward the sink, and my eyes dart to my phone on the table. 7:57.

I finish my tea, then set down the mug and head through the kitchen door to the shop. Charlie meows and follows me to the cabinet where I grab window cleaner and a rag, then we head to the front of the shop.

I spray the window and scrub the panes, gazing outside, the clock ticking in my head. I check my phone again. 8:12. Marcus usually leaves by now. He pushes out of his apartment building and strides down the street, earbuds in, his hair waving in the breeze. I imagine how he smells as I watch him until he turns the corner.

Maybe today is his day off. Or maybe he's running late. Or maybe he left early? I spray the window, clean the same spot, my eyes flicking between the building's door and his window like they'll give me clues about where he is today.

I glance over my shoulder when Guo Mama's walker creaks toward me from behind. "The very cleanest window in all of San Francisco." She nods and smiles, her eyes disappearing into her cheeks. "You will be able to see everything."

"Will you please just tell me what you know?"

"Bah. That would take too long." She chuckles, her eyes scanning the street beyond the window. "Remember to clean the outside window, too, Xiao Mei. It's been very windy."

I nod and she stands there, her eyes watchful until she makes a little yelp and whips her walker around, headed toward the back of the shop at record speed.

I watch her, then finish cleaning the inside of the glass before heading outside. Spraying the glass, I take my rag and scrub, stopping when there's movement in the reflection and glance over my shoulder toward Marcus's building.

My breath snags in my throat, and I snap my head back toward the window, watching him in the reflection as he stands across the street, hands shoved deep inside the pockets of his jeans, like he's been there all morning, waiting.

I yank at my sweater where it's slipped off my shoulder, terrified Marcus saw my newest tattoo from where he's standing and will tell me I have no right to make that date permanent. He's probably coming to tell me to stay out of his life and his neighborhood.

I glance over my shoulder and his eyes slide to mine over passing cars. Heat pools in my stomach, my legs going weak as I turn to him, gripping the door handle behind me to steady myself.

We stare at each other, the world slowing to a stop. My breathing rustles in my ears as he glances both ways, waiting for a steady stream of traffic to pass before darting across the street, his eyes never leaving mine.

He slows and steps onto the curb, the endless expanse of sidewalk between us adding to my uncertainties of what's about to happen as the lump in my throat grows.

"Hey," he whispers, glancing at me from beneath his eyelashes. I haven't heard his voice since Taiwan and it carries a million moments in time, all sacred, and I want to drop to my knees.

My eyes roam his to find words, but there's only clear blue.

He looks down at his feet, hands still shoved in his pockets, then closes his eyes. I can't do this. I can't listen to what he's about to say or even look at him when he tells me we have no chance.

I turn my back on him, not caring that my sweater has slipped off my shoulder again, not caring that he has a close up view of 6-21 branded on my skin. I fumble with the doorknob to go inside, be anywhere but here.

"No more running, Mei." His words grab me from behind, hold me tightly, and I press my forehead to the door, waiting for the blow. "Because…Magic 8 and I were talking last night and…" He hesitates and I hold my breath, unable to face him as he continues. "It was the weirdest thing because he only has 20 possible responses but somehow managed to tell me how much he misses you." His voice breaks, and I slowly turn to face him. He keeps his head down but lifts his eyes to mine and they speak the rest. *"And it's crazy because…I've been thinking the same thing for months."*

I see blue—blue sky, blue hoodie, blue eyes. Relief pushes out a gasp, and my hand glides to my trembling mouth, the other pressed to my heart to hold it in place.

He runs a hand through his hair, and my eyes land on his wrist where a red, swollen patch of skin peeks from under his jacket sleeve. With my eyes, I outline the numbers tattooed on him: 6-21.

My heart jumps, and I swallow as he steps toward me, his body so close I feel his heat. He reaches for the hem of my shirt, pulling me into him and I roll onto my tiptoes, wrap my arms around him and tuck my head into his neck.

His arms pull me against him, our hearts finding each other again.

He pulls back just enough to rest his forehead against mine, the breeze squeezing between us as he takes my face in his hands, then draws in a deep steadying breath, letting it out slowly. "That was close, Mei."

Nodding, I grip his hand, pressing his tattooed wrist to my lips. "I thought I'd lost you for a third time." Tears cling to my lashes before giving up and falling.

"We've tried all the sides of being together and apart, and they keep leading us back to each other, so…I'm kinda getting the feeling we should do that whole you and me, 365 forever thing, especially since we're us now and have matching tattoos to prove it." His smile glints in the morning sunlight and steals my breath.

"You saw," I whisper.

"Oh, I saw." His eyes spark. "And word on the street is, you're married to Darius Bromley, but I was wondering if…" He pauses, smiles down at me, searches my face, then throws his thumb over his shoulder. "I've got a bike. A different one —with pedals. But we could still run away together on it, I bet. Maybe go get married for real this time? As Marcus and Mei?"

I release the wild, hopeful breath I was holding back and fling my arms around his neck again. He lifts me and I wrap my legs around his hips, his hands holding me against him. It's finally us on the same side of the street, the same side of the world.

Wordlessly—first with my eyes, then with my lips against his—I tell him yes.

CHAPTER 57

AFTER EVERYTHING

One week later

f the satellites are watching me through the rain clouds today, they'll see that my personal dot is right where it's supposed to be.

As soon as I'm off the bus, I zip my hoodie and hit the sidewalk, puddles splashing my bare legs that were sweaty from practice minutes ago. Slipping my earbuds in, I call Mei, immediately talking when her end clicks. "Hey, Pegs."

She pauses, laughs, and I can practically hear her eye roll which makes me wanna call her Peggy every time I talk to her.

"Hey, Darry." Her voice sends laser beams of light through the fog and drizzle, and I put my hand over my heart as I turn the corner, dodging a dog sniffing its way along the side of a building.

"Hang on." The other end rustles before her voice comes back to me. "I had to slip into the hallway to talk. Too many eyes and ears around me. I think everyone might suspect something is up. I mean, your dad's a detective. You almost here?"

"I'll be there so soon, promise. Almost home. Just gotta shower."

"You always like to make an entrance."

"You nervous?" I ask, jogging under Dragon's Gate.

"A little, I guess. But mostly, I'm second-guessing because I've totally fallen in love with Darius all over again this last week. What if Marcus is just a disappointment?"

I smile, panting as I slow-run up the steep hill toward our street. "I was talking about the dinner, but you should know, Darius is gonna share all his secrets with Marcus so when you marry him tomorrow, there'll be no disappointment. Marcus might even have a few new tricks up the ol' sleeve."

"It's just so hard to choose between two incredibly attractive men."

"Not the first time you've done it." I scan the street over my shoulder before crossing, waiting for her reaction to my mention of Leo.

"Oh. Right. I'm in a tough situation."

I laugh and turn the final corner toward Guo's. "Good thing you can't resist me. At least that's what I got from last night. Maybe I misread the message you were sending when you—"

"I need to check on the food," she interrupts, her words squeezing through the grin so big I can hear it.

"Come on. Just let me relive the magic." I slow to a walk. "Or, if you're having a hard time resisting me right now, you can always meet me at the apartment. I'll be the one in the shower."

"Tempting. But I can't risk the food burning, not even for you."

"Boring," I sigh dramatically, "but I'll hurry because I can't wait to see you. Today's been our longest time apart in a week."

"Seven hours and…thirteen minutes."

Something on her end hisses and my stomach rumbles. "Be there soon, Pegs. Love you like crazy."

I end the call and break into a run again even though my legs are angry after three hours of practice. But even tight, sore calf muscles can't convince me to stop smiling. Think it might be a permanent feature now that Mei's back in my life and nothing makes me run harder or faster than knowing the faster and harder I go, the sooner I see her.

Stopping in front of the back entrance to Guo's shop, I punch in the code, then shove my way through the storage room, kicking off my shoes and sliding into slippers before heading upstairs to Mei's and my room. Something I never thought we'd share again.

Charlie greets me at the door with a high-pitched meow that's not very manly but makes me pick him up every time. I give him a good ear scratch before setting him on the bed and dropping my soccer stuff on the floor next to Mei's school bag. I peel off my clothes and bend to pick up her bra from where it landed on the floor last night, mentally reliving the whole sequence of events that put it there. Gratitude and hormones rush through me, and I rub my chest. Mei's really here. We're together, and tomorrow, we're gonna make it official in front of all our favorite people. No sneaking around. No lying or hiding. No more running away from anything or each other.

I take the fastest shower of my life, smiling at my shampoo bottles lined up beside Mei's. Forget USF dorms—I'll stay in Guo's tiny, cramped upstairs apartment forever if it means my shampoo bottle and I are next to Mei.

Ten minutes later, I jog through The Clubhouse building door, take the stairs two at a time, my wet hair flopping against my forehead. Stopping in front of the apartment door, I collect myself, breathe, then slip through it into a room bursting with excited chatter.

Dad and Kenna, Johnny and Lin, Meemaw, Audrey, and

Guo who greets me with a smile, nod, and raised eyebrows; she's the only one who knew about Mei and me from the beginning and she's the only one who knows about tonight's big announcement. Everyone else squished into The Clubhouse thinks this is a celebration dinner for Mei's return. They have no idea that right now, Mei's mom is being personally escorted to the states by Leo and will be here tomorrow morning for the real celebration.

Mei rushes to me, throws her arms around my neck, and I hold her against me, burying my face in her neck. Darius won first, but Marcus is about to win bigger this weekend. Yeah, Darius planned a better honeymoon than Marcus can right now, but he'll make it up to her. Especially now that he'll have forever to do it.

———

Audrey's laughing so hard she chokes on her dumpling and Dad sets down his napkin, ready to jump up and do the Heimlich, but she waves her hand, her face red from laughing.

"Choking's usually not a compliment to the chef, Drey," I say around a mouthful of sweet and sour pork. Mei made enough to feed the whole building, but I'm doing an impressive job of making it disappear. This is the first Mei Meal I've eaten since Indiana and just when I didn't think it was possible for her to get any better than she was, she surprised me yet again.

"Sorry, sorry," Audrey says, taking a drink, and Kenna continues her story about how many shopping bags she and Mei carried up the stairs to create all this food.

The most important people in our lives, minus those currently flying, are elbow-to-elbow around a table piled with so much food, the white tablecloth is barely visible. Two weeks ago, I was putting pieces of myself back together. Then

Mei showed up, busted my life open again, and we found a better one on the other side. And here we are.

I slide my hand under the table, rub Mei's thigh, lean over just far enough to whisper, "I love you," in her ear.

Her fingers slip between mine and when our eyes meet, my whole body goes numb in the most magical way. It's been a week of not being able to keep our hands off each other, and I consider all the places we could disappear for a few minutes as she smiles, knowing exactly what I'm thinking and how hot she's making me just by existing.

Johnny gives me the side eye, like he has a radar for under-the-table shenanigans, and I kick his foot. At least he and Lin are keeping their hands off each other during dinner, but honestly, at this point, it's kind of convenient to have my best friend dating Mei's best friend.

"*Should we do it?*" Mei asks with her eyes.

Mine widen. "*By 'do it,' do you mean—*"

She pinches my side, and I laugh and squirm away from her, then nod and scoot back my chair, maneuver around the table and casually stroll toward the kitchen and the bowl of fortune cookies.

Snatching it from the counter, I slide between the wall and back of chairs, setting a fortune cookie in front of everyone. When I hand one to Guo, I lean down and kiss the top of her head, then do the same to Meemaw who reaches up and squeezes my arm. I'm so crazy glad she got a flight on short notice because I wouldn't wanna do this without her.

"Love you, my big ol' grandbaby."

I slide into my chair next to Mei again, drape my arm across the back of her chair, casual. The very picture of relaxation.

"Hope you left room for dessert," she says, her voice pushed from behind by excitement. "Marcus and I have been looking forward to this night for a whole week." She glances at me, sends me love with her eyes, and it tingles all the way down. "We have a surprise, so go ahead and open your fortune cookies."

"Is something going to jump out at me?" Audrey asks, holding up hers, tilting her head at me from across the table.

"When was the last time something jumped at you from a fortune cookie?" I arch my eyebrows and take a long drag on my water.

She points at me, then runs her thumb across her throat before cracking her cookie, giving me the evil eye.

I smile, my heart pounding as I grab Mei's hand under the table again.

Lin squeals and everyone's head snaps toward her as she jumps out of her chair, holding the crumbled pieces of her fortune cookie to her chest. "Does this mean what I think it means?"

Mei laughs. "What do you think it means?"

Lin holds up the paper, reads it out loud. "We're doing this the right way this time. See you at Palace of Fine Arts tomorrow, 1 PM. Look for the dino blanket."

———

Guo's shop is dark except for the window display lights, shining on the dangling folded notes. Spotlighting the beginning of Mei and me. But it's the Mei and me right now that I'm most interested in.

Trying to stay grounded, I fumble with the lock, but Mei's all over me and my focus flies backward through Chinatown. When we're finally inside, I lower the security gate and lock the door, Mei's arms around me from behind, slipping beneath my T-shirt.

My stomach tenses as I set the alarm and when her hands move to the button of my jeans, she sets me on fire.

I lead her around shelves and racks toward the backroom, our dishwater shriveled fingers tangled around each other.

Dad walked Guo home awhile ago while the rest of us cleaned up, so I really hope she's upstairs sound asleep and snoring.

We slide off our shoes but don't make it to the stairs before I turn, press Mei against the nearest wall.

Her mouth is hot on mine as my hands move down her body, my mouth on her neck.

"Not sure I can wait until after the wedding this time," I breathe as I kiss my way to her ear.

Her hands grip my hair. "Good thing Darius and I are already married. I'll deal with Marcus tomorrow."

Her mouth gets frisky again, her teeth catching my lower lip, and my toes curl into the tile, my legs flooded with heat when she ducks under my arm. She tugs my shirt, taking me with it as she walks backward toward the stairs. Her smile is a white heatwave I willingly follow, quietly rushing upstairs behind her, a stupid smile on my face as I close and lock the door behind us.

Charlie startles where he's curled on our bed and jumps off, sauntering toward the window seat, completely annoyed. I grab Mei around the waist from behind, bend over her, kiss the side of her neck. When she yelps, I cover her mouth, and we whisper-laugh as I straighten and she twists toward me, grabbing my shirt and pulling it up and over my head. It drops to the floor and hers follows.

My hands slide down her body and when she gasps, I lift her. Her legs wrap around my hips, and I press her against the door, lips exploring places that were only painful memories until last week.

Clutching her, I take two steps to the bed, grateful for the bathroom between our room and Guo's.

When her back hits the mattress, Mei pulls me down to her, eyes glossy from the streetlights reaching through our very open curtains. I hold her gaze, slowing things way, way down because I mourned every moment I'd ever spent with

Mei for so long, and now that she's back, I don't wanna rush through any of them, even if my body disagrees.

Her eyes share her deepest feelings while she runs her hands through my hair, down my back, sending ripples through me and the last night we'll ever spend as Darius and Peggy.

CHAPTER 58
THE BEGINNING...AGAIN

One week and a day later

Mei and I huddle together, peeking around one of the massive pillars holding up the dome at the Palace of Fine Arts. We watch everyone settle on the blankets we laid out on the very spot we had our first date. The dino blanket that started it all is in front, empty except for a RESERVED FOR MARCUS AND MEI LI MILLER sign. We got here early to set up and put a picnic basket on each blanket so once the ceremony's over, we'll take off and let everyone have a chilly picnic. We don't wanna waste any time since neither of us can take off work or school and only have two days. We don't have any money either, so when Dad gave me a nice wad of cash, I booked a hotel to surprise Mei. At least that part will be exactly like our first time around. There's nothing more "Us" than making the most out of nothing, and our second but official wedding is definitely embracing the theme. Honestly, it couldn't be more perfect.

I adjust my tie that's going to choke me before the ceremony even starts, Mei's fingers gripping my side as she peers around me and the pillar.

"It's going to be so hard not to run out when Mama gets here." Excitement sparks in her words.

"What about when you see Leo?" I smirk, watching Dad and Kenna help Guo settle into her minister chair we decorated with a bunch of gold streamers. She and Meemaw cackle about something I'm glad I can't hear.

"Maybe I'll give him a long, lingering hello kiss," Mei says. "Technically, I'm not married to Marcus Miller yet."

"He kind of deserves one since it seems cruel that we're making him watch you marry someone who's not him."

She reaches up, pulls my neck toward her, kisses me, slowly and deeply before leaning back. "He never asked me to marry him. And he never would have because he knew I was too in love with you."

"Yeah, but still." I lean my forehead against hers. "I feel bad for the guy because I know what it's like to lose you, and he's coming around the world to watch it happen before his eyes."

"Are you feeling so bad for him that you'd offer him your spot?"

I grab her around the waist, pull her to me, and back against the pillar. "I'm saying…I won, but that doesn't mean I can't feel bad for the guy who lost big. But it's nothing special; I feel bad for every guy who doesn't have you." I run my hands down her back, hips, her white dress smooth and silky under my palms. "Especially you in this dress."

"You mean the dress we got at your girlfriend's favorite vintage store?"

"Right now, I love her so much for introducing me to that store so you could look like this."

"Supposedly, it's bad luck to see me in my wedding dress before the ceremony, but I think our bad luck is exhausted, so I'm not that worried."

I tilt my head, raise my eyebrows. "Should I take it off you instead? That seems like my luck would increase."

"As much as I would love to be thrown in jail by Detective Miller for indecent exposure, I'd rather get married. Again. Right now. For the last time." She peeks around the pillar again, tensing in my arms. "Oh my gosh. She's here. Mama's here."

Mei's mom and Leo walk toward Dad and Kenna, shaking hands, giving hugs. He's once again wearing a shirt that stretches around his biceps. Maybe I don't feel that bad for him.

I look down at Mei. "Go see her."

"No." She straightens, swipes at a tear. "After. Right now, it's you and me. Marcus and Mei Li almost Miller."

Once everyone we love is sitting on their blankets, I start the song we chose on my phone and blast it through the speakers beside Guo's chair, laughing when she jumps in surprise.

I turn to Mei, smooth my hands down her arms. "You ready, Pegs?"

She grins up at me and rolls onto her toes to kiss me, hard and decisive. "Beyond ready. So you can never call me Pegs again."

Holding hands, we walk down the sidewalk toward our family and friends, stopping in front of a waiting Guo who beams up at us from her chair.

I turn toward the half circle of our family. "We had this spot all to ourselves on our secret first date and, back then, we were very careful not to get caught together."

Meemaw whoops, her laugh rolling toward us. "Not careful enough with some of us."

I laugh to the ground and Mei covers her face. No one else knows the story. At least that I know, but I shrug. "Love you, Meemaw, for hopefully keeping that a secret and for whatever magic you put into this dino blanket that started this whole thing."

Dad looks around Kenna at Meemaw for clarification

about the secret, but she mimics zipping her mouth shut and throws me a kiss.

"Thanks for coming, everyone. We love you all." I turn back to face Guo, who grabs Mei's hand, then mine.

"I was told to keep this brief, but I am not good at brief. But I am great at keeping promises so let's just get to the good stuff, yes?" She clears her throat. "Marcus and Mei Li, do you both promise to love and adore each other as you do now, laugh as you always have, and make mischief and many beautiful babies together, just as you have been practicing?" She chuckles to herself and Lin's laugh bursts into the air behind us. I don't wanna know what Dad's face is doing, so I shake my head at Guo, smiling.

"Do you promise you will never, ever again be apart for the rest of your lives and for as many lives that follow?" She looks at me, waiting.

"Yes, to all of it," I say as I look down at Mei. "And I'm hoping for a lot of lives together after this one."

Mei nods, her eyes on mine. "Yes, to everything. Definitely, yes. Forever and ever."

Guo sighs through a smile, then pulls a Magic 8 ball out of a bag beside her chair and hands it to us. "See if Magic 8 agrees."

We take it from her, shake it, then flip it over to wait for the answer to float to the surface. We read it at the same time and shout "Without a doubt!" through smiles, holding it up and turning to show the rest of our family.

Johnny whistles and Lin shrieks and covers her mouth while everyone else claps and cheers.

"Then I pronounce you, Marcus and Mei Li Miller, husband and wife again but for good this time."

I pull Mei to me, kiss her deeply, slowly, until groans float toward us and we're surrounded by our favorite people, wrapped in hugs, congratulations, and flowing tears and love.

My face aches from smiling, and after I've hugged everyone, I look for Mei and see her wrapped in her mom's arms, tears rolling down their cheeks. Leo stands beside them, smiling and watching, so I walk toward him.

"Hey," I say, holding out my hand when I get closer. "Leo?"

He looks at me, then my hand before taking it and offering a smile. "Marcus, nice to meet you."

"I'm not sure how you're feeling right now, but I'm feeling grateful for you, man. Thanks for everything you did for Mei so we could be here doing this today."

"Yeah. Definitely. I'd do anything for her although she's pretty good at taking care of herself." He rubs his forearm, looks at the ground before looking back at me. "Congratulations. Looks like your luck turned."

I shake my head and want to ask the guy who's obviously in love with my wife a few more questions but Audrey walks up and intentionally bumps into me.

"So where are you two headed for your honeymoon?"

"None of your business, Drey, but thanks for asking. We're actually saving up to go to Rhode Island this summer."

"That's...perfectly random," she says as Dad walks up beside her.

"Rhode Island?" His eyebrows meet. "Why Rhode Island?"

I twist, grab Mei's hand where she stands squealing with Lin. "Hey, Mei. Wanna tell everyone why we're going to Rhode Island this summer?"

She steps over to join our conversation, her mom beside her. "I'm going to meet my biological father."

Her mom grabs Mei's arm. "What did you say?"

Mei puts her hand over her mom's and smiles. "I said... I'm going to meet my dad. You told me I should know him. So I messaged him and after he got over the shock, he wanted to meet. He said he'd come here but Marcus and I think it would be fun to go there instead."

Her mom blinks like words are stuck in her throat.

"Turns out, he has three kids that look nothing like me and are a lot younger, but I'm not an only child after all." Mei leans into her mom. "Also turns out, he's very single. And I casually mentioned you're in Taiwan. Single." Mei smiles at the sky. "And casually gave him your number."

The blinking continues but I swear this time, there's extra pink in her mom's cheeks, and Mei laughs and throws her arms around her, telling her she better answer when he calls before turning and grabbing my hand. "Let's get out of here, Marcus Miller."

"You can boss me around anytime, Mei Li Miller." I turn to everyone. "Enjoy the food. We've got better things to do."

Mei squeals and flings herself at me. Laughing, I catch her as Audrey fake vomits, Lin and Johnny cat call, and Leo becomes incredibly interested in the grass.

I swing Mei around so she's piggyback, my hands on her thighs, which are covered in dress but won't be for long.

We wave goodbye to everyone and head across the grass toward the motorcycle parked at the curb. Dad offered it to me again and this time, I said yes like I have to a lot of things recently. A bunch of white balloons are tied to the seat, bobbing in the breeze. When we reach the bike, I notice Sharpie messages written on every balloon, and I set Mei on the ground before we take turns reading them out loud.

Meemaw's says how happy she is for her original grand-baby and her beautiful new one. Mei shrieks when she reads Lin's and I easily find Johnny's, swearing through a laugh. Kenna's makes my throat oddly itchy, and I blink away tears, but they flow without shame when I read Dad's. He's come a long way from hating all women and wanting me to. Looks like we both kinda like them now.

Guo's is way too suggestive for an old lady to think or

write and Audrey's is an insult loaded with love. Leo's says he can see we were meant to be together. But it's the message from Mei's mom that has me wrapping her in my arms as we read. They endured years of abuse together only to come out on top and stronger. She thanks me for loving Mei, but if it weren't for her, I wouldn't even have a Mei to love.

We take a selfie of us with the balloons, then slide on the bike, Mei pressing close just like she used to. I grip the handlebars for all kinds of reasons as I rev the engine a few times, then pull away from the curb toward the newest and permanent version of Us.

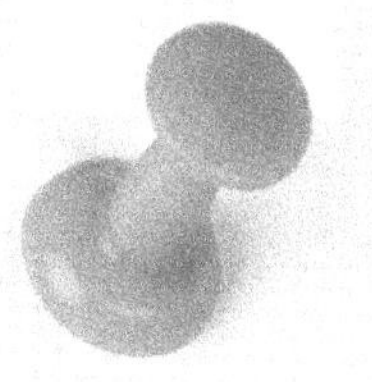

ACKNOWLEDGMENTS

Hey Reader!

We, Marcus and Mei, would like to thank this very long list of people who helped give us our happily ever after. It was a close one, but you really came through for us.

Monster Ivy and its Team Trifecta: Michelle, Mary, and Cammie

Devoted ARC readers who genuinely seemed to care when we weren't sure anyone would: @beastreader @ohshebookish @kricklereadsbooks @bbookmylife

Siri Burgess and her 20+ readings (Note from Marcus: If it hadn't been Mei, it would've been you.)

Emily's and Nicole's real-life people who were often ignored for our benefit: Jake, Liam, London, Mei, Christopher, Miles, Bennett. Also, just a word of warning: your wives/moms have a lot going on inside their heads that should probably worry you.

The calm, steady influence of The Fluffy Boys: Lucky and Bucky Allen, Higgins and Marlowe Cox, Charlie Miller

Brainstorming sessions, Thought Portal revelations, and plain, old-fashioned determination.

Editing. We love your company.

God and Jesus who absolutely put Emily and Nicole where they needed to be so we could finally (finally!) have a story between book covers.

ABOUT THE AUTHORS

Emily Cox is a fast-walking cloud watching, big thinker who believes in aliens, has superior hearing, a mostly-titanium face, and a rhyming maiden and married name (Box-Cox). She lives in Utah in a house of all boys and two fluffy writing assistants. She had a hard time choosing only one dream job, so she has three: school counselor, therapist, author. She loves to plan all kinds of trips, then take them, read multiple books at a time, and explore new places, cultures, and ideas. The inside of her head is the craziest place she's ever dared explore.

Nicole Allen is a crime podcast junkie, travel enthusiast, and Diet Coke addict who not-so-secretly hopes heaven looks exactly like Disneyland's Main Street U.S.A. She fills her head with and likes to share useless, random facts and news headlines, has crazy-vivid dreams almost nightly, believes in karma, but is skeptical about dinosaurs (sorry paleontologists). When she's not writing novels, she loves acting in and watching live theater, is president of a local theater company and runs a youth theater group. She resides in Utah with her supportive rockstar husband (and webmaster), three amazing kids, and two adorable cats.

CONNECT

with us

STAY CONNECTED BY
JOINING OUR MAILING
LIST AND RECEIVING
UPDATES!